Nikki Mottram has a psychology degree from The University of Queensland and has worked in London and Australia in positions protecting and promoting the welfare of children at risk of harm. Her first book, *Crows Nest*, was published in 2023, and her work also appears in the Boroondara Literary Awards anthology. She has been shortlisted for the Fish Short Story Prize and the Hal Porter Short Story Competition. In 2018, she was the recipient of a Katharine Susannah Prichard Writers' Centre Fellowship. She grew up and resides in Toowoomba, and brings to her work an understanding of rural communities.

For Barry and Frances Mottram

KILLARNEY

NIKKI MOTTRAM

UQP

First published 2024 by University of Queensland Press
PO Box 6042, St Lucia, Queensland 4067 Australia

University of Queensland Press (UQP) acknowledges the Traditional Owners
and their custodianship of the lands on which UQP operates. We pay our respects
to their Ancestors and their descendants, who continue cultural and spiritual
connections to Country. We recognise their valuable contributions to Australian
and global society.

uqp.com.au
reception@uqp.com.au

Copyright © Nikki Mottram 2024
The moral rights of the author have been asserted.

This book is copyright. Except for private study, research, criticism or reviews,
as permitted under the *Copyright Act*, no part of this book may be reproduced,
stored in a retrieval system, or transmitted in any form or by any means without
prior written permission. Enquiries should be made to the publisher.

Cover design by Christabella Designs
Cover photograph by Shutterstock
Author photograph by Syd Owen
Typeset in 12/17pt Bembo Std by Post Pre-press Group, Brisbane
Printed in Australia by McPherson's Printing Group

 University of Queensland Press is supported by the Queensland Government through Arts Queensland.

  University of Queensland Press is assisted by the Australian Government through Creative Australia, its principal arts investment and advisory body.

A catalogue record for this book is available from the National Library of Australia.

ISBN 978 0 7022 6581 5 (pbk)
ISBN 978 0 7022 6735 2 (epdf)
ISBN 978 0 7022 6736 9 (epub)

University of Queensland Press uses papers that are natural, renewable and
recyclable products made from wood grown in well-managed forests and other
controlled sources. The logging and manufacturing processes conform to the
environmental regulations of the country of origin.

Johnny Buckley hurries down the steps of the Killarney Hotel, oblivious to the scent of wattle and rain in the air. He skids on the wet pavement, and with a flash of teeth beneath his moustache, strides down the footpath. His mother complains that he walks too fast – always in a hurry – but he's spent the evening with his mates and now it's time to go. If he didn't have Friday nights to blow off steam, he doesn't know what he'd do. He could be a bloody robot for all his job requires. Cut. Saw. Push the wood along the conveyor belt. But for the moment, with the alcohol in his veins, he is free.

He's been working overtime at the sawmill as he needs the money for his daughter – for the scooter he's bought for her fifth birthday. He pictures her face light up when she sees the purple streamers for the first time, the grin blossoming on her shy, gentle face. His little girl's been through a lot this past year, what with their separation, and her mum's new boyfriend. Amber's never been very good at being on her own, but he has to admit, he wasn't expecting to be replaced this soon, and he's not sure he likes the feeling.

He leans against a telegraph pole, contemplating this, then with a jolt remembers where he is, what he's doing. He steps out onto the road, a desperate need to get home and sleep off the hangover which is sure to follow.

George and Frank, friends since primary school, sit on the porch outside George's house, his kelpie at their feet. Dire Straits plays on the stereo and beads of condensation drip down their beer bottles in the humid evening. A motorbike speeds up along their street – seventy, eighty, ninety kilometres per hour. The two men look at each other. *Here we go again.* The rider's been putting on a show at the same time every night for the past week. They have no idea who it is – which is strange for a town the size of Killarney.

They don't see the bike as much as they hear it. And later when they're asked, they will say it sounded like a high-pitched scream, getting louder and louder. Until it wasn't. They will recall metal scraping bitumen. Orange sparks against a black sky. The dull thud of impact.

They leave their drinks and run. A man lies crumpled on the road, a halo of blood beneath his head. The smell of burnt smoke stings Frank's nostrils as he leans over to see if the guy's breathing, and that's when he realises it's Johnny Buckley from down the street. George sprints back to the house to call triple zero.

A hundred metres away the motorbike has stopped sliding. The rider, in a helmet and black leathers, stands up in a daze, then retrieves the motorbike and limps away into the shadows.

On a verandah in a cottage in the next block, a scooter is propped against the balustrade, its ribbons flying in the breeze.

1

Dana sank into the leather Chesterfield that had become like a well-worn pair of shoes and nibbled on leftover Christmas cake. She stared at the empty grate of the fireplace. The house was silent in the early January afternoon, save for the low rumble of a plane overhead, and she began to wonder when Angus would drop by. For the first few weeks of the school holidays she'd been taking him to the library and they'd been having lunch together. Now that she was back from Sydney and her bags had been put away, the house felt empty without him.

She was about to put a CD on when the doorbell rang. Her neighbour, Susan, stood before her, fiddling with the ceramic stone of her necklace. She was trialling a new hair style and wisps of hair had escaped from the combs pinned to the side of her head.

'Hi,' said Dana with a rush of goodwill. 'Where's Angus? I thought he'd have stuck his head in by now.'

A flicker of pain darted across Susan's eyes. She stood

awkwardly on the front step, her collarbones sharp in the vee of her blouse. 'That's what I've come to talk to you about – he's still with Tina.'

'Why don't you come in?' suggested Dana, ushering Susan down the hallway to the kitchen. 'I'll make us some tea.'

Dana switched on the kettle and retrieved the good set of china from the lounge room cabinet. She set two cups with painted butterflies on matching saucers, the aroma of spice filling the air as she steeped the tea in boiling water.

'Let's take these out to the verandah,' she said, handing a cup to Susan, sensing that whatever she'd come to say would be easier sitting side by side looking out over the garden and the park across the road. The cane chair creaked as she eased into it. She blew on her tea as she waited for Susan to speak.

'How was your Christmas Day?' asked Susan.

'It was nice. I spent the day with Mum and we relaxed and watched *It's a Wonderful Life*. Then we had a glazed ham for lunch.'

Susan looked at her pointedly. 'Did you end up talking to Hugh?'

'Uh-huh.'

'And how did it go?'

'Ahh, look, we've decided to leave things as they were … in that we're still separated.' She sipped her tea. 'I used to hear the statistics, that after the death of a child your marriage has only a five per cent chance of survival, but I never thought it would apply to us.' She paused, watching the hydrangeas sway in the breeze. 'My counsellor agrees that ultimately it's been hard to heal myself within the confines of our relationship.'

'It sounds like seeing her has really helped you clarify things.'

'It has. And how about you? How was Christmas here?'

'Jason came out for the day. He's lined up a new mining job in Saudi and flew out a few days later. It's the opportunity of a lifetime – I've never seen him so happy. Angus was pleased to see his uncle, but I'm going to miss him.'

'And what about Tina?'

'She called saying she had a Christmas present for Angus and begged to see him, so she finally showed up with an enormous soft gorilla from god knows where and handed it to him like it was the best thing since sliced bread.' Susan shook her head. 'And against my better judgement, I said she could take him back home with her for a week or two. She's off the drugs and her AA counsellor in Warwick gave me his word about that, so in the end her sobriety was the reason I said yes.' She glanced at her watch, her forehead creased. 'They were supposed to be back this morning.'

'I'm sure they won't be too much longer,' Dana said, suddenly feeling jittery and wishing she'd added honey to her tea. 'How did Tina seem when you saw her?' she asked tentatively. 'Was she looking healthy?'

'Well, I've always hated all that get-up she wears, short skirts and ripped jeans, like she's thirty-seven going on sixteen, but she has some meat on her bones, so that's a step in the right direction.'

'And what about Angus?'

'He lights up when he sees her. It's like the millions of times she's disappointed him just never happened.' She paused. 'I'm just worried. He's finally settled down, he's got an academic scholarship to Grammar next year, and he's even started playing tennis. I don't want to risk her blowing it all up again.' A muscle clenched in her jaw. 'You should have seen his face when he saw her again. He was so happy.'

Dana leant back in her chair. 'And has Tina told you what her plans are? Is she still living out near … Warwick, is it?'

'She's working at the corner store out at Queen Mary Falls. Angus says they've been letting him help out too. But aside from that, no. And there's a part of me that doesn't want to know.'

A neighbour with a pram waved up at them as she strolled along the street.

'I often wonder,' Susan continued, 'if she inherited her father's schizophrenia genes. She was always one of those kids who got herself into scrapes. Honestly, if there were five kids sitting in a tree, she'd be the one who'd fall out. Or, if there was a group of them running in the bush, she'd be the one who'd get bitten by a snake. I know that she loves Angus with all her heart, and I really want her to start doing better – and I feel terrible for saying it – but after all the overdoses I'm just not sure I trust her.' Her cup began to clatter as she returned it to the saucer.

'Are you okay?' Dana asked gently.

'I'm fine.'

Dana recognised Susan's fierce independence in her terse response.

'Sorry to burden you with my worries. I should be heading back and getting dinner on.' She took a final sip of tea and placed the cup on the cane table beside her.

As Dana walked Susan down the path she bent over to pull a tuft of grass from the base of the lavender bush in the garden bed. 'With all the rain we've had, the weeds are growing back overnight,' she observed.

Susan followed Dana's lead and reached down to pull a weed. She straightened up and threw it onto the lawn. 'Strange weather we've had lately. So much rain and then the odd freezing day. It got down to nine degrees here on Christmas day.' As Susan bent over to pull another weed her legs buckled and she doubled over, collapsing into the bush.

'What's wrong?' Dana asked, her heart beating faster as she reached down to her friend.

Susan's face was white as she took Dana's arm and allowed herself to be pulled up to rest on the brick fence.

'I don't know.'

'Should I call an ambulance?' Dana was alarmed. Susan was usually so robust.

'No, just a bit dizzy,' Susan insisted, but Dana wasn't convinced. She hurried next door and grabbed Susan's car keys, kicking herself that she hadn't bothered to replace her Mercedes after crashing it the year before. She'd reasoned there was no point having a car of her own given her proximity to the office, but now she regretted it.

After helping Susan into the passenger seat, she drove at breakneck speed through town and skidded into a loading zone outside the Emergency Department of the Toowoomba Base Hospital. Five ambulances were moored against the kerb as she hastened around the side of the car to help Susan, who was still looking pale and withdrawn.

Inside, the reception area was packed. As they stood in line waiting to be triaged Susan clutched her stomach and stared at the pale linoleum of the floor, clearly in pain. Dana felt the stares of other patients as they progressed towards the reception desk. A man in thongs and a hoodie crouched against the wall, a red-cheeked toddler slumped against his mother's chest. Dana had a vision of her holding her own baby son, Oscar, who'd been eight months old when he died. She did her best to banish the image of him from her mind and focus on Susan.

A large television was anchored on the wall opposite. As they inched forward in the queue, they watched in silence as the news bulletin came on.

A man has been seriously injured in a hit-and-run involving a motorcycle last night, in the small Queensland town of Killarney. Witnesses said the thirty-two-year-old man was knocked unconscious, sustaining serious head wounds on Arbutus Street after the bike collided with him. He was taken to Warwick Hospital and is in a critical condition. Police have appealed for any witnesses to come forward.

'God, how awful,' said Susan, a sheen of sweat glistening on her brow. 'Maybe you should move the car?'

Dana shook her head. 'I'll wait until we've seen a doctor and sort it out afterwards. We're almost there.'

When the receptionist finally waved them forward and asked a brief series of questions they were ushered into a small cubicle. Susan lay on a bed while a nurse took her pulse and palpated her stomach. There was a thinness to Susan's face that Dana hadn't noticed before and she had a flashback to Susan saying how exhausted she'd been before Christmas. When Susan mumbled something to the nurse about having a colonoscopy a few days earlier, Dana stood up. 'I'd better go and move the car.'

'Maybe you could duck home and leave a note on the door for Tina and Angus?' Susan suggested. 'She doesn't have a mobile, and I'm worried they're going to get home and have no idea where I am.'

Dana made her way back through multiple heavy doors until she was standing outside under an ominous sky. At Susan's house, she taped a note to the door letting Tina and Angus know they were at the hospital. By the time she'd returned, parked on a side street and managed to speak to someone in Emergency, an hour had passed. Susan was lying sedated in the same room in which Dana had left her.

'What did I miss?' Dana asked, taking a seat.

'Oh, nothing much. They're just waiting on the results of some tests. Apparently I should know later on at some point.'

Dana spent the next two hours listening to beeping machines and the chatter of medical staff on the other side of a curtain as Susan dozed. She slumped in her chair, her head against the wall, wishing she'd brought a book. She was just about to get up and try to find a magazine to read when a woman burst into the room, her white face blazing in the stark fluorescent light. The woman, who could only have been Susan's daughter, Tina, rushed to her mother's side, Angus on her heels.

'God, Mum, you scared the shit out of us,' the woman said, collapsing dramatically into the vacant chair beside her mother.

Angus gave Dana a hug and she wrapped her arms around him and pulled him close. Despite the fact that he was now twelve and his white-blond hair had darkened over the summer, he looked pale and anxious. As Susan introduced them, Tina picked at the long sleeves of her turtleneck bodysuit and adjusted her harem pants, avoiding meeting Dana's eyes.

'What happened?' Tina asked, reaching for her mother's hand.

Susan winced. 'Nothing to panic about. I just had a bit of a fall. They're running some tests, but I'm sure it will end up being nothing.' She gestured for Angus to give her a kiss.

'Mum, I've told you before, if you keep working like a maniac, you're gonna die of a heart attack'

'As I said, Tina, it's probably nothing, just a stomach bug.

They're running some tests and I should know in the next day or two.'

'Anyway, Mum, you need to slow down.' Tina stretched her arms in the air and let out a loud yawn. 'So do I, I'm so freaking tired today.'

'Why are *you* so tired?' Susan replied irritably. 'I would have thought you'd be well rested after the Christmas break.'

'Paid employment is hard, man. I've got to be at work by nine and they glare at me every time I go out for a smoke.' She winked at Angus. 'It's not all bad though. There's some hot guys, they've got this, like, rad hippy vibe with dreddies and flannelette shirts.'

Susan's mouth was a thin line. 'You know how much it pains me to see you working in that shop, when you could have done anything. If I had your brains, I would have done something really worthwhile, like finance or law.'

Tina nodded emphatically. 'Great, Mum, maybe you should do law. They're accepting mature age students now, so you can totally sign up. It's never too late to live out your wildest dreams.' She cackled loudly at her own joke.

'Honestly, Tina, the only thing I've ever wanted is for you to be happy.'

'That's bullshit, Mum.' The volume in Tina's voice began to rise. 'The only thing you've ever wanted is for me to be less embarrassing. You just wish you had a daughter you could show off to the CWA ladies, so you don't have to lie and change the subject every time someone asks how I'm doing. Remember that time you told Rosemary I'd gone on a six-week trip to Europe while I was in rehab? When I bumped into her at Kmart and she asked about my trip and I was like, "Fuck off, Rosemary, I wouldn't go to Europe if you paid me."'

'Okay, Tina, that's enough.'

'Mum,' Angus interrupted, giving his nan's hand a squeeze. 'Do you mind if we go to the canteen and get some chips? I'm starving.'

'Sure, baby,' Tina cooed and ruffled his hair, 'Just let me get my purse.' She groped around in her pockets, then grimaced. 'Hey, Mum, I don't suppose you have five bucks you could lend me?'

'Yes, Tina,' Susan said through gritted teeth. 'My handbag's on the table.'

As Tina stood up the curtain swung open and a nurse stuck her head in. 'I need you to keep it down in here,' she said with a look of annoyance. 'The patient needs her rest and if you can't be quiet, I'll have to ask you to leave.'

'We were just going.' Tina rolled her eyes. She retrieved a ten-dollar note from Susan's handbag and waved it in the air. She hesitated before giving her mother a peck on the cheek. 'I'm going to hang out with Liz tonight, then head back to Killarney in time for my shift tomorrow morning. I hope your stomach ache, or whatever, gets better.'

'I'll be fine, darling.'

'Nan, do you mind if I go with Mum? Edith at the cafe said that I could have another few days of work if I wanted.'

'That's fine, sweetheart.' Susan gave Angus a hug and stroked his cheek. 'Be good for your mum, please. I'll give you a call tomorrow night and let you know how I'm getting on.'

As they disappeared behind the curtain divider, a doctor in navy blue scrubs swept into the room. She stood at the end of Susan's bed, a chart in her hand.

'So, how are you feeling this evening, Susan?' Her brown eyes were earnest beneath tortoiseshell glasses.

Susan attempted to straighten up against the pillow. 'In all honesty, I've felt better.'

'Would it be okay if I sat on the bed?'

Susan nodded.

'So your results have come back.' The doctor flicked a glance at Dana. 'Do you need some privacy or are you happy to have company?'

'I'd like Dana to stay – apparently it helps to have someone clear-headed with you if the news isn't good.'

The doctor put the chart by her side and frowned. 'Well, I'm afraid you're right about it not being good news.' She ran a hand through her fringe, looking as though what she was about to say had leached every remnant of her energy. 'So we've tracked down your colonoscopy results and, as your doctor would have discussed with you, a number of polyps were found on your bowel and further testing has confirmed that those polyps are cancerous. Today's CT scan showed that the cancer has spread to your lymph nodes and liver.' Her eyes were bright with emotion as her hand shot across to Susan's.

The blood drained from Susan's face.

'I'm afraid there's no easy way to say this, Susan. You have stage four bowel cancer.'

2

Dana sat in front of her work computer staring blankly at the screen. She sipped from a mug of instant coffee, desperately hoping it might revive her as she clicked through the backlog of emails. Her eyes filled with tears every time she thought about Susan. She'd been spending the last week of her holiday visiting Susan in hospital and was amazed by how well she was holding up.

It was nearly lunchtime when she looked up to find Lachlan draped over the top of their office pod.

He gave her a lop-sided smile. 'Hey stranger! How's things?'

'You mean, besides Susan having stage four bowel cancer?' she replied, too miserable to continue.

'God, that's terrible,' he said, clearly shocked. 'When did this happen? What have the doctors said?'

'It's an end-of-life diagnosis, so it's about making sure she's comfortable with the time she has left.'

'Oh god,' he repeated. 'And what's going to happen with Angus?'

'That's the thing. His mother's never been a consistent presence in his life and after the consultant left last night Susan told me that she'd really like me to look after him. She doesn't want anything to jeopardise his scholarship and thinks that living with me will give him the best chance of succeeding.' She sipped her coffee to hide her storm of emotions. 'I mean, I love him with all my heart, and I knew that Susan wasn't going to live forever. At some point my role in his life was going to increase. I just didn't realise it would be quite this soon.'

They sat for a moment in silence until Lachlan's phone started to ring.

'Yes, yes. I'm looking for him. I'm going to head out to Killarney so I can track him down. I'll let you know.' He hung up the phone and closed his eyes.

'What was that all about?'

'Jayden Maloney. No-one's been to visit him for months. Beloved in the community, and by me for that matter. The family he's been placed with are worried about him, so I'm heading out there today.'

'Killarney? Where that hit-and-run took place?'

'That's right.'

'Where exactly is that?'

'About a hundred kilometres south of here. An hour and a half in the car.'

'I had no idea we covered that area. No wonder you haven't managed to see him lately.'

At that moment a young man with a beard came over. 'Excuse me, Lachlan, do you have any idea where I'd find the Hooke file?'

'I don't know, Vaughan. Have you tried the compactus?'

'I've searched the whole lot. It's not there.'

'Maybe it's lost? It's been known to happen. Ask one of the admin workers – if you can find one. Hopefully they can help.'

They watched as Vaughan wandered off down the corridor.

'I'm sensing a level of frustration,' said Dana.

'It's this new team leader from the Department of Corrections, Judy. She's *content-free* so I'm basically running the show.'

'Really?' Dana raised an eyebrow, well aware of his tendency to exaggerate.

'Yes.' He smirked. 'People are feeling stretched – they spent hours at the tavern last Friday night, and there was a lot of complaining. There seems to be a bullying problem with Judy that no-one is addressing. She's loud and intimidates everyone. She needs to be moved on but no-one has the balls to do it. Morale is low and, frankly, I'm glad we're getting the hell out of here today.'

'We? I was planning on spending my first day back catching up with Shivani and getting my head around my new cases.' Shivani had started work five months earlier and she and Dana had become fast friends.

'The truth is, we need to find Jayden.' He handed her a manila folder. 'Have a read of his file. I put tabs on the important bits.'

She opened up the folder. The first tab was a photo – a posed shot in which a teen boy with an upturned button nose and close-cropped hair was leaning against a tree with a Michael Jordan backpack slung over his shoulder. His arms were tanned and muscular in his tank top and he had a calm and open face. The second tab was an Affidavit:

Jayden Maloney is sixteen years and two months old. He loves religion and working with his hands. He's described as a kind boy who is loved by everyone in his community. Jayden was subjected to a difficult childhood, which involved abuse and neglect, yet despite this he has remained a gentle and caring young person.

'Anyway, you can read the rest later,' said Lachlan. 'What do you say I grab my keys, you sign us out, and we'll see if we can find him. There's a bit of water on the roads so we'll take my Rangie instead of one of those puny work cars. Oh, and Judy's going to have a thousand questions, so if she spots us on the way out, pretend you don't know anything.'

They crept along the corridor and had almost made it past Judy's door when a voice boomed from inside. 'Lachlan! Is that you? Can you come here for a minute?'

Lachlan grabbed her by the elbow and they made a run for it, ducking behind a tradesman and heading for the fire escape.

Fat drops of water ran down the windscreen and the wipers swung back and forth as Dana and Lachlan drove south along the highway. On the outskirts of Toowoomba purple and yellow flowers were dotted through the green fields that sprawled before them. Despite the beauty of their surroundings, Dana's mind soon returned to Susan – the tragedy of what was happening and the unfairness of it all. Susan had finally managed to get custody of her grandson and was enjoying the peace and happiness of retirement only to have it cut short. Not to mention Angus. *How is he going to cope?* Dana swallowed the knot in her throat and blinked hot tears from her eyes.

Lachlan glanced over at her. 'Thinking about Susan?'

'Uh-huh.'

'Well, hopefully this road trip to the place of my birth might take your mind off it for a bit.'

'Killarney's your home town?'

He grinned. 'Not only that, but it's also the birthplace of the entire O'Malley clan. One of my relatives decided to settle here after he saw the green pastures and rolling hills that reminded him of his native County Kerry in Ireland. I still have family there – half the town's population are my cousins.'

Dana held her breath as Lachlan sped past an enormous flatbed truck. 'What about your parents?' she asked, once they'd made it safely past. 'Do they still live there?'

'Thankfully, no. Everyone still refers to the O'Malley clan as the Irish mafia, but my parents were one of the few who made it out.'

'What do you mean?'

'They're from a generation of people involved in family feuding and a bunch of other dodgy stuff. Ultimately, they decided to pack up and move to Stanthorpe.'

'And are they happier?'

'Definitely.' His brow crinkled. 'But I have to admit it's been months since I last caught up with them. We had Christmas with Rachel's family this year.'

'And this teenager we're going to look for, what's his story?'

'In his younger years he was sent back and forth between his parents, but in the end both of them rejected him and he went to live with his maternal aunt. And that was going quite well until he was about twelve and she started to fall back into her old habits – drinking, spending hours playing the pokies. Even still, the Department put in a lot of support and with the help of the community and the school we were able to keep him out of foster care. But then one day the school called up saying that he was turning up with no lunches, bursting into tears and was found fast asleep on the steps of the office one morning. We looked into it, and Jayden was basically being kept alive by the meatballs given to him by the publican at the Killarney pub while his aunt succumbed to her alcohol addiction. We bit the bullet and took him into care.'

'So, what's the plan for finding him?'

'Well, I thought we could grab some afternoon tea at the cafe in town and then head out to speak to the foster carer, Trevor McClusky. He called this morning and said that Jayden hasn't been home for a few days. Trevor oversees Jayden's apprenticeship at the sawmill and has been letting Jayden stay in his caravan since the previous placement broke down. At that time, Jayden told me he was done with school and I said if he could organise work and somewhere to live, then he could leave. And he did exactly that.' Lachlan drummed his fingers on the steering wheel and took a deep breath. 'And I want to be clear, even though it's been a few months since I've seen him, Jayden's case was one of the first ones I was ever given when I started at the Department. He's been on my caseload for four years and during that time I've gotten to know him really well. He works hard, he's good with his hands. He's really social and he reminds me a lot of myself when I was younger.' Lachlan shook his head as though he was trying to focus. 'What I'm trying to say is, this kid means a lot to me.' He rubbed the back of his thigh, grimacing.

'You okay?' asked Dana.

'Just the bloody sciatica from the car accident. It'll go away in a sec.'

KILLARNEY

A wave of guilt descended on Dana as she remembered the previous year when she'd pushed Lachlan into driving late at night to investigate a case. The car had rolled and he'd been in rehabilitation for months. In that moment she made a promise to herself to do whatever it took to find Jayden. Helping Lachlan out was the least she could do.

They wound down the hill into Warwick, the spire of a church rising up from the centre of the town. As they neared the train tracks she could see the road was covered with water. Lachlan changed gears and powered through, brown sludge spraying out from under the wheels and hitting the windscreen.

A sign beside the road announced that they were thirty-two kilometres from Killarney. Lachlan fiddled about in the glove box then shoved a disc into the CD player.

'Hope you don't mind, but I brought some tunes for us to listen to.'

In the next instant, 'Heartache Tonight' was blasting from the stereo.

She frowned. 'Is The Eagles the only music you ever listen to?'

'What?' He cupped his ear. 'Music attained perfection in the seventies? I couldn't agree more.'

She smiled and leant against the cool glass of the window as they passed fields of white sheep and dairy cows, rusted sheds and bales of hay. In the distance, the Border Ranges were clipped by low-hanging clouds. They soon descended into a valley ringed by mountains on all sides and were greeted with the spectacular view of the Condamine River.

Lachlan pointed at a farmer mowing his lawn before the next lot of storms forecast to sweep through. 'With all the rain we've had lately, Killarney's about as pretty as you'll ever see it.'

Dana wound down the window as they drove through an avenue of London plane trees and daisies springing up through the thigh-high grass. Cool air rushed in and she had the distinct feeling she was entering another world. The breeze was chill on her skin and the song of currawongs filled the air.

In the town centre, the old Co-Op Dairy Association building sat on the corner beside a supermarket and petrol station. They pulled up in front of the Killarney Hotel

'Great, Finn's here,' said Lachlan, nodding in the direction of a lanky red-headed man who disappeared into the small cafe across the road. 'He'll be sure to fill me in on what's been happening.'

Inside, a Black Forest cake with morello cherries was displayed in a backlit cabinet. Paintings by local artists hung from the walls. A young woman was humming to herself as she wiped down the espresso machine.

Lachlan and Dana stood at the counter where a donation box had been set up. It read: *Please give generously to the family of Johnny Buckley involved in the hit-and-run tragedy.*

Lachlan dropped a two-dollar coin into the slot of the cardboard box. 'That poor guy. How's he doing?' he asked the young woman.

Her face clouded with confusion. 'He was killed in that hit-and-run near the bowls club.'

'Oh god, I saw that on the news. I thought he was only injured?'

'He didn't make it. They had to turn off his life support.'

'Jesus. Would you mind telling Finn I'd like a chat?'

'Just a sec, I'll go get him.' She disappeared into the kitchen and returned with an apologetic smile. 'Sorry, he's not here. He ducked out a few minutes ago to get milk.'

Lines of consternation formed between Lachlan's brows. 'What do you mean? I saw him come into the shop two seconds ago.'

Colour rose in the young woman's cheeks. 'You must be mistaken. There's nobody out there.'

Lachlan leant over the counter towards the kitchen door, shouting, 'Tell Finn O'Malley that if he doesn't want to see me, he should have the guts to tell me himself. Not send his twenty-year-old employee out to do his dirty work.'

They took their cake and coffees and sat at a table in front of the glass windows facing the street.

'Bloody hell,' said Lachlan. 'We grew up together ... I'm sorry, I should have known coming here would be problematic. Still, I thought with Finn it would be different. None of this, *if you leave the clan you're dead to us*. He's my cousin for god's sake.'

'I thought you said everyone in Killarney was your cousin.'

He smiled ruefully. 'They are, yeah. Look, I hate to do this to you on your first day back, but I think I should transfer this case to you. Fact is, I'm too close to everyone. If there are any issues it's going to make it impossible for me to make decisions from a neutral point of view. I'll have to let Judy know, and I'll be here to assist, but you take the lead on this one.'

'You know I'd do anything to help, right? But I want to remind you that the last time I took one of your cases two women died and I almost lost Angus, too.'

'Seriously, Dana, this is nothing like that. In all likelihood, Jayden's gone camping and he'll show up this afternoon.'

On Lachlan's advice they headed to the sawmill next. As they entered the old timber shed they were met with the sweet, almost wine-like scent of freshly cut wood. They made their way up the stairs to a mezzanine office overlooking the work floor. Lachlan paused, his hand on the door handle. 'Now's probably a good time to mention that my brother works here.'

'You have a brother? How did I not know this?'

'You never asked.' He smiled at what was a repeat of an old joke between them.

Inside, a man was talking on the telephone as he sat beneath a wall calendar featuring a model in a high-cut swimsuit. He was wearing a soft chequered shirt like the ones Angus's mother, Tina, had enthused about, but with a suit jacket and pants that grazed the tops of his work boots. As he put the phone down her gaze met his and a jolt of electricity passed through her. Her cheeks burned with self-consciousness.

'Lachy! The return of the prodigal son,' said the man.

'Long time no see, Sean,' said Lachlan.

'I know, what's it been … like, two years? He turned his attention to Dana. 'And who's this young woman?'

She was flattered, but at forty-two there was no way she'd be considered young. 'I can see that like your brother, you're not short on charm.'

'Yes,' Sean said in a conspiring whisper. 'But unlike me he wore braces until he was sixteen and the only way he could attract girls was to yell out, "Show us your map of Tassie!"'

Lachlan looked worried. 'None of that's true by the way.' He nodded at the wall behind Sean. 'Nice calendar.'

'Not my sort of thing, but the boss seems to like it.'

Lachlan squinted at the swimsuit model. 'She looks a bit like that friend of yours – Vicky.'

Tension crackled in the air between them. 'You'd have a lot

better idea than I would,' Sean shot back. 'I'm guessing you're here for work since you'd hardly grace me with your presence for any other reason. Or was it to return my denim jacket? Or my Pink Floyd album?'

'I'd really love to bring up all this stuff from the past, but right now we need to speak to Trevor about his apprentice, Jayden Maloney.'

'I thought you were going to grill us about Johnny's hit-and-run?'

'I work for the Department of Families, Sean, not the police.'

Dana was taken aback by the animosity between them. 'Perhaps you two can take off the gloves for a while so we can talk to Trevor?'

'I'll contact one of the men and get them to send him up. I'm very busy here, we're about to have a team meeting to order new stock, so I'd better get back to it. It was lovely to meet you ... I'm sorry, we didn't get an introduction.'

'I'm sure it was just an oversight – Dana Gibson.'

He put his hand out and she shook it. When he smiled something warm and soft bubbled up inside her. There was a mischievousness in his grin that was hard to resist.

'If you're ever in Killarney again, maybe you'll let me show you around? We have many fine establishments with a full complement of wines, succulent steaks and whatnot.'

'Lay off it, Sean,' said Lachlan.

Sean winked at her before disappearing through the door that led to the workshop.

'Sorry about that. He's the youngest brother so he always gets away with murder,' said Lachlan.

'You two have an interesting relationship,' she said.

'I shouldn't have mentioned Vicky.'

'Who is she?'

'A girl we both liked in high school. He's always been annoyed because I ended up dating her.'

'And what about the record?'

He looked sheepish. 'I did borrow his Pink Floyd album. But only because he stole my AC/DC one first.'

Five minutes later a short man with olive skin and a nose that looked like it had been broken a few times came through the door. He took his hard hat off and tucked it under his arm.

'Lachlan, mate. Long time no see.'

'Trevor. At least you're talking to me.'

'Don't be so sure.' Trevor chuckled, eyes darting nervously. 'Anyway, let's go outside – I need a smoke.'

They walked to an undercover area outside and sat at a pale pine bench. 'Thanks for coming,' said Trevor. 'Look, as I said on the phone, I'm worried about Jayden. He's one hundred per cent reliable and shows up for work on time every day. Then Thursday and Friday last week, nothing. It's not like him.'

Dana took a pen from her handbag and began to jot down some notes.

'You don't think ... I don't know ... that he's gone camping or something?' suggested Lachlan.

'I don't.' Trevor lit a cigarette and blew smoke from the side of his mouth. 'Some of the guys are unmotivated, but Jayden is committed, he works hard because he likes the money. In the end that's why I let him stay at my place. I knew he came from nothing and thought if I gave him a headstart, let him live with us for free, then maybe he could save up and get something of his own.'

'And what did Connie think about that?'

Trevor looked sheepish. 'She wasn't happy at the start, but he's a good kid. He's pulled his weight – does the mowing, helps with the kids, goes to church every weekend. He won her over.'

'What church does he go to?' asked Dana.

'There's only the one.' He glanced at her as though she wasn't very bright. 'The Catholic one, up on the hill. Very devoted he is, spends a bit of time there and is always talking about God, which I always find a bit hard to get my head around.'

Dana was intrigued. Most of the teenagers she'd known over the years kept their beliefs well and truly under wraps.

'There's still one thing that's not really clear to me. Aside from the meagre foster-carer allowance, what were you getting out of it?' asked Lachlan.

Trevor flicked the ash of his cigarette. 'It's hard to get decent help out here. Half the time you train these young guys up then they take off and go backpacking or whatever. I thought, maybe if I made it worth his while he'd be more likely to stay.'

'Have you told the police any of this?'

'I did, but it's such a small station and all their time's being taken up with investigating Johnny's death.' He dropped his smoke and ground it into the dirt with the heel of his boot. 'Awful business that. We're just having a run of bad luck lately. I've just lost one of my best workers and now Jayden's run off.' He stared off into the distance to the green field on the other side of the road. 'The best-case scenario, and the one I'm hoping for, is that he's gone off with a girl or something. Then I can give him a major bollocking and he can come back to work.' Trevor paused. 'But something tells me that isn't going to happen. All his stuff is still in the caravan.' Trevor checked his watch. 'Anyway, I need to get back. I'll let you know if he shows up.'

Dana and Lachlan stood up, watching as Trevor went through the door and into the shed.

She turned to Lachlan. 'Is it just me or did he seem nervous about having you here?'

'Most of my cousins, and Trevor is one of them, are into small-time drug trafficking, you know, moving a bit of weed over the border. And for some reason they can't seem to get it into their heads that working for the government is not the same as working for the police.' His phone started ringing and he reached into his pocket, rolling his eyes when he saw the screen.

'Seriously?' he said after he'd answered. 'No, thanks for telling me. We'll figure something out.'

'Who was that?'

'Judy. Apparently, there's been an accident outside of Warwick. A bunch of horses got loose on the highway and a car crashed into them, then the ambulance driving out to assist also hit a horse.'

'Jesus.'

'Anyway, the highway's blocked off till midnight.' He sighed. 'I know it's unorthodox, but how would you feel about spending the night at my parents' place in Stanthorpe? No-one's really talking to me here and we may as well make the best out of a bad situation. I reckon Dad can give us some info on Jayden. He knows everyone in the community, so he's bound to have some pointers on where to look.'

3

They took the Mount Lindesay Road turn-off, passing an absurd amount of roadkill on the way. Dana winced at the sight of a youngish kangaroo with bloody entrails, its head perfectly intact. Further along was an older kangaroo in the throes of rigor mortis, hind leg pointed at the sky. There was no dignity in death, thought Dana, as visions of Johnny Buckley's hit-and-run swam in her mind.

The road became steeper as they neared Stanthorpe and the air grew crisp. They drove down High Street, past an avenue of poplars, the clock tower and Quart Pot Creek. When they turned into McGregor Terrace and pulled up in front of a white Queenslander, Dana could hear a barking dog and half expected the blue heeler Lachlan had told her about to come flying out of the house to welcome them.

As they made their way up the front stairs under a rose-covered arbour, Lachlan's silver-haired mother opened the door and pulled him into a hug.

'What a lovely surprise!' She drew back, her hands on his waist.

A dog with a grey-speckled coat came skidding down the hall on a Persian runner rug. 'Rex!' said Lachlan. The dog jumped up with its paws on Lachlan's knees and he bent down and pressed his face to its coat. 'I've missed you, buddy.' Lachlan gestured to the dog as they stood in the hallway beside a basket filled with umbrellas and gumboots. 'Dana, meet Rex. Rex, Dana.'

Lachlan's mother gave him a withering look and turned to Dana. 'And I'm Ruth.' She glanced back at Lachlan with raised eyebrows. 'Luckily, there's enough carbonara to go around.'

'Maybe we should have called before dropping in?' Dana whispered to Lachlan as they followed Ruth down the hall.

Ruth led them into the kitchen where the adjacent dining room table had been set with napkins and a crystal vase of roses. A younger, female version of Lachlan sat on a day bed with her legs tucked under her. Her hair was wet, and she was wrapped in a long cardigan.

'Anna!' said Lachlan.

'Lachy!' she exclaimed and threw her arms into the air for a hug. She whispered in his ear, 'Thank god you're here. Mum's giving me hell about not having a boyfriend, saying I should join some clubs or put an ad in the paper.'

Ruth opened a bottle of wine. 'I'm a mother. It's my job to worry sometimes,' she said, laying out two extra settings on the table.

Thoughts of Lachlan's younger brother floated into her mind as she tried to picture Sean fitting into this domestic scene. She took a large sip of pinot noir, comforted by the blue walls of the old-fashioned kitchen and the copper pots hanging above the oven. Her gaze came to rest on a framed photograph on the wall, a family portrait with everyone in their best clothes. Ruth was in the centre of the picture, her teased mass of blonde hair partly blocking an older man – presumably Lachlan's father – huddled in behind. Lachlan, Anna and a chubby-cheeked Sean sat smiling in front of them.

Ruth grated parmesan over the pasta she'd dished into bowls. She beamed at Lachlan. 'It's so lovely having you visit, darling,' she said. 'We missed you at Christmas this year – it's not the same without you.'

'I know, but things have been hectic lately. Anna,' he said, clearly wanting to change the subject, 'have you heard about the hit-and-run in Killarney?'

'Oh my god. Brooke Buckley is one of the kids in my kindy class.' Her eyes brimmed with tears. 'I was devastated when I heard what happened. Johnny's such a lovely guy. He and Amber were separated, but when she and Brooke moved from Ipswich, he moved too. He just couldn't bear to be away from them. I can't believe it.'

'Any rumours about who was responsible?' Lachlan asked.

'Not really. The story is Johnny was legless drunk, he'd been at the pub before it happened.' She chewed her pasta. 'He still didn't deserve to die that way though.'

Dana's curiosity got the better of her. 'What do people think happened?'

'Well, Eve from the gym said there were witnesses. Eve heard from a guy at the bank that a bloke on a motorbike came flying down the street near the bowls club and when the bike hit Johnny he flew up into the air like a crash-test dummy.'

'It's terrible alright.' Lachlan wiped his mouth with a napkin and sat back in his chair. 'And now Jayden's gone missing.'

'Jayden Maloney?' asked Ruth, a look of concern on her features.

Lachlan nodded.

'He volunteered at the hospital last summer and was great with the kids.' Ruth turned to Dana. 'He had an incredibly rough upbringing, but he was a delightful boy. Just delightful. What's happened?'

'That's the problem,' said Lachlan. 'No-one seems to know.'

A heavy silence settled over the room and Dana pondered how beloved Jayden had been in the community, and how extraordinary it was that no-one had a bad word to say about him.

'When's Dad getting home?' asked Lachlan, interrupting the quiet. 'Not like him to miss a meal.'

Anna looked to Ruth, her eyes wide. 'You haven't told him yet?'

'I'm telling him now,' said Ruth. 'Your father and I separated a few months ago. I've called multiple times, but you never answer your phone!'

Lachlan's complexion turned grey. Rex trotted over to him and he stroked the dog's silky ears.

Dana squirmed in her seat, feeling like an intruder.

'Where's he living now?' asked Lachlan.

'Drowning his sorrows in the shack in Amiens.'

'You've been married forty years. Why would you pull the plug now?'

Anna butted in before Ruth had a chance to answer. 'So, Mum, met any nice men yet?'

'I have no intention of meeting other men.'

'That's a defeatist attitude. Maybe you should join some clubs? Put an ad in the paper?' Anna grinned, clearly enjoying herself.

Ruth pushed her half-eaten meal away and stood up. She brushed past Anna and shoved her feet into some gumboots by the door. 'I'm taking Rex for his walk.' The door slammed as she passed through it and the photo on the wall shook, swinging precariously from the nail before tilting to one side.

'Anna.' Lachlan held his empty glass aloft. 'Could you pass the wine, please?'

Dana did not feel like visiting Lachlan's father, Pat, the next morning. She was out of sorts from the wine the night before, and despite the cloudy sky outside the spare bedroom window, it was already humid and her shirt, which she'd slept in, clung to her back and armpits. She thought about stuffing a valium down her throat, but knew that if she did, she'd be back to her previous level of addiction in no time.

When she got into the car she flicked the radio on before Lachlan had the chance to play his Eagles CDs. On the way they stopped at the Quart Pot Bakehouse for an apple pie to share with Lachlan's father. After fifteen minutes of negotiating potholes as he drove north-west to Amiens, a small property came into view. Lachlan slowed down and glanced over at her. 'I'm worried about what kind of mood Dad might be in today. When I was younger, the word bipolar was bandied around but his legendary stubbornness meant it was impossible for him to ask for help.'

'Mental health problems aren't something you need to be ashamed of.'

'I know, I just wanted to warn you about what we're walking into.'

The worker's cottage they arrived at was little more than a shack with peeling paint and a rusted corrugated iron roof. The blinds had been pulled tight across the front windows and a stack of Bushmills whiskey bottles glinted in the morning sun beside the doorstep. They walked around the side of the house, passing a newish looking dog kennel, and Lachlan banged on the back door. A kelpie puppy came bounding out from the shady trees up the back. Lachlan tried knocking again but there was no answer.

The dog butted its nose against Dana's hand and it took her a second to realise what it wanted: *water.* She jogged back to the side of the house and grabbed a bowl, placing it under the tap and filling it to the brim. The dog stuck its face in, lapping as though it had wandered out of the Sahara.

By the time she returned to the back of the house she didn't need to knock – the door was already open. The blinds were drawn in the kitchen and it took her eyes a moment to adjust as she stood in the doorway. An elderly man was at the sink with a jar of instant coffee.

The man looked over at Lachlan with the groggy, slow grinding gaze of a hangover. 'I wasn't expecting you.'

'Dad,' Lachlan said angrily, 'your new puppy was out the back dying of thirst when we arrived. You need to make sure it has water.'

He was irritated. 'Of course it does. There's a bowl in the bedroom and another one at the side of the house.'

Lachlan shook his head. 'The one outside was empty and it couldn't get into the house because it's locked up like a tomb.'

'Why are you here, son?' Pat stopped stirring his coffee and looked at Lachlan, strangely paranoid. 'Did your mother send you?'

'Get real. I think she'd rather I didn't come at all.' Lachlan's features changed and he went over to him and kissed his father's stubbly cheek. 'Sorry to hear about you and Mum,' he said in a more conciliatory fashion.

His father's forehead was lined with creases, tributaries ran from the corners of his eyes and pooled in his sunken cheeks.

'Dad, this is my colleague, Dana,' Lachlan added, turning to introduce her.

As she stepped into the kitchen and Pat noticed her for the first time his demeanour changed.

'Good to meet you.' He gave her a warm smile. 'Where are you from, Dana?'

'Sydney.'

'That makes sense. You're much more cosmopolitan than folks around here. And such beautiful eyes.'

'Give it a break, Dad.' Lachlan pushed the apple pie into Pat's hands.

'Have a seat, we can have this after I've made us some tea. You'll have a cuppa, won't you, Dana?' asked Pat.

'That sounds lovely, thanks.'

The kitchen was small and poky. Spots of mould dappled the ceiling and a sour smell hung in the air. Dana tried to imagine Ruth's reaction if she'd known about Pat's living situation.

Pat put the kettle on and removed a knife from a drawer. 'So, how've you been, Lachy?' He cut the pie into neat slices.

'Good, Dad.' The puppy sat sphinx-like, staring at the food. 'Work's work, so I can't complain, and Rachel and the kids are good, too.'

The dog's head popped up over the table.

'Beau! Get away.' Pat said. 'What brings you two down this way? It's been months.'

'A local boy's gone missing. His name's Jayden Maloney, he's in the care of the Department. We were in Killarney yesterday and he's a member of the church. Seeing you were on the pastoral council for all those years, I thought you might be able to give us an idea of who we could talk to.'

'That's a shame. I remember Jayden. I think he's training to be an altar boy.'

'Do you remember anything about him?'

'Not really. Well … no, it's nothing.'

'Come on, Dad.'

'Look, I probably shouldn't mention this, but Blair, you remember him, don't you? He transferred back up from Sydney at the beginning of last year and there's been some complaints.'

'Such as?' asked Dana.

'He gets too involved with the boys. One of the parents complained when he took a group of them to the city without their knowledge, that sort of thing.' He leant down to stroke Beau's head. 'I was always worried about Blair when you kids were younger. There were all these rumours about his father, Phil Hadley. It all came out after he and Lynette split up.'

Hadley. Dana made a mental note of Blair's surname so she could search his name in the client database when they returned to the office.

'What rumours?' Lachlan grabbed for the butter knife. 'What kind of gossip have you been listening to now?'

'Lynette confided in me at one stage – this was years ago – she was worried that Phil had been sexually inappropriate with Blair when he was younger.'

'Sexually inappropriate? What does that even mean?'

'Lynette wasn't real specific, but she told me that she definitely didn't want Phil getting custody. After they finished in the Family Law Court and she won, he just up and left and no-one ever saw him again. With these new allegations about Blair, I just hope it's not going to be a case of history repeating itself.'

'Anything else?' asked Lachlan.

'Well, he was at the Catholic church in Rose Bay. Then the next thing you know, he's back up here living in Warwick. Not what you'd expect.'

'What's your point, Dad?'

'What's a single man his age doing back here? I'm telling you, he came back because something went wrong.'

'Not necessarily. Maybe after he'd lived there for a while, he realised that he wasn't a fan of the big smoke.'

Pat tapped his nose. 'You know what they say. Never ask a Brother where he's going, or where he's been.'

'You really do thrive on gossip, Dad. Makes me wonder what you're doing out here, all by yourself. Don't you get lonely?'

'I'm fine,' Pat said gruffly. 'Beau keeps me company.'

'I was referring to human company.'

'My mate, Pete, comes out sometimes. That's all I need. What I don't need, is you trying out your social work on me.'

An uncomfortable silence fell and Dana focused on her pie. Lachlan looked across to a framed photograph on the windowsill, of an older woman with bold red glasses and a straw hat. She was flanked by two men with their arms around her and a couple of younger boys crouching in front.

'What are the cousins up to these days?' Lachlan asked Pat.

'The usual – drinking and driving trucks. And other

proclivities which I'd rather not mention. They're still under Edith's thumb and doing exactly what she tells them.'

'And how is Aunty Edith?'

'The same. I keep asking her when she's going to retire from the family business, but I don't think she will. She can't help herself.'

'What business is that?' asked Dana.

'Transport,' Pat said quickly.

'Transport?' asked Dana, curious about the sudden electricity in the air between Lachlan and his dad.

Pat smiled. 'Killarney's had trouble moving into the twenty-first century because it's lost a lot of core farming business. Drug crime is up and I know Edith is worried about it. Not to mention, a lot of bad people have moved into town these past few years because of the border crackdowns.'

'Lachlan did mention that,' she said.

'It's a shame, because Killarney's a beautiful place and has a wonderful community spirit.'

When they finished their morning tea, Pat gave Dana a bag of freshly picked apples and plums and walked them to their car.

'Maybe you can drop by again soon, Lachy,' he said, patting his son's shoulder.

'Sure thing.'

'Feel free to bring your beautiful friend.'

'Work colleague, Dad.'

Lachlan started the engine and Dana watched in the rear-view mirror as Pat waved until they reached the bottom of the driveway.

'What were you so worried about?' she asked, noticing Lachlan's expression once they'd pulled onto the highway.

'Don't tell me you didn't see the stack of empty whiskey bottles?'

She nodded and was silent for a moment. 'Do you think there's any truth in what he said about Blair?'

'No, I don't. I've known Blair since primary school and there's no way he'd be involved in something like that.' Lachlan sighed. 'I have to say, it always depresses me when people make out that there's something sinister about the church. I've always found that the people who go to church in Killarney are just genuinely nice folks.'

'Still, it might be worth following up on?'

'Not worth it,' he said, as large splotches of rain hit the windscreen. 'And anyway, I need to get back to the office. I've got to organise a social assessment this afternoon, then pick up the kids and be home in time for our anniversary dinner, otherwise Rachel will kill me.'

Her eyes turned to the endless fields of green. His blank refusal to talk to Blair surprised her. Why was Lachlan so dismissive of his father's suspicions? It was clear that Lachlan was overly attached to the case, and to Killarney and the people who lived there. If Blair knew Jayden from church then it made sense to at least talk to him. It was better than telling their new manager that they'd lost track of a child who was supposed to be in the Department's care.

When they got back to the office, Dana spent a few hours at her desk reading Jayden's child protection history and the struggle of his young life. She was impressed by what a hard worker he was; against the odds he'd managed to find himself a home with

Trevor and Connie and stable employment at the sawmill. She ruminated over what else might be going on and hoped he was alright, wherever he was.

By the time she finished for the day and headed across Queens Park, the rain had cleared. She strode up Godsall Street admiring the glistening dew drops on the flowers and shrubs. As she drew closer to her house she heard raucous laughter and could just make out two people sitting on the verandah. One of them was Susan, but the other person – a man – had his back turned. Who could it be? She wasn't expecting anyone.

When she reached the fence she could hear Susan's voice. The man she was with turned and waved, giving her that broad grin. *Lachlan's brother.* Dana opened the latch on the gate, trying not to trip over her feet as she walked up the path.

'Sean?' Her heart hammered as she took in his glittering blue eyes. 'Fancy seeing you again.'

4

Dana raised an eyebrow at Susan, who shrugged. Clearly, Susan had no idea what Sean was doing there either, but judging by her smile, she was clearly enjoying herself. She stood up and smoothed the material of her coral pedal pushers. 'Oh well, I'd better be going. Great to meet you, Sean.' She headed down the front steps, where the blue star creeper was in bloom among the bricks.

'So, what brings you here?' Dana tried to pretend she wasn't rattled that he'd made himself at home on her verandah. She took a seat next to him; it would be easier to talk without the requirement of eye contact.

He threw his arm over the back of the chair, crossing his legs in a way that reminded her of Lachlan. 'I know it seems weird, but having Lachy visit made me realise how little I've seen of him and what a terrible uncle I've been. I thought I'd drop by and give Patrick the birthday present that's been in my spare room for the past six months. I was really looking forward to seeing them, but when I arrived their place was empty.'

'He did say that he couldn't be late for his anniversary dinner with Rachel tonight, otherwise his head would be on the chopping block – his words not mine. Nice bike by the way, is that a Harley?'

'Triumph Thunderbird. I bought it at an auction in South Australia. Dad and I spent five years doing it up. Mum hates it. She was a nurse before she retired and she's convinced I'm going to have a terrible accident and never walk again.' Sean smiled and she grinned back as though she'd known him for years.

'How'd you know where I live?'

'When I realised my brother wasn't home I swung by his work, hoping I'd catch him. One of your colleagues – Vaughan, is it? – thought he might be with you. He said you lived on Godsall Street, so I took a punt and that's when I bumped into Susan in her garden. She pointed me in the right direction. Lovely lady by the way.'

Dana tried not to think about the cancer diagnosis. 'Yes, she is.' A gust of wind whipped the branches of the neighbouring camphor laurels and she shivered. 'I can't imagine that Lachlan will be home for hours yet. It's been a long day so I'm going to head inside for a drink. Would you like to join me?'

'That would be great.'

Inside, she took Sean's leather jacket and hung it on the rack near the door, then grabbed the wineglasses from the display cabinet and headed for the kitchen. She stopped, almost bumping into him as she turned back for a bottle of Penfolds. The colour rose in her face. 'You can sit here if you like.' She gestured to the Chesterfield before hurrying to the kitchen, relieved to have some space. *Pull yourself together.* She returned with a platter of brie and an assortment of dips and crackers, then poured the wine and handed him a glass. 'Cheers.'

'Yes, cheers.' He grinned at her over his wineglass. 'Thanks for taking pity on me. If it wasn't for you, I'd still be sitting on Lachlan's front doorstep.' He hesitated. 'And sorry about letting my emotions get the better of me back at the sawmill earlier. With Lachlan being the older brother and all, it always sets off my competitive instincts. Ever since we were young I've felt like he's gotten everything – the better clothes, the better grades, the better girlfriends. Sometimes I just need to pull my head in.' He helped himself to the food. 'Did you have any luck finding Jayden?'

She shook her head. 'How well do you know him?'

'In Killarney you can't even duck out for milk without running into five people you went to school with. And Jayden works at the sawmill. He's a nice kid. Always says hi when he comes into the office.'

She found herself drifting into fantasy as he spoke, wondering what it would be like to be close to him, feel his breath on her neck.

His expression clouded with concern. 'Am I boring you?'

Heat scorched her cheeks. 'It's been a long time since I had lunch and this wine is beginning to go to my head. I was thinking of cooking up some steak and salad for dinner, if you're interested?'

'Sure, but let me help. It's the least I can do for crashing your night.'

In the kitchen, she took the meat and salad ingredients out of the fridge and poured more wine. She turned and leant against the bench, watching as he ground salt and pepper over the steaks.

'So, have you always lived in Toowoomba?' he asked, massaging some oil into the meat and taking a copper pan from the wall. 'You don't give me the impression that you're someone who's grown up here.' He turned his head to look at her before switching on the gas.

'I grew up in Sydney, but took a secondment here last year.' She had a fleeting desire to tell him about losing her son, Oscar, then changed her mind. 'But I've landed on my feet here. I've become good friends with Susan, who owns this house and rents it out to me, and I've also become close to her grandson who lives with her, Angus.'

He placed the steak in the hot pan, prodding it with the tongs as it began to sizzle. 'Why isn't the kid with his parents?'

'He's never really known his father and his mum's had mental health and substance misuse problems so she's never been stable.' Dana stared out the kitchen window as diagonal sheets of rain began to fall. 'Problem is, Susan's just found out she has stage four bowel cancer.'

Sean turned to her, holding the tongs mid-air. 'God, that's awful. Poor Susan. What's going to happen with the kid?'

'She's asked me to look after Angus. Which is fine, he's become like a son to me. It's just that I'm worried about what happens when he hits adolescence. What if he becomes this stony-faced, brooding teenager who won't listen to me and is struggling with the fact that all of his family have gone at the exact moment his hormones have kicked in. I'm worried that it's going to end in disaster.' She took a deep breath. 'I think that what he's really going to need is a strong male role model. Someone with parenting experience who can talk to him about what it's like to be a man. I have no idea how I'm going to give him that.'

She paused, realising that whatever gift Lachlan had for getting people to spill their secrets, Sean also had it in abundance. 'Sorry, I didn't mean to burden you with all my problems.'

'It's fine, at the sawmill the only thing anyone ever talks about is how the Broncos are playing and how much booze they drank on the weekend. Believe me, this is a refreshing change.' He reached for the knob of the gas and turned it off. 'Okay. These are ready.'

'God, sorry. I've been talking so much I forgot to make the salad.' She grabbed a bowl and threw together spinach leaves, grape tomatoes, olives and crumbled feta, then mixed in balsamic vinegar and placed the bowl on the table.

She topped up their wine as they sat down. 'This is amazing,' she said savouring the tender meat. 'Really.'

'Thanks. It's the one aspect of cooking I'm actually good at.' He nodded at the Breville coffee machine in the corner. 'I've been thinking about getting one of those.'

'When I moved to Toowoomba I quickly realised that if I wanted a decent coffee in the morning, I was going to have to make it myself.'

'If you think the coffee in Toowoomba's bad, you should try it in Killarney.' He smiled, elbows bent as he sliced through his steak.

'Lachlan and I had one at the cafe yesterday. He described it as tepid brown water.' She laughed. 'Actually, we took a drive to Stanthorpe after we were in Killarney and I ended up meeting your mum and sister. And your dad.'

He looked up from his meal. 'That would have been interesting.'

'They were quite lovely actually,' she said, finishing her wine. She felt a golden glow as they talked and told jokes. After they cleaned up their plates, she served them some ice cream for dessert. It was nearly midnight when Sean stood and walked over to the bay window, staring at the street lights shining onto the wet park. 'Geez, I might have had one too many. It's going to be a while until I'll be right to drive. I should probably call a taxi.'

'You can stay over if you like.' As soon as the words were out of her mouth she wanted to bite them back. 'In the spare bedroom, of course.'

'Of course.'

When she snuck a glance at him she was relieved to see that he was grinning. Everything was going to be fine, she told herself, repeating the mantra her counsellor had given over during the Christmas holidays: *I am happy. I am healthy. I am safe. I am loved.*

He nodded at the Breville and smiled across at her. 'Looks like I'll get to try that coffee after all.'

Sean left early the next morning and Dana drifted around the house with the glossy sheen of the previous night still on her. She listened to her Des'ree CD as she got dressed and then headed across the park to work, careful to avoid the swimming-pool-sized puddles that had formed on the oval overnight.

When she arrived at the office she was surprised to find a dozen long-stemmed red roses on her desk. The card staked in the centre of the bouquet read: *Thanks for all your kindness last night. And for the coffee. Let me make it up to you with dinner Friday night? Sean. X*

She pressed the velvety petals to her face and breathed in their scent. A feeling of warmth spread through her chest as she marvelled at how quickly he'd been able to arrange a flower delivery. She hurried to the tearoom for a vase and water, but when she got back to her desk she stared at the bouquet wondering what to do with it. She didn't want to draw too much attention to herself on the second day back in the office.

Shivani rounded the corner and came into their pod. 'Dana! Welcome back!' she exclaimed, throwing her coat over the back of her chair and leaning against her desk. 'Oh my god! Who are they from?'

Dana peered over the top of the partition to make sure there was no chance of them being overheard. She turned back to Shivani. 'They're from Sean – Lachlan's brother.'

'I didn't even know he had a brother.'

'Me neither, to be honest. He's never really spoken about him.' Dana stashed the flowers under her desk before any of her other colleagues had a chance to comment.

'So, how'd you two meet?'

'Lachlan introduced us when we went out to Killarney to make enquiries about Jayden. Turns out that most of Lachlan's extended family live in Killarney.'

'Wait, you were at work with Lachlan and Sean asked you out on a date?' Shivani's green eyes narrowed.

'Not exactly.'

'Come on. Don't hold out on me!'

'I still don't know what to make of it, really. When I arrived home yesterday, I found Sean on my verandah chatting to my neighbour. Apparently, he'd been hoping to catch up with his brother, but Lachlan wasn't home.'

'Sounds a bit suss to me,' Shivani murmured. 'Has it occurred to you that his sole reason for visiting Toowoomba might have been to visit you?'

'It did cross my mind.' Dana tried to keep the smile from her face.

Shivani threw out her arms in a Roy Orbison rendition. 'He drove all night, to get to you!'

'It was only an hour and a half, but still …'

They collapsed in front of their computers with laughter.

At that moment, Lachlan came into the pod looking expectant. He placed his thermos of coffee on the desk. 'What's all the hilarity about?'

'Nothing,' Dana said flatly. There was no point getting him involved in a relationship that might not last till the end of the week.

'Oh hey, Lachlan,' said Shivani. 'I was just telling Dana that a nice firm massage is exactly what she needs. It'll loosen her up a bit.' She let out a shriek of laughter as Dana shook her head and turned back to her computer.

The entire office had filed into the conference room for the monthly team meeting and Dana stared across the table at Lachlan as he gave an overview of the upcoming team planning day. Again, she pondered whether she should be telling him what had happened with Sean. They'd only had dinner together, she told herself, it wasn't as though she'd entered a life-long commitment.

When the meeting was over, she strolled into the kitchen for a glass of water trying to remember the last time she'd felt this happy. She promised herself that this year she was going to enjoy herself. Allow herself to be vulnerable. Not take life so seriously.

When she returned to the pod and sat down at her computer Lachlan came over and perched on the edge of her desk. 'I just picked up a Notification from the Intake team. It's from the kindy. About five-year-old Brooke Buckley.'

Dana felt a flicker of interest. 'The daughter of the hit-and-run victim your sister mentioned?'

'Yes. It looks like the mother, Amber Lanaski, might be struggling with her mental health and addiction issues. She and Johnny used to lead a bit of a druggie lifestyle before they had Brooke, but once their daughter was born they cleaned up their act. They separated last year. Yesterday, Amber had a meltdown when she was dropping Brooke off at kindy. She screamed at the staff and told them to get out of her face. They're worried she's slipping back into old habits. We'll need to leave in the next half-hour and head out to Killarney to do an assessment.'

'No problem,' she said, beaming up at him, knowing that being back in Killarney would give them another shot at finding Jayden, and another chance to redeem herself. Perhaps they'd even bump into Sean again. Her good mood continued in the car and she tolerated Lachlan's Eagles CDs for the duration of the trip.

When they reached Killarney, they pulled up in front of a small worker's cottage with a wildly overgrown lawn. Christmas lights were still dangling over the fence beside four crooked candy canes. Further up the road there was a man sitting on his front steps singing a Johnny Cash tune. The house was painted green and stood out in the street.

Lachlan waved. 'Sounding good, Arthur!'

'Great to see you back in town, Lachy,' Arthur called out.

'There's another person who's still talking to me,' Lachlan said to Dana as they made their way up the front path. 'Arthur's a local legend. He's out on those steps rain, hail or shine.'

'Hard to miss that house,' Dana observed as they approached Amber's house.

A woman with dangly earrings and a long floral skirt opened the door before they could knock. There was a tightness in her face – he look of someone who wasn't sleeping.

'Amber?' asked Dana.

'Seriously?' replied Amber, before Dana had the chance to introduce herself. 'Like I haven't got enough going on without the bloody Department coming around.' She waved them inside. 'I'm stressed out of my head and some bastard has made a complaint that I'm neglecting Brooke.'

'That's not why we're here,' said Dana, evenly. 'The father of your child has just died under tragic circumstances, and we thought we'd check in and see how you're doing. I'm Dana Gibson. My colleague is Lachlan O'Malley.'

Amber rubbed her eyes. 'Fine,' she said, with resignation. 'But do you mind if I smoke? No offence, but the sight of you people after all these years makes me nervous as hell.'

They walked through a lounge room with children's toys stacked neatly in the corner, across the lino floor of the kitchen and out onto a small deck with a table and chairs. Amber sat down and reached into her pocket for a slim packet of Winfield Blues. She gestured to Lachlan and Dana to sit as she lit a cigarette and stared at a wall of grass growing along the back fence.

'I've been meaning to fix the yard and get some mowing done but it hasn't stopped raining in weeks,' said Amber.

Dana smiled at her. 'Don't worry, I've had the exact same problem.'

Amber's foot jiggled nervously as she exhaled smoke from the side of her mouth. 'What did you want to talk about?'

'We wanted to have a chat about how you and Brooke have been coping since Johnny's death?'

'Pretty shit, really. Brooke keeps asking me when her daddy's going to come back from heaven and she's started having nightmares.' She shook her head. 'Johnny might have been a shit boyfriend when we were together, but he'd really got his act together since she started kindy.'

'How were you getting on when he passed away?' asked Dana, noticing that Lachlan was silent and presuming it was because she'd managed to establish a connection with the mother.

'We broke up last year.' Amber took a drag on her cigarette. 'We were just arguing all the time and decided that we'd be better parents if we were separated.'

'That sounds wise.'

Amber shrugged. 'We went off the rails after Brooke was born, but after you guys threatened to remove her from us it scared the shit out of us, so we went and got help. He's been great with Brooke and tried to see her every other day.'

'And do you feel …' Dana could see Amber was on the brink of tears and chose her words carefully '… like you might be about to go off the rails now?'

'No,' Amber said with a level gaze. 'There was a blow-up the other morning at the kindy and I know they dobbed me in, but they were hassling me about Brooke's speech and I hadn't slept all night and just wasn't in the mood.'

'Do you think Brooke needs help with her speech?'

'Maybe.' She chewed her thumbnail. 'But taking her to a speech therapist is bloody expensive and there's no way I'll be able to afford one – especially now that we won't have Johnny's income to rely on.'

'We can look into it for you,' said Dana. 'See if there's anything we can do.'

'Is there anything else you think we might be able to help with?' asked Lachlan.

Amber pursed her lips. 'I'd like to have a babysitter occasionally. Mum helps out a bit but Dad's not very well – it's hard for her to get up here, so I always feel bad that I'm piling it on when I ask her to look after Brooke.'

'Okay,' said Lachlan, 'there should be something we can arrange.'

Amber ground her cigarette into the step. 'What's going to happen now?'

'I think that under the current circumstances, you're doing everything that you could possibly be doing, so aside from making a few referrals and offering you a support service, I don't think we'll need to be involved. But I'll give you my card, so if you have any issues or you feel like you need some more support with Brooke, just let me know.' Dana took a Departmental business card from her purse and scribbled her name and number on the back.

'Thanks,' said Amber, her body sagging with what appeared to be relief.

Lachlan, Dana and Amber returned inside to the dark alcove between the kitchen and bathroom. 'Do you mind if I do a quick check of the house before we go?' added Dana.

'Do what you have to do.'

Dana took a tour of the house while Lachlan chatted to Amber on the front verandah. After noting nothing of concern she made her way outside.

'Have you heard whether the police have made any headway in finding out who was responsible for Johnny's death?' Lachlan was asking as Dana joined them.

'Nope.' Amber shook her head. 'They spoke to me once and I haven't heard from them again. It pisses me off. Johnny and I might not have always seen eye to eye, but at the end of the day he's Brooke's dad and I want to be able to tell her that the bastard who killed her father is now behind bars and won't be coming out for a very long time.' She stared down at the government car. 'But I'm not holding out much hope. To them Johnny was just another one of those guys from the sawmill who liked to drink too much and was a pain in the arse they needed to put in the cells every second Friday night.'

'Still,' said Lachlan massaging the back of his neck. 'They should be able to give you an update. I can call the sergeant for you, if you like? See if I can find out what's going on?'

'Thanks,' she said. 'He might actually listen to you. Pretty sure this wouldn't be happening if we were one of the posh families in town who go to church.'

Lachlan was silent, making Dana wonder if he agreed.

'Well, lovely to meet you.' Lachlan gave her a reassuring smile. 'Take care and get in touch if you need anything.'

'Thanks,' said Amber standing on her front step and watching until they were in the car.

'What did you think?' asked Lachlan as he started the engine.

Dana pulled the seatbelt across her body and waited until she heard it click. 'She was reasonably insightful. Of course, we'll have to sight Brooke and do a check with the kindy, but given her ex-partner's basically just been killed and she's got almost no support, I think she's doing about as well as can be expected.'

'Agreed,' said Lachlan as he did a U-turn and headed out of Killarney. 'So, what's the plan now?'

'First stop is the kindy. Then I thought we could swing

through Warwick on the way back and pay Brother Blair a visit. See if there's a grain of truth in those rumours that he has something to do with Jayden's disappearance.' She looked pointedly at Lachlan. 'Seeing as I'm taking the lead on this one now.'

They were buffeted by the wind as they ran up the stairs of St Mary's Catholic Parish and through the heavy wooden doors. Dana was met by the scent of incense as she stepped inside. Though it had been years since she'd attended mass she felt strangely emotional under the high vaulted ceilings and large stained-glass windows. Out of childhood habit, she dipped her fingers in the holy water and crossed herself before following Lachlan down the scarlet carpet between the pews. The wind whistled through pillars of marble as they passed the grave of an Irish priest and a set of stairs that led to the bell tower. When they reached the altar, Lachlan called out to Blair, his voice echoing through the cavernous space.

When it was clear there was no-one around they retraced their steps. They were heading down the front stairs when a man got out of a car in a black clerical shirt and white collar. 'Can I help you?' he asked.

'We're after Brother Blair,' said Lachlan.

'He's at the old butter factory in Killarney with some boys from the youth group – he's trying to find a missing kid.' He frowned and shook his head. 'I told him he was crazy, that it was a police matter, but he wouldn't listen. Said the mother of one of the kids had told him that her son had been squatting there for a week with a group of teenage boys and was refusing to come home.'

Dana grabbed at the sleeve of Lachlan's shirt and tugged it. 'Jayden.'

They ran for the car.

Half an hour later they arrived at a dilapidated brick building where the windows that weren't boarded up sported jagged holes through the glass. They parked out the front beside a swamp-green VW Golf.

After a few determined yanks Lachlan managed to open the sliding door and they stepped into a pitch-black room smelling of mould.

'Whose bloody great idea was this?' Lachlan joked as they waited for their eyes to adjust.

Dana took a step forward and something furry brushed against her ankle. The hackles on her neck rose and she stifled a scream. She had a flashback to the year before when Angus had been held hostage in a darkened shed in Crows Nest as she had pleaded for her life. She turned and pushed back through the door, waiting in the bright light until Lachlan joined her.

He followed her back outside, his eyebrows knitted together with concern. 'You okay?'

'Fine.' She shook her head, annoyed with herself. 'Just a bit claustrophobic. There's a lean-to attached to the back of this building. I think we should check there.'

They went around the side through waist-high grass and wildflowers to the rear of the building. Lachlan knocked on the door of what appeared to be a small office and when no-one answered, he pushed it open. They were met by the powerful smell of hot chips and three boys lounging in ancient low-set sofas.

A man with large ears and a balding head, who reminded Dana of a marsupial, was sitting at a table and eating a burger from a white paper bag. When he looked at Lachlan his face broke into a grin. He wrapped up his burger and stood up.

'Lachlan O'Malley,' he said, arms outstretched for a hug.

'Blair!' Lachlan pulled him into a bear hug and slapped him on the back.

'What are you doing here?' asked Blair. He adjusted his glasses and stared at Lachlan. 'It's been years.'

'I'm working for the Department of Families these days.'

'I heard you'd thrown in the carpentry and had gone back to uni. Good on you.'

'Thanks.' Lachlan's expression turned serious. 'Blair, this is my colleague, Dana Gibson. The reason we're here is that a young boy in foster care has gone missing. Jayden Maloney. You haven't seen him, have you?'

Blair took off his glasses and rubbed his eyes. 'We've spent all morning looking for him. We just came back here for a break and a bite to eat. We searched the area around Browns Falls, Queen Mary Falls and the school, but no luck.'

Dana recognised the name from her conversation with Susan. Queen Mary Falls was where Tina had been working, where Angus was staying with his Mum – she hadn't realised it was so close to Killarney. She had a sudden pang of missing him.

'The last time I saw Jayden,' Blair went on, 'was on Wednesday afternoon when I gave him a lift out to the waterfall.'

Dana's heart swooped with disappointment, but she looked at Blair with renewed interest. 'Do you have much to do with Jayden? The people he worked with at the sawmill said he is a regular at church.'

'He's a member of our youth group and he's training as an altar boy. Lovely kid. I hope nothing's happened to him.'

'Well, that's what we're trying to find out. Would you mind if we asked the kids a few questions?'

'Be my guest.'

The three boys looked up at them wearily as Dana and Lachlan entered the room. Dana was shocked by their fresh, soft faces. The youngest looked about eleven; the eldest couldn't have been more than thirteen. The hideaway was well set up with a heater in the corner, beanbags on the floor and an old television on a crate against the wall. Dana glanced at the pile of blankets and clothes under the window and wondered how much time they spent there.

'Do any of you know Jayden Maloney?' she asked.

The youngest of the boys, with a wide pale face, shoved a chip into his mouth. 'Yeah, he's our mate.'

'Well, at least he was till he took the job at the mill and didn't have time for us anymore,' said the older boy with glasses. 'We were dragging him down.'

'That's not true,' the moon-faced boy shot back. 'He was just busy because he wanted to buy some cool stuff when he got older. He used to sleep at the clubhouse before he moved into the caravan – on that beanbag over there.' He pointed to a deflated brown beanbag. 'It was pretty much his bed.'

'When was the last time you saw him?' asked Dana.

'Dunno. Probably out at the falls.'

'And when was that?'

The boy shrugged. 'A couple of weeks ago.'

'Do you guys spend a lot of time out at the falls?'

'Yeah, Browns Falls has been epic with all this rain. We've been doing backflips, front flips and just hanging out there.'

'Sometimes we go there with a few beers and that's when it's really fun to jump in.'

Lachlan's neck was red above his collar. 'You realise that years ago a girl called Marnie Lisotte jumped into the swimming hole from a high rock and fractured both her legs? She's paralysed from the hips down. In a wheelchair for life.'

The older boy looked at Lachlan with disdain. 'That's because she didn't know how to jump properly. We've been going there since we were little so we know where it's safe to jump and where it's not.'

Dana suddenly had a thought. 'Do you think Jayden might have gone for a swim on the day he disappeared? After he was dropped off at the waterfall?' she asked the moon-faced boy.

'We'd done it a few days earlier and it was our best day ever. We took some ham and cheese sandwiches Mum had made us. We hung out there for hours.'

'Sandwiches your mummy made,' mocked the older boy.

'Shut up, pizza face.'

'Okay, boys, that's enough,' said Dana. 'If you see him, please let us know.' She held up her business card and placed it on the crate in front of the TV. 'And we'll have a chat with your parents about the underage drinking.'

The boys groaned in unison, then returned their gaze to the TV.

Outside, Blair walked with them to the car.

'So what's the story with the boys?' she asked Blair.

'They've been shoplifting and getting into a bit of mischief. Just last year one of their brothers was sniffing a can of Rexona and died of a heart attack. They have no idea how dangerous it is. I'll never forget that poor kid being loaded into the ambulance – it was the worst thing I've seen in my life.'

'Was Jayden into chroming?'

'No, never.' Blair shook his head. 'It's not something he was interested in at all. I would say he was focused for a teenager. Wanted to make his fortune and get out of here. At least, that's what he told me.'

'Look, I should probably let you know,' Lachlan said to Blair, 'I'm a bit concerned that as you were one of the last people to see Jayden, you're going to end up being scapegoated for his disappearance. You know what this town's like. People get an idea in their head and it's hard to convince them otherwise.'

Blair stopped dead, his spine bolt upright. 'What do you mean?'

Lachlan turned to face him. 'There's a rumour that there were previous complaints about your involvement with a boy, when you worked in Sydney.'

'But they looked into it.' His voice rose an octave. 'It was unsubstantiated!'

'Sorry, mate. I wanted to give you the heads-up.'

Blair's shoulders slumped. 'What am I supposed to do? I work with these kids day in, day out.'

'Make sure you have professional boundaries in place. No giving kids lifts or buying lunches.'

Blair's eyes bored into Lachlan's. 'If a kid comes to me from a disadvantaged background saying they haven't eaten since the previous day, I'll buy them food. If they tell me they can't get to football training, I'll drive them there. For the love of God, what's the world coming to?'

'I know, mate, just …' he placed a steadying hand on Blair's shoulder. 'Be careful.'

Dana noted the sharpness in Blair's eyes, his tight, pinched mouth. As Lachlan backed the car out of the driveway, crunching over gravel, she tried to assess if the man with high colour in his cheeks was telling the truth. Perhaps it was the pallor of his skin or the look in his watery blue eyes, but she didn't trust him. But Lachlan *did* and that made her doubt herself. Maybe she'd worked so many sexual abuse cases that her radar was broken.

'I know Blair's your friend and you've known him a long time,' she started, 'but I'm not sure you should be tipping him off about people coming for him if Jayden has done a runner.'

Lachlan's eyebrows were raised as they headed back into town past the co-op and petrol station. 'I can tell you with full assurance, it's fine.'

'I really don't think you should let your personal relationship with this man cloud your judgement.'

'My personal relationship with Blair *is* my judgement.' He shook his head. 'Blair's biggest problem is that he's one of those guys who's always been a bit clueless. Like the time he put an ad in the Warwick paper in the Lonely Hearts column before he joined the ministry. Said he wanted the companionship of a woman with a passionate commitment to Christ and a love of good clean fun. Boy, did he cop it that time.'

'I'm just saying, you need to be careful. How does that saying go? *We are all savages on the inside.*'

'I think you're taking that quote out of context and I'll tell you something for nothing – Blair is not a savage. Not even close. In fact, he's one of the kindest, most thoughtful people I've ever met. When I'd just finished high school I was flat broke and couldn't afford to get my car fixed after I cooked the engine. Well, he paid for the mechanic to repair it. And he never expected me to give him the money back – just told me to pay it forward. Not only that, but he used to volunteer as a phone counsellor for Lifeline. It really used to get him down at times, but he told me he'd never quit because of the regulars who relied on him. He's a good guy.'

'Okay, I won't say anything more.'

Lachlan pulled onto the highway, his foot on the accelerator until he sped up to a hundred and twenty kilometres an hour.

'You might want to slow—'

'It's *fine*.'

Back in the Toowoomba office, Lachlan and Dana traipsed up the stairs from the car park and into the lift. When they heard the chime at the fourth floor they stepped out into the foyer and were confronted by a burly security guard, arms crossed as he stood in front of the reception counter.

'Can I help you?' He gave them a hard stare.

Lachlan sauntered over to him and flashed his ID. 'We work here, mate.'

The man nodded and Lachlan used his security swipe to enter the side door.

'Since when do we have security?' Dana asked, pausing at the door and addressing the guard on her way through.

'Since a disgruntled dad burst from one of the interview rooms last week and tackled one of the admin workers.'

'Yikes.'

Lachlan turned back to her. 'I'm just going to grab a coffee. Do you want anything?'

'I'm fine.' As she waited for him down the corridor Dana took the opportunity to type Blair Hadley's name into the child protection database. She knew she'd get a serious rap over the knuckles if she was found out, but if it helped locate Jayden, then so be it.

The only results that came up were a female Blair Hadley, aged sixty-seven, from Mount Isa and an eleven-year-old, Briar Hope, residing in Far North Queensland. She clicked out of the database in frustration, just as Lachlan returned to their pod. The phone at the empty desk next to him started ringing and he ignored it. After it finally rang out there was a short pause before it started up again.

'Aren't you going to get that?' asked Dana.

'Not my job,' he said over the insistent chirp of the phone. 'Keely's been on stress leave for the past couple of weeks and they still haven't transferred her calls. I'm fed up with being her receptionist.'

Dana wondered whether he was still annoyed at her for questioning him about his allegiance with Blair. 'Keely's on stress leave?'

'She was here one day, did a morning on the intake line, then just walked out of the office. No-one has seen her since before Christmas.' His phone started ringing and he gave Dana a dark look as he picked it up.

'Sure,' he said. 'Transfer him to the phone in interview room two.' He hung up and turned to Dana. 'One of the detectives from the Killarney Police Station wants to talk to us – says it's about the drug task force.'

Not long after they had seated themselves in the private interview room the red light on the phone flashed. Dana opened her notebook as Lachlan picked up the call and put it on speaker. 'Ryan!' he said, his hands flat on the table after the officer introduced himself. 'I heard you'd joined the force. Didn't know you were back in the area. How's things?'

'Yeah, good. It's been a few years. Look, I'm heading up Operation Border Control for the drug task force and we're trying to infiltrate the drug trade that's coming through Killarney since we cracked down on the east coast.'

'I'd heard rumours about that,' Lachlan said, rubbing his beard and looking to Dana.

'Anyway, I got word that you lot had been in town this week, and I thought I'd reach out to get a lay of the land. How's your folks?'

'Look, mate, as you probably know, ever since I quit the O'Malley clan people haven't been very willing to open up to me.'

Ryan chuckled. 'I'm not sure they're going to talk to me either.'

'There are worse things than getting divorced, mate.'

'Try telling it to the Catholics.' They laughed.

'I'm trying to find out if that recent hit-and-run might be linked to the drug trade. There's been a few incidents in Killarney recently. I've been working out of the station here for the past few months.'

'Well, maybe. I know that some of the employees at the sawmill liked to party. We spoke to Buckley's ex-partner, but she didn't seem to think that the police were very interested in finding out what had happened.'

'That's not true, there's just been some difficulty establishing who the rider was and who was the owner of the motorcycle. Between you and me, the investigation stalled after we realised it had false rego plates.' Ryan expelled a large breath down the other end of the line. 'The plates on the motorcycle at the time of Johnny's death belonged to a quad bike.'

'Sounds complicated,' said Lachlan. 'Anyway, the main reason we were in Killarney was that a child in our care, Jayden Maloney, seems to be missing. No-one has seen him since last week.'

'Have you filed a report yet?'

'Trevor out at the mill had a chat with the local police. We were in Killarney on Monday and again earlier today, checking if anyone had seen him, but no luck.'

'Actually, this is ringing a bell now. I overheard the constable saying that Jayden's backpack had been found in the barbecue area of Queen Mary Falls yesterday.'

Dana gave Lachlan a quizzical look.

'I hate to say this,' said Ryan, 'but an abandoned backpack may be evidence that we're dealing with foul play.'

'I hope not,' he said. 'That's our worst-case scenario.'

'It's something we'll need to consider.'

Lachlan raised his eyes to the heavens and shook his head. 'Anyway, mate, I'll be in touch tomorrow and we'll talk about next steps if Jayden still hasn't been located.'

'We'll wait to hear from you.'

'And sorry I couldn't be more help this time, but I'll keep an ear out and let you know if I hear anything.'

Lachlan hung up and rubbed his temples. 'I really hope that's not true. After everything that kid's been through, for something terrible to happen to him would be tragic.' He pushed back his chair and stood up.

'Agreed,' she said, concerned by how personally Lachlan seemed to be taking the matter. She closed her notebook and followed him from the room.

Back in the pod, he turned to her. 'Sorry if I was a bit grumpy earlier. The kids kept me up all night and I didn't get much sleep.' He peered out the window, dark grey clouds building on the horizon. 'How about you let me buy you dinner at pub trivia Friday night? Reckon I'm going to need a few drinks after this week.'

She hesitated. 'I'd love to, but I have a date.'

'With who?'

'Your brother.'

'Sean?' He gave a strangled laugh and stepped backwards.

'I didn't think you'd have a problem with it.'

'I don't.'

'Okay then.'

'Okay.'

Perhaps she'd underestimated the rivalry between the brothers. But Lachlan was married, she reasoned, surely he didn't care who she was dating? As he sat down and shuffled papers on his desk without meeting her eyes, it was clear she'd made a mistake by not telling him sooner.

Dana dropped in at Susan's house on her way home from work and found her in the backyard retrieving the washing from the line. When Susan looked up from folding a shirt, her eyes were red and puffy and she hastily wiped the tears from her face.

'Is everything okay? Not more bad news, I hope?' asked Dana.

'Nothing like that. I just got off the phone from Tina.'

'What's happened?'

'She's pleading with me to let Angus stay with her. She's asked if he can go to school in Killarney and live with her. Permanently.'

Dana walked over to the line and unpegged a pair of jeans, not trusting herself to meet Susan's eyes. 'What did you say?'

'I said, no. She knew the deal was that he'd only be there for the school holidays. He's got a scholarship to one of the best schools around and is all set to start in a few weeks. It's infuriating. I used to call her Hurricane Tina. She has this way of manipulating people so it's impossible to say no, but I've learnt that the best way to deal with her is head on, otherwise everyone else gets hurt and she comes out untouched.' Susan let out a long sigh. 'Anyway, I'm not sure when I'm going to be able to get him – I'm not feeling well enough for a long car drive right now.'

'We're heading down that way again tomorrow morning. I'm happy to bring him back with us?'

'Would you? That's perfect. If he's home tomorrow afternoon I can organise his books and uniform. Then he can head back to Tina's and spend the final week of the holidays with her before school starts.'

Dana felt her body sag with relief. She took a white linen shirt from the line and folded it against her chest. 'I've missed him, you know. Since he's been away I've felt like I don't know what to do with myself. I can only imagine how it feels for you.' Dana watched as Susan folded a pair of socks. 'Have you told Tina about your diagnosis yet?'

'No, and I have no plans to, for the moment. As soon as she hears it will be just one more reason why she should keep him.' She gave a resigned smile. 'On a brighter note – what happened with that lovely man last night?'

'It was a really good night, actually. Sean ended up staying for dinner and asked me to go out again on Friday night.'

'How wonderful!' Susan touched Dana's upper arm. 'Make sure you enjoy yourself. Life's not meant to be all work.' She gave Dana a meaningful stare. 'One day you turn around and suddenly you're in the twilight of your life.'

5

A crowd had gathered in the shadow of the Warwick Court House, a sombre sandstone building silhouetted against a dark sky. The first raindrops fell and umbrellas came out, black with a sprinkling of vibrant colours. Spectators huddled together on the stairs. At the front of the pack, journalists with microphones jostled each other beneath the clock tower.

Dana inched towards Lachlan so he could share her umbrella. As he ducked his tall frame to take shelter, he nudged her with his elbow. 'I heard about your visit from my brother the other night?'

She looked up at him, trying to figure out whether he was still annoyed. 'We had dinner at my place after he realised you were out for the evening, and that was about it really.'

'Did he stay for breakfast?' Lachlan asked.

She ignored him. 'Why are they holding the media conference here, instead of at the police station?' In actual fact, she was thankful for the cool air.

'They made a huge mistake treating Jayden like someone who'd absconded from his placement and now they're trying to be professional. And as for making us all stand out here in the rain – they're probably hoping it'll prevent the journos from asking too many questions.'

'Well, I'm glad they're finally treating this with the seriousness it deserves.'

A woman in a navy pantsuit came through the door with a photo of Jayden mounted on a stand. It was the one Dana had seen in his case file – a side-on shot of him with his Michael Jordan backpack slung over his shoulder. The woman was joined by a male police officer. A hush fell over the crowd as she asked for silence. The only sound was the steadfast patter of rain.

'My name is Della Baldwin, Media Officer for the Queensland Police. We are gathered here today to hold a media conference in relation to the disappearance of Jayden Maloney. With me is Senior Sergeant Vince Maretti of the Warwick Police, who will provide his address shortly. Can I please ask respectfully that any questions are left until the end?'

Sergeant Maretti stepped forward. 'The Queensland Police Service are asking for public assistance to locate sixteen-year-old Jayden Maloney who has not been seen for eight days now – which is very concerning for us.' He cleared his throat. 'Jayden is from Killarney and was last seen outside the Queen Mary Falls store on the eighth of January at approximately four pm. He is described as being Caucasian in appearance and one hundred and seventy-two centimetres tall with a medium build, light brown hair and blue eyes. He was last seen wearing a dark-coloured work shirt, brown-coloured pants and black work boots. Anyone with information is asked to contact the police or Crime Stoppers on 1800 333 000.'

'We will now open up to questions,' the sergeant announced.

A female journalist with a glossy black bob and grey steel-framed glasses shot her hand up.

'Yes, Bronwyn.'

'Firstly, the obvious question – why did it take so long for you to treat this as a missing person case?'

'There was some confusion in relation to who had the authority to publicly release information given he is a child in state care.'

Dana whispered to Lachlan, 'Is that true?'

He nodded. 'Apparently there was a lot of back and forth between the Department of Families and the Queensland Police because of the confidentiality provisions regarding the media release of information with respect to children in foster care.'

The same journalist put her hand up again before anyone else had a chance.

'Yes, Bronwyn,' said Sergeant Maretti.

'Is it true that a current member of the clergy in Warwick is under suspicion and that you're in the process of gathering evidence against him?'

'I can't comment on specific persons of interest in this case.'

'Okay, well, is the disappearance of Jayden Maloney in any way linked to the hit-and-run death of Johnny Buckley two weeks ago?'

The sergeant's face gave nothing away. 'At this stage we do not believe there is any logical connection between the incidents and we're treating them as separate enquiries.'

As Dana looked around she noticed a familiar face at the fringe of the crowd. Angus was standing with his mother, her arm circling him protectively. Dana was momentarily confused about what they were doing in Warwick, until she remembered Tina's AA meetings. Dana felt a jolt of resentment towards the woman who'd monopolised Angus's time during the Christmas holidays, but tried to tell herself that perhaps it was a good thing he was spending more time with his mother.

The volume from the crowd increased as a volley of questions were fired from the journalists.

'This is a small town. Why have there been two serious incidents in a week? Is this a case of police negligence?'

Dana and Lachlan both turned as Amber Lanaski started waving her arms and calling out. 'What are you doing to find out who killed Johnny? Why's it taking so long?' She launched herself at the podium and it almost toppled over. 'My daughter needs to know what happened to her dad.'

Della raked her fingers through her fringe and held up her hand in an attempt to restore order. 'That's all the questions we'll be answering today. We thank you for your time.' She spun around and hurried into the courthouse, Senior Sergeant Maretti holding the door open for her and closing it firmly behind them.

Dana scanned the crowd looking for Angus as people started drifting off. When their eyes locked across the crowd he gave her a half-wave, half-salute. A deep melancholy radiated through her as she felt him slipping away from her. She waved back, and for a brief moment it was just the two of them amid the chaos.

Then Tina pulled him away and he was gone.

The interior of the Warwick Police Station looked the same as the other headquarters Dana had visited – carpet tiles, computers, walls with procedural charts, high-vis vests thrown over the backs of chairs. Lachlan fist-pumped the sergeant by way of greeting and then introduced Dana to the man who had made the statement at the media conference earlier that morning.

He showed them to his desk and dragged two additional swivel chairs over, then reached into his satchel and pulled out a white paper bag. The scent of warm cinnamon and dough drifted through the air as he opened the packet.

'Doughnuts, Vince?' Lachlan laughed. 'Really?'

'Mate, stereotypes exist for a reason. I pulled a late shift last night, so I reckon this breakfast is as good as any.' He chewed his food, staring at them with protruding eyes and a hypertensive flush that made Dana wonder whether he had thyroid problems. He gulped the last of an iced coffee then made an elaborate shot for the bin, which missed.

'So, what have you got for us?' asked Lachlan.

Vince reached into his in-tray and slapped a folder on the table in front of them.

Lachlan picked it up and opened it. 'Blair Hadley,' he said, peering at a head shot of Blair in which his ears were particularly prominent. He read from the file. *'Brother Blair charged with four counts of indecent assault.* So, you're working the paedophile priest angle?'

'You betcha.'

'Mate, that's low hanging fruit, even for you.'

'He's got form!'

'What for?'

'Touching someone's low hanging fruit, if you know what I mean.'

Lachlan shook his head and Vince turned his face away, a schoolboy trying to suppress his laughter.

Anger flared inside Dana like a blowtorch. 'Before this descends into complete depravity, what's he supposed to have done?'

'He caught one of the boys at the school smoking in the sports shed. Instead of reporting it, Blair said he'd turn a blind eye if he could put his hands down the kid's shorts. Then Blair asked the boy to do the same to him,' said Vince.

'Come off it,' said Lachlan.

'See for yourself.' The sergeant reached over and turned to the criminal history section in the file, pointing it out to Lachlan.

'I've known Blair since primary school. He's a good guy. If this turns out to be true, I'll eat my hat.'

'Mate, you know as well as I do that if a kid tells you someone's been abusing them, then you have to believe them.'

'How old's the kid?' asked Lachlan.

'Fifteen.'

Dana frowned. 'What's that got to do with anything?'

'Just trying to get some context.'

'Is there any information on why Blair wasn't convicted?' asked Dana.

'It says that the teen made a complaint and gave clear disclosures, but the court process hasn't taken place yet.'

'So that's it then. The matter's progressing through the courts,' she said.

'Looks like it. And then the Catholic Church did what it's been known to do from time to time – geographical solution by moving him to Warwick.'

'That's terrible.' She remembered a priest who'd been transferred to Papua New Guinea only for the abuse to start all over again.

'*If* it's true,' said Lachlan. 'So, you think that he's sexually abused this kid and now he's kidnapped Jayden, or worse?'

'Every rock spider has to start somewhere.'

'Seriously, Vince? You've known Blair since he entered the church. Did you ever get the feeling someone like him would end up a criminal?'

'Nothing surprises me anymore. And you should have more sense than to associate with him given his record – you're supposed to be smart.'

'If standing up for a friend you've had since primary school is stupid, then call me the world's biggest dummy. When are you bringing him in? I'll act as his support person,' said Lachlan.

Vince sighed. 'Don't say I didn't try to talk you out of it … we're having a strategy meeting this afternoon; we'll be doing interviews tomorrow morning.'

'Do you think there's any truth in that journalist's question about the hit-and-run being connected?' asked Dana, like she was being forced to mediate.

'I don't know how you can link a drunk man wandering onto the street with a missing teenager, but some people can find conspiracy in anything,' said Vince.

'And have you been making any headway in finding the perp of that hit-and-run?' asked Lachlan.

'Keep to your side of the fence, mate.'

'We're doing some work with Amber, the mother of Johnny's child, and we said we'd ask you on her behalf,' Dana interjected, trying to calm the situation.

Vince pointed to the blinking red light on his landline. 'I've got no doubt that about half of those messages are from that woman. We're having a few problems tracking the owner of the bike. These bikies use fake rego plates so they can speed through the winding roads to Brisbane in the middle of the night and never get caught. But you can tell her we'll get to the bottom of this, don't you worry.' Vince's phone beeped in his pocket and he dragged it out of his pants and stared at the screen. 'I'll have to go in five, I've got a meeting with the big boss.' He stood and eased himself into a coat with the QPS insignia on the breast pocket. 'How's your aunt these days?' he asked Lachlan.

'Haven't see her lately, but Dad tells me she's well. Still the matriarch of the family. No signs of retiring any time yet.' Lachlan paused. 'I'm surprised you haven't had more contact with her.'

'As you'd know, she's been on our radar from time to time but we've never been able to lock anything down.'

'Always was a sly old bird.'

Vince gave Lachlan a strange look. 'Must have been hard cutting ties with the O'Malley clan. How'd you manage to get out of it.'

'Nothing a career change and a move to a different town couldn't fix. As well as accepting that none of them are ever going to speak to me again.'

'Come on, Lachlan. I think it's time we were heading off,' said Dana.

'Anyway, it's been good to catch up.' Vince smirked and reached out to shake Lachlan's hand. 'Even if you do have some crackpot ideas these days,'

'You, too. I guess I'll see you tomorrow during the interviews. And let me know if you get any real leads on Jayden. I'm worried about him.'

'Aren't we all.' He gave them a weary look then opened the bag of doughnuts. He offered it to them. 'Sure I can't tempt you?'

Lachlan patted him on the shoulder as they walked out the door.

Dana and Lachlan headed south out of Warwick to pick up Angus. After they passed through Killarney they headed out along Spring Creek Road and crossed a small bridge at Browns Falls Park. 'I had my first kiss in the culvert under this bridge.' Lachlan pointed down as they drove across. 'Her name was Jane Higgins. I was twelve and she was a whole two years older than me.'

'You must have been very mature,' Dana said, surprised by how quickly he'd recovered from Vince's accusations against Blair, but happy to be discussing something else.

'Not really. After that kiss she never spoke to me again. I never figured out if it was because I was a bad kisser or if it was just super creepy down there. I had no idea when I took her hand and led her into that tunnel that it was going to be so damp and echoey. I think there might have even been a dead bird in the water. Not exactly the romantic setting I was hoping for.'

They continued uphill along the winding road until they arrived at the car park of the Queen Mary Falls picnic area. Dana unclipped her seatbelt while Lachlan sat with his hands on the wheel staring out the window.

'Do you want to come in?' she asked.

'Not really ...'

'Why?'

'I had a falling out with my Aunt Edith a while back. She runs the place.'

'This is where your aunt works?' she asked. She hadn't realised just how far-reaching Lachlan's family was, or that his aunt was also Tina's employer. 'What was it about?'

'A few years ago, I lent her my car so she could keep it ticking over while I was overseas. She drove it all the way to Cairns and back.'

'Cairns!' Dana let out a horrified laugh.

'It was terrible. Added thousands of k's to the odometer and wrecked the engine, but that's the sort of person she is.'

'Is Sean okay with her?'

'Yeah. They have more in common, I suppose.'

'Like what?'

He rubbed his temples. 'I don't want to get into it.'

She let it drop but made a mental note to ask Sean at the first opportunity. Lachlan remained in the car and made some calls while she headed across to a wooden building with wide front stairs nestled between bottlebrush trees. A sign out the front proclaimed *Edith's Corner Store*.

She passed an elderly couple throwing seeds to squawking rainbow lorikeets as she peered around the side of the shop. A couple of wooden cabins were dotted along a road, and she surmised this must be where Angus and his mother had been staying.

A bell rang over the door as she stepped into the darkened shop. Angus darted out from behind the counter when he saw her and threw himself into her arms, almost knocking her off her feet. She savoured it, relieved that any distance between them had only been in her imagination but understanding his lack of self-consciousness wouldn't last forever, that adolescence was just around the corner.

'How've you been?' she asked.

'Really good. I can show you around if you want?' The pride in his face tugged at her heartstrings.

'That would be great. Where's your mum?'

'She said something about hating goodbyes and not wanting to get too emotional, so she went to the warehouse to get supplies.'

'It's only for a few days,' Dana reassured him. 'Just so Susan can get your uniforms organised.'

'I know, but Mum really loves me, so it's hard for her when I'm away.' He said this without irony as if Tina's previous year-long absence had never happened. He grabbed Dana's hand and dragged her to the cash register. 'What are you having?'

She stared at the drinks list above the counter. 'How about a sparkling mineral water?'

'Edith lets me have drinks for free so you can have one of mine.' He took a small bottle of Schweppes from the fridge and gave it to her. 'But choose something else so I can show you how good I am on the register.'

'Okay, how about a Mars Bar?' She could give it to Lachlan on the drive back.

'That'll be eighty cents, thanks.'

She handed him a five-dollar note and he rang up the amount.

'And here's four dollars and twenty cents change.' He beamed at her.

She smiled. His industriousness was one of the things she loved most about him. 'So, what else have they got you doing while you're here?'

'I serve the customers, refill the paper bags with seeds for the bird feeding, and I've just started filling in the logbook, which is how Edith keeps track of everyone's hours so they get paid properly.' He reached under the counter for a large black leather-bound notebook and laid it in front of her, opening it on a page with a grid detailing the days of the week. 'See, I fill out the employees' start and finish times and the total hours they worked.'

'Very impressive.'

'I have to make sure they put in their hours properly, so they can get paid the right amount.'

'And how much are you getting paid?'

'I'm underage, so I'm not in the book, but Edith gives the money to Mum and then she gives it to me.'

'And have you been saving it?'

'Yes.' His pale eyebrows knitted together. 'Except when Mum needed to borrow some for smokes – but she said she'd definitely pay me back.'

'I see.' Dana tried to keep the judgement from her voice.

'I'm saving up for a Nintendo Game Boy, like Jayden's.'

Dana felt like she'd been struck by lightning. 'Jayden Maloney?'

'Yeah, we take our cokes and chips out the back and feed the rosellas on our breaks.'

'He works here, too?' asked Dana, feeling as though she was still catching up.

'Only a couple of afternoons a week, after he finishes his shift at the sawmill.'

'Why did he want two jobs?'

'He was saving up for his own car. He said he'd take me somewhere once he got it. It sounds really cool. But he never writes his hours down in the book, Edith says it's easier that way – for tax purposes.' He paused. 'I hope he comes back. I really like hanging out with him.'

She knew how hard it was for Angus to make friends and the look of concern in his eyes made her even more determined to find Jayden. 'The police have started a search now, so hopefully he'll be found soon.' She steered the conversation back to what he'd said earlier that had piqued her interest. 'So how many other people who work here are off the books?'

'That's all. Everyone else has to write their hours down normally.'

The bell rang and his back straightened as a woman and two children entered the store. Dana stepped aside as they ordered three Hava Heart ice creams.

Dana checked her watch as the customers went back outside. 'Do you want to tell your boss that we're ready to leave now?'

'Okay, but you'll have to watch the store.' He jogged in the direction of the back door and called out over his shoulder, 'Don't let anyone buy anything until I'm back. You don't know how to use the register!'

Eventually he returned with a woman with short silver hair and a linen shirt with an upturned collar. Her lips were thin, painted an arresting shade of red. She sized Dana up with an arched eyebrow, giving the impression that she didn't suffer fools.

'I'm Edith.' Her voice had a gravelly quality, like that of a seasoned smoker.

'Dana. I'm just picking up Angus and dropping him back to his nan's in Toowoomba.'

'Does Tina know?'

'Yes, it's all been arranged.' Dana removed her ID badge from her handbag and held it up. 'Sorry to blindside you, but I work for the Department of Families. I'm Jayden Maloney's caseworker. I'm just wondering whether there's anything you can tell me about him?'

'Technically he didn't work here, just helped out two afternoons a week.'

'I gather he wasn't on the books?'

'I knew he had the sawmill job. It seemed so cruel that he should be taxed so heavily because of his second job.'

'And I suppose it worked out well for you too?'

Edith's eyes narrowed. 'He was a great worker and a lovely boy. I swear, if I find out that anyone's done anything to hurt him, I'll kill them.'

Dana was taken aback by her threatening tone and fought to keep her expression neutral. 'Do you have any idea what might have happened to him?'

Edith shrugged and shook her head.

'When was the last time you saw him?'

'He worked last Tuesday. I remember because one of the customers spilt a heap of bird seed on the floor and he had to clean it up.'

'And have you ever seen him in the company of Blair Hadley?'

'No, I haven't. Most of the town folk go to the Catholic church in town, but I've never had much time for religion.'

The bell rang as a man entered the shop and Edith turned to him and smiled. 'Hi there, how can I help you?'

When Dana and Angus got back to the Range Rover, Lachlan was leaning against the bonnet waiting.

'Angus, my man!' He grinned and ruffled Angus's hair. 'What's been happening?'

'Not much. Just working in the shop.'

Lachlan opened the boot and stashed Angus's bag.

'He's got some pretty interesting news actually,' said Dana, once they were in the car. 'You wouldn't believe it, but Angus here has become good friends with Jayden Maloney.'

Lachlan's eyebrows rose so high they almost reached his hairline. 'How'd you end up meeting Jayden?' he asked Angus.

'He works in the shop two afternoons a week.'

'Off the books,' Dana said pointedly.

'I hate to say it, but that sounds exactly like the way Aunt Edith operates. How've you been finding the work there, Angus?'

'It's good. She lets us have free drinks from the fridge and twenty-five per cent off food. So that's the best thing.'

'I bet it is.'

Dana fiddled with the radio as they drove along the road to Killarney and when Jewel's 'Foolish Games' began to play Angus put in the headphones for his Walkman.

Lachlan looked over at Dana, his face serious. 'I've just spoken to Blair. I'm going to be his support person when Vince interviews him.'

'You don't think it's a conflict of interest?'

'I'm not Jayden's caseworker anymore – you are.'

Dana was silent. 'I think you need to be clear on your professional framework versus your personal framework. And how you're going to separate the two. I mean, do you really think the police in New South Wales would bother charging Blair if they didn't have a reasonable file of evidence against him?'

'Blair says he was muddled when the police originally interviewed him. He was in shock over the allegations.'

She pinched the skin between her eyes as a headache came

on. 'I just think where there's smoke there's fire. You've got a man who's been charged with indecent treatment of a minor *and* your dad said that Blair's father was sexually inappropriate, *and* the research tells us that perpetrators of sexual abuse are often abused themselves as children. What I do know is, it's going to kill your career if it comes out that he's guilty and you've been supporting him.'

'I'm doing this, Dana. I know he didn't do it and if it makes you feel any better, Blair has agreed you can watch the interview tomorrow morning. He's got nothing to hide. He wants Jayden to be found as much as we do – this way you can be apprised of the situation and can make up your own mind.'

'I guess it's all been arranged then.' She crossed her arms and glanced over at him, his face unreadable as he stared straight ahead at the dark clouds gathering on the horizon.

6

Dana sat behind a one-way mirror looking into the interview room at the Warwick Police Station. Vince was on one side of the table with Blair and Lachlan on the other. Blair had a spot of colour on each cheek and his eyes bulged as he clasped his hands.

'For the purpose of the tape, please state your full name and date of birth.'

'Blair Thomas Hadley. Eighth of February 1961.'

Lachlan glanced at the glass where he knew Dana was sitting, then looked away.

'Do you agree for the record that the date is the seventeenth of January 1997, and the time is ten am?' asked Vince.

'Yes,' said Blair.

'And do you agree that you've been advised that any statements you make during this interview may be used in court at a later date, and that you've been advised of your right to legal representation.'

'I do.'

Dana had a vision of Lachlan schooling Blair on the need for short, direct answers.

'What do you currently do for work?' asked Vince.

'I'm based at St Mary's Catholic Parish, Warwick. I run a few of the local youth groups in the district.'

'How long have you been employed in this capacity?'

'Just over a year. I started in January 1996.'

'And prior to that?'

'I was employed in Sydney at St Mary Magdalene in Rose Bay. I worked there for five years before I came back to Queensland.'

'And what were the circumstances of your transfer?'

Blair blinked. 'There was an allegation.'

'What was the allegation about?'

'That I'd ... inappropriately touched a fifteen-year-old boy on his private parts, and then asked him to do the same to me.'

'You touched his private parts?'

'Yes, I mean, no! That was the allegation, but it wasn't true. I was naive. I befriended a boy who I thought I was helping, but I was wrong. He took advantage of me.'

'*He* took advantage of *you*?'

'He told me he needed money for food, school books and clothes, so I helped him out. But then he started asking for more and more, showing up at the youth group with brand new Nikes and the latest Nintendo games. By the end I was giving him fifty dollars a week – that's when I had to say "no" and put a stop to it. A week later, he put the complaint in.'

'What was the outcome of his complaint?' Vince's double chin bobbed up and down, a toad ready to pounce on its prey.

'I was questioned by the police, they charged me, and put me in a cell for a few hours.'

'You were put in jail for a few hours? For something you didn't even do?'

'I've forgiven him now, I've made my peace with it. He's a very confused kid.'

'That's big of you.'

Blair looked confused. 'Is that a question?'

'So, what was the outcome of the court case?' asked Vince.

'I'm not sure yet. I'm due to appear in the Tweed Heads Court House next month.'

'And what are the charges?'

'You mean, you don't know?'

'I'm asking you to confirm them for me.'

'Four counts of indecent assault.'

'And what does the church think of these allegations?'

'Initially, they were supportive, they knew how much of a toll it had taken on me and my mental health. I was very upset about it, so it was decided that I needed a break from the city. There was an opening at Warwick and they knew I'd grown up here and that my family were still here, so they helped me move. But last week they suspended me, pending the outcome of the case. They said it's untenable for me to be working until …' he coughed '… until the charges have been dealt with.'

'And when did you first meet Jayden Maloney?'

'Shortly after I moved to Warwick. He was a regular at our Friday night youth group in Killarney. He was also training as an altar boy.'

'And how was the training going?'

'He was exceptionally good at it. Most boys his age get distracted, but he always had the hymn books out before I asked, the communion wine and wafers ready to go.'

'How would you describe your relationship with him?'

'As I said, he regularly attends the youth group out at Killarney and I assist with his training as an altar boy. Occasionally I would give him a lift to church because he didn't have a car.'

'So, you gave Jayden lifts, just like you gave money to the boy in Sydney? Do you see a pattern here?'

'It was different. Jayden was genuine. He didn't have parents and he's a good kid. I knew he'd never use me in that way.'

'And when was the last time you saw Jayden?'

'On the eighth of January. I gave him a lift out to Queen Mary Falls – he said he was meeting a friend.'

'Did he give you a name for the friend?'

'No.'

'And how was he during the lift?'

'He seemed nervous, as though he had something on his mind.'

'Did he tell you what it was?'

'No.'

Vince began to drum his fingers on the table. 'What happened when you dropped him off?'

'He got out of the car, stepped over a wooden fence railing, gave me a little wave, then disappeared down the path.' A shadow passed over Blair's face. 'I haven't seen him since.'

'And when did you first learn that he had disappeared.'

'He wasn't at youth group on Friday night, which was unusual. But then when he didn't show up for church on Sunday I thought something was amiss – it was out of character. I checked in with Trevor at the mill the next day and he wasn't at work. We've been trying to get the community involved in searching for him ever since.'

'Do you have any theories on what might have happened to him?'

'No.'

'None at all?'

'No.' Blair's hands were shaking and he clasped them together in an effort to keep them still.

'May I remind you that anything you do or do not say, may be used against you in court?' He paused. 'So, I'll ask you one final time. Do you have any idea what happened to Jayden Maloney on Wednesday the eighth of January, the day he disappeared?'

'No.'

'I'm ending this interview at eleven-forty am.'

Vince was fuming. Flowers of sweat had bloomed under the arms of his pale blue shirt as he crossed his arms tightly across his chest. He struck the stop button on the recorder so hard that it almost flipped.

Blair's mouth was turned down as he stared at the table. He put his hands over his face and began to sob.

A downpour started at the exact moment Lachlan and Dana stepped out of the police station. A splash hit Dana's forehead and she reached into her handbag for an umbrella. She offered to share it with Lachlan, but he shook his head and made a run for it. Dana joined him in the car a moment later.

'That came out of nowhere,' she said, as she stashed the umbrella in the footwell. 'How was Blair after the interview? Did he seem okay?'

'Not really – he was upset. He wanted to head straight back to the priory.' Lachlan wiped the water from his cheeks, his face as dark as the storm clouds. 'What did you think of the interview?'

'Look, I know you're friends, but I've never had a good feeling about him ... especially with his history.'

Lachlan's eyes narrowed. 'So, you're basing your dislike of him on women's intuition?'

'Well, when you think about it, my intuition is really just the sum total of my experience and learning in the field. So maybe I am.'

'You told me that you were a lapsed Catholic. Are you sure you're not projecting your feelings about the church on to him? Making him seem worse than he actually is?'

'I don't think that's it. I'm worried that he might be one of those perpetrators who insert themselves into the drama of a child going missing, make a big ruckus and get everyone involved, when he's actually responsible. It's been known to happen. Some predators get a secondary thrill from outsmarting everybody.'

'You could not be more wrong about this. Truly, this is why they can't get men to be primary school teachers anymore. Or kindy teachers. Or swimming instructors. It's because as soon as you show an interest in working with children, you're labelled as a paedophile.'

'That's slightly dramatic.'

'I swear, last week I was at a kid's birthday party and I took a few snaps of my daughter. I looked up to see a group of mothers staring at me like I was the spawn of Satan – just for taking photos!'

'It must be extremely hard being a man. I can see how you drew the short straw there.'

'You can laugh, but working with children has got us all absolutely terrified. In fact, next time I go to a park, or a sporting fixture, or a family gathering and I want to take photos of my own child, I'm going to wear a sign that says *Not a Paedo*. And I'm going to buy one for Blair too.'

'I can see this is something you feel strongly about. Maybe we should talk about something else?'

'Of course I'm upset! I'm basically the only guy left in our office. And I want to be clear that you're wasting your time if you're trying to suggest Blair is responsible for Jayden's disappearance.'

'Okay, we'll just have to agree to disagree.'

'Fine, but before you say anything else, I'm going to swing past St Mary's before we leave and have a word with the priest – it's just not fair how he's being treated.'

'That's such a bad idea, Lachlan! Blair's now a suspect in Jayden's disappearance and you're his support person. How's it going to look if he's responsible?'

'I've known him for nearly thirty years. I'm going to drop by and see if I can help, because that's what friends do.'

Lachlan pulled into a diagonal park in front of the church and yanked on the handbrake. He stared straight ahead out the window, anger emanating from him in waves. 'You can come in or stay in the car – up to you.'

'I think I'll just go for a wander,' Dana said, hoping that having some space from each other would give him a chance to calm down. 'Stretch my legs.'

As he jogged up the stairs of the church she hoisted her umbrella and headed down Palmerin Street in the rain. She steeled herself against the wind, unable to believe how badly things were going – their inability to see eye to eye about Blair. If she could just find Jayden, then the animosity between them would disappear. With the lapels of her jacket clutched to her chest, she hurried down the wide street, the palm trees in the church yard offering little shelter. She ducked into a coffee shop on the corner, swinging the door open and dumping her wet umbrella in a basket by the entrance. A woman in a cardigan with streaks of grey through her jet-black hair was at the counter, flicking through a *Woman's Day*. She leapt to her feet when Dana came in.

'Terrible weather, isn't it?' she said in an odd, high-pitched voice. 'Can I get you anything?'

'A latte would be great, thanks,' said Dana.

The woman smiled. 'We don't do those new-fangled drinks, but I can get you a filter coffee? And a slice of apple crumble, if you'd like?'

Dana contemplated the drip machine with uncertainty, figuring that if nothing else she was sure to get a caffeine hit. 'That would be lovely, thanks.' She pulled up a seat at the counter and reached for a newspaper.

The woman took the glass jug from the warming plate and poured coffee into a mug. There was a stiffness to her manner. 'So, what brings you to Warwick? I'm guessing you're not a local.' The woman eyed Dana's suit with suspicion. 'You can't get slacks like that here.'

Dana had no desire to discuss what she did for work, so tried to keep her answer vague. 'My colleague's at St Mary's having a chat to one of the brothers.'

The woman's head snapped up. 'Which brother's that?'

'Brother Blair.'

'How interesting.'

Dana couldn't help herself. 'Why's that?'

The woman lowered her voice. 'Folks have started to get

suspicious of him – you know, after word got out about what happened in New South Wales.'

'And what was that?'

'I don't like to spread rumours, my brother-in-law is a police officer, you see ...'

Dana nodded sympathetically.

'But he said that Blair Hadley had been abusing a teenager. And that Jayden Maloney was about to tell on him too.'

Dana was shocked that news of Blair's alleged crime had already spread and that the Warwick locals appeared to be just as outraged by Jayden's disappearance as they were in Killarney. 'Did your brother-in-law say anything else?'

'Not really. Blair used to come in on Tuesdays for my tea and pikelets.' She looked agitated as she watched a branch outside being swept along by a gust of wind. 'But one day he got very angry and asked for a refund on the stew.' She set the cup of coffee and slice of apple crumble down in front of Dana. 'He said it was disgusting.'

Dana took a sip of the coffee and immediately regretted it. She pulled her mobile from her handbag and made a show of frowning. 'I'm so sorry, but can I please get this to take away?'

'Yes, of course. You must be very busy.'

Dana stood and took the take-away coffee and plastic container from the woman.

'If you're ever in town, you should come along to one of our CWA morning teas. It really is a lovely group.'

As Dana made her way back to St Mary's she threw the take-away in the bin. For the first time, she stopped to appreciate the grandeur of the gothic-style building, the octagonal spire reaching into the sky above the parapet. She recalled the white marble of the altar inside, the stained-glass rose window. How had such an awe-inspiring church, on par with those she'd seen in Sydney or Melbourne, come to be built in such a small town? She could only assume that the locals at the time had offered up serious money for its construction.

She went up the front steps through the double-panelled timber doors, crossing herself as she stepped into the cool space, a refuge from the wild weather outside. Once again, the church was deserted, the scent of frankincense drifting through the air. She found Lachlan up the front near the altar.

'Did you talk to the priest?' she asked, hoping they could hurry back to the car and retreat for home.

'Yes, I had a chat to the guy we spoke to the other day. He's very worried. He said that when Blair came back from the interview he was extremely distressed. Father Gleeson said to try in here, apparently he often comes in to pray when he's troubled. Could you look in the office? I'll check out the back.'

Dana strode past the stations of the cross, irritated that they were wasting so much time on Blair when they should be searching for Jayden. She took a deep breath and ran her hand across the polished wood of a pew, remembering the midnight mass she had attended with her parents each Christmas. Staying up late to sing hymns with her mother had brought joy and comfort. She poked her head into the door of the empty office, still thinking about the self-reflection of church that had once brought time and space to think, to be a better person. She'd just started contemplating whether she should return to confession when she heard raised voices. She stood silently among the pews trying to figure out if she'd imagined it. A loud cry jolted her into action. She ran towards the back of the church to a set of dark wooden stairs. A shaft of light sliced through a flower-shaped window creating a complex and shifting pattern on the wall. Above her, a wire with a wooden handle hung from the ceiling. The bell tower.

Her footsteps echoed as she jogged up the wooden steps and through a door with a sign: *No Entry.* Inside was an old spiral staircase. She paused when she heard the sound of wailing – a man in distress – and the low tones of Lachlan attempting to provide comfort. She bounded up the last of the stairs, her chest growing tight as her breathing constricted. Gripping the low railing, she made the mistake of looking down, at the now distant scarlet rug. Her stomach lurched and a sweat broke out on her forehead. She flattened her body to the wall, closed her eyes, then forced herself onwards.

When she got to the top landing she could see Lachlan through the partially open door, his back to her.

'I can't do this,' Blair's voice was trembling. 'I went through it last time and it almost killed me. Now it's happening all over again. I gave them my whole life, then they turned on me.'

'Not everyone—'

'And this time the betrayal is so much worse because it's happened in my home town, where everyone knows me. I could deal with it in Sydney, no-one knew me there, they hadn't seen how much of my life I'd devoted to others. But in Killarney they all know that, and they've chosen to ignore it.'

Dana's palms were sweating as she pushed the door open and stepped onto the landing. Open arches were cut into each side of the tower and above her, thick wooden beams supported a brass bell that hung from the roof. The heavy din of wind and rain whirled around them.

Blair looked pale and gaunt as he stood at the furthest arch, his back to the town as it spread out behind him.

'Go away,' Lachlan mouthed when he registered her standing there. He put his hand out to stop her coming any closer.

She ignored him, deciding that Blair was less likely to hurt himself if he knew she was there. 'We need you to come with us Blair.' She took a step towards him. 'So, we can chat. Nothing's ever that bad that you can't talk about it.'

'It is that bad,' Blair said, unsurprised to find her in the bell tower. 'It doesn't matter what I do, it always turns out the same – with me being accused of something terrible, being called a blight on the body of Christ.'

'But surely God wouldn't want you to—'

'God doesn't give two shits about me!' Blair turned and looked behind him, contemplating his next move. 'Even Dana doesn't believe me. And you've told me how much you respect her. She's tarred me with the same brush as everyone else, like she's judge, jury and executioner. Look at her – judgement rising off her in waves.' He edged backwards.

Dana held her breath, panicked.

'Come on, mate, think about what it will do to your mum,' said Lachlan. His voice was calm, but his forehead creased with anxiety. 'The death of her only son. It'd devastate her.'

'She'll be better off.'

'You don't mean that.'

'It's true. It'd give her a break from the small-town gossip, the endless speculation about why I never had a girlfriend after I left school.' He stared past them as if they were no longer there. 'I don't care about me anymore. I just want this to be over. And when it is, everyone will be happy.'

Blair backed away from them, terrifyingly close to the drop below. Dana's heart was racing. She wanted to reach out to him, but the slightest movement could send him free-falling.

When Lachlan spoke again his voice was low. 'Are you questioning your faith, Blair? Is that what this is?'

Blair laughed bitterly. 'On days like today when it feels like the whole world is against me, sure. But before all this happened, I had a vocation, I wanted to be a priest.'

'You'll get your purpose back, mate. I know you will. Pretty soon these ridiculous complaints will be a thing of the past.'

There was silence. For a moment all Dana could hear was the wind rushing through the tower. The sound of her own beating heart. She inched forward.

'Please, Blair. Please don't do this,' pleaded Lachlan. 'Remember what it was like when Phil died? What it did to everyone?' Lachlan took a step towards him. 'Do you remember being so sad you couldn't even speak at his funeral?'

Blair's shoulders sagged and he leant against the arch for support. Lachlan rushed forward, grabbing him and propping him up as his legs gave way. Dana went to help, but not before seeing the look of rage Lachlan directed at her as he put his arm around Blair and helped him across the landing.

They drove back to Toowoomba in silence under a mauve sky. In the end they'd driven Blair to Warwick Hospital where he'd been admitted to the mental-health unit overnight.

'How dare you barge in like that,' Lachlan had yelled at her in the hospital corridor, his face contorted with anger. 'I had the situation completely under control.'

'Maybe you should be thinking about Jayden instead of obsessing about Blair,' she'd yelled back. She'd only been trying to help. She wondered if Blair's suicidal ideation was an indicator of a guilty conscience, but didn't want to get into it with Lachlan again. She had tried to change the subject, but the only thing that came to mind was Sean, and whether she was going to make it back in time for their date.

When Lachlan flicked on the headlights and glanced in the rear-vision mirror, she could see the irritation in his eyes. She wondered when their relationship had become so strained. Last year he'd been one of her closest friends, she could have trusted him with anything. Now they were standing on opposite sides of a fast-flowing river. Unable to bridge the gap.

7

Dana skidded around her bedroom, trying on clothes. She settled on a navy shift dress and heels before checking her appearance in the bathroom mirror. She put on some blush and mascara then grabbed her handbag, rushing through the front door and bolting across the park.

In the end she was five minutes early. She sank into the cushions at the front of the Tatts Hotel, ordered a whiskey, and tried to regain her composure. She'd just finished her drink when she spotted Sean across the road. He stood outside the PF Chicken Bar checking for traffic and cocking his head in side-to-side movements. The decisiveness in his stride as he crossed the street made her stomach flutter.

She thought about what Susan had said earlier – that life shouldn't all be about work – and decided that she was going to cast off the shackles of the awful day she'd just had and throw caution to the wind. It would be nice to just relax and enjoy herself for a change.

Sean spotted her as soon as he walked into the pub. He came over and kissed her on the cheek. 'Nice dress,' he said.

'Thank you.'

'Is it something you've just bought?' His line had the ring of rehearsal and he gave her a sheepish grin.

'No – but thank you. How's work?' she asked.

'Busy. We've had to fill some orders but they've been delayed because of the rain, so I've been running around like a lunatic trying to catch up. What about you? How was your day?'

'I spent the morning talking to the police about Jayden Maloney, then there were all these other dramas at the church.' She remembered Susan's advice about life beyond work. 'Anyway, enough about that. Tell me, how do you find living in Killarney?'

'I grew up there, so I've always had a soft spot for the place,' he said with a wistful look. 'I travelled for a bit when I was younger, lived in Scotland for a few years, but the homing instinct was strong so I returned to the coop.'

'What drew you back?'

He gave her his best travel guide impersonation and flashed her a cheeky grin. 'Killarney was named after the town in County Kerry, Ireland, because it has similar scenery. It's a beautiful part of the world.'

'Sorry, but Lachlan beat you to that one. He told me that piece of trivia on our first visit.'

'Does he have to one-up me at every turn? Okay, I've got more. You may or may not know that David Malouf wrote a book called *Harland's Half Acre*, which was set in our beloved town.'

'Ooh, a literary reference. That's good!'

'And of course, there was the tornado in 1968 which smashed the town while everyone was watching speech night at the local theatre.'

'I see.'

'And in terms of tourist attractions you can't go past Queen Mary Falls. If you're free on Sunday, I could take you out to enjoy the majesty of a thousand litres of water rushing down a mountain.'

Her heart leapt when he alluded to a future date. 'Sounds incredible,' she said, trying not to get ahead of herself. 'So, what was it like growing up with Lachlan?'

'I could tell you about what he used to do to me as a child.'

'What did he do?'

'There were a lot of big hills behind our house when we were growing up and he used to put me in a sawn off forty-four-gallon drum and roll me down them.' He paused. 'If you come closer you can see my scar.'

Dana leant in to look at the raised lump above his eye and he surprised her with a kiss. She was caught in the undertow, her head spinning. She pulled back, struggling to focus. 'If I don't stop now I'm not going to be able to drag myself away,' she whispered.

'Fine by me.'

'Yes, well.' She laughed. 'We don't want to get kicked out of here just yet – we haven't had dinner.'

They ordered some drinks and read the gold-embossed menus.

'Should we share a bottle of wine?' Sean asked, turning to signal the waiter.

'That would be lovely.'

Once they'd ordered their meals, Dana sat back in her chair and looked across at him. 'So, what's the story with you and

Lachlan? Are things really as strained as they seem?'

'The problem with Lachlan is that he's always believed he's the alpha dog. But what he's never understood is that *I'm* the alpha.'

'Can't there be two alphas?'

'No, Dana, there cannot be two alphas.'

'It'd be a nice concept if it helped you two get along?'

'You clearly have a limited understanding of pack mentality.'

'I'm hoping you're not too much of an alpha, that I'll get to see your soft underbelly at some point.'

He patted his rock-hard stomach. 'I think you'll find it's not exactly soft.' He winked at her.

She shook her head and laughed despite herself. When they finished dinner they wandered upstairs to the dance floor, which was buzzing with people. They sank into a couch and ordered another bottle of pinot noir. A crowd of teenagers seized the table behind them, shrieking with laughter. Frankie Valli's 'Grease' wafted from the speakers. Dana hummed along as the night air began to cool. She nuzzled into Sean's chest and drifted in a golden glow of happiness.

'Should we go back to your place?' he asked when last drinks were called.

She laughed at how confident he was. The thought of leaving alone was inconceivable. They stumbled outside, arm in arm, and caught a taxi back to Godsall Street. Somehow, she found her keys and they stumbled through the house into the kitchen. She poured two glasses of chilled water and led him to her room before excusing herself to go to the bathroom.

When she came back, he pulled her close. His eyes flashed and she felt the thrill of electricity as his mouth met hers. She slid her hands into the back of his jeans and tugged his hips towards her. He smelt good, a mixture of sweat, laundered shirt and cologne.

'Let's get you out of these clothes,' he whispered as he unzipped her dress and pulled his arms from his shirt. He kicked off his jeans and boxers. She was surprised by his body, the powerful chest and definition of his biceps. His hands went to the hem of her dress and he yanked it over her head. She fell onto the bed and he moved on top of her. She ran her fingernails down his back as he kissed her and began to push inside.

'Sean,' she panicked. 'I'm not on the pill.'

'I've got a condom on,' he said.

She touched the latex pulled tight over his penis and giggled awkwardly.

She felt a rush of pleasure as he slid inside her, his mouth dipped to her neck, his stubble grazing her skin. She rocked against him until he moaned quietly in her ear as he came.

When they were done, he pulled himself onto her chest and stared at her with awestruck wonder. She baulked at the sudden intimacy and reached to the bedside table for a singlet. The spell was broken and he rolled onto his back and shut his eyes. As she nestled under his arm, her mind replayed the events of the night, and she was suddenly riddled with doubt. *What would happen now? Had she slept with him too soon?* She wished for a jar in which she could detach her brain like a pair of false teeth. *Why on earth had she drunk so much?*

She was still awake when the birds started squawking beyond the window. She propped herself up and gazed at Sean as he slept, drinking in the coffee colour of his nipples, the silken hair of his chest.

He woke up and looked at her with one eye. 'Morning,' he said.

'Morning to you, too.'

'Did you sleep okay?'

'Not too bad,' she lied.

She prepared him a coffee and made a beeline for the shower. When she was dressed she found him on his phone in the lounge room, wearing his clothes from the previous night. He hung up when she came in. They parted on the verandah and he smiled and waved before disappearing down the street. When she returned to her room, she saw that he'd folded the clothes she'd left on the floor and stacked them on her bed.

Dana spread the newspaper on the table in front of her and lingered over a breakfast of poached eggs and hollandaise sauce. She contemplated heading into the office – it would be quiet on a Saturday so she could catch up on work – but was diverted when she heard pounding on the front door. She padded into the hallway, wondering if Sean had returned. When she opened the door, Angus pushed past her, flinging himself on the lounge and sobbing into the cushions.

'What's wrong?' She had a terrible feeling she knew what he'd come to tell her.

'Nan's dying.'

She put her hand on his shoulder, trying to hold back the surge of her own emotions. 'I'm so sorry, Angus.'

He sat upright, his face red, his cheeks wet. 'Why didn't you tell me?'

'I thought she should be the one to break it to you.'

'She didn't. I found a letter from the palliative care team,' he said, stumbling over the pronunciation of palliative. 'I wasn't sure what palliative meant so I looked it up in the dictionary. It said, palliative care helps people live as comfortably as possible when they have a life-limiting illness. That means she's going to die.'

Dana was at a loss for what to say. 'No-one knows for sure when that will happen. It could be weeks, or it could be much longer than that.'

'I know.' He was trying to act tough, but his bottom lip was wavering. 'I figured out something was wrong. She's always sleeping in and she hardly eats anymore. We had Chinese last night, which is her favourite, and she hardly touched it. So, what's she got?'

'I think this is something your nan should discuss with you.'

He booted the coffee table with his feet. 'I'm sick of you both treating me like I'm stupid. I'm not stupid!'

'C'mon, sweetie, you know I don't think that. It's okay for you to feel sad and angry because it's just ...' She blinked to keep herself from crying '... It's very sad'.

He stared straight ahead, his face hard. 'I should just get used to it. Everyone I love leaves me. My grandfather, my dog, Jayden and now Nan.'

'I don't think that's true. I'm here for you and I'll always be here. I'm not going anywhere.'

'People always say that at the start, but something always comes up and they leave. Then when I ask why, they say they had no choice in the matter.'

His words cut to the bone. So many people had let him down and she was determined not to be one of them.

'Anyway, it'll probably make Mum happy,' he said, before she'd had the chance to reassure him.

'Why's that?'

'Because she's been hassling Nan to let me live with her. She always says that it's not right that she gave birth to me and now she doesn't even get to bring me up. She said we could stay in the cabin in Killarney. I could keep my job at the shop.'

'And what do you think?'

'I would like to try and live with her again.'

Dana let his admission wash over her. Maybe he would be better off with his mother. What did she know about raising a teenager? What little claim she had over him would surely be gone once Susan was no longer alive. She forced herself to speak. 'Maybe we could do something nice this afternoon, after I've put in a few hours at the office. We could go to the park or get one of those Nintendo games you're keen on.'

He shook his head. 'I've got a better idea, I thought we could do some investigating today – and find Jayden.'

'I really don't think it's a good idea. The last time we—'

'It's not the same as last time. Trying to find a friend is totally different from investigating the murder of two ladies we didn't even know. We can just drive to Killarney and talk to Jayden's friend, Brian, who lives at the pub.'

'I'd love to Angus, but last year when I let you investigate with me, I wasn't really in my right mind and I've promised myself I won't put you in that kind of danger again.'

'But there was no problem, I was perfectly fine. Nothing even happened to me.'

'Angus, you almost died!'

'Fine. I'll just go home and do nothing then.' His shoulders slumped and before she could stop him, he'd trudged out of the room, his head bowed with a dejection that almost broke her heart.

At the office she swiped her card and entered the security code to turn off the alarm. The air inside was stuffy and as she rounded the corner into the pod she found Shivani at the computer, sipping from a can of Red Bull.

'God, Shivani, energy drinks on a Saturday morning? You're going to die of a heart attack.'

'This affidavit isn't going to write itself. I'm going to pump it out this morning so I can see *Jerry Maguire* at the movies with Jody after lunch.' She looked up expectantly. 'You should come with us – I hear Tom Cruise is to die for.'

'See how I go.'

She rolled her eyes. 'Yeah, sure. Have you given any thought to the Noosa mini break?'

'It sounds amazing, but I'll just have to wait until this Jayden stuff dies down.'

'Fair enough. Any news on what's happened to him? You must be worried.'

'No.' She felt a queasiness deep in her gut as she sat at her desk.

While she was waiting for her computer to boot up, she opened the compactus and located the McCluskys' foster-carer file. She flicked through the pages until she came to the foster-carer assessment. For the next thirty minutes she was engrossed in reading: Trevor owned the sawmill business and he and his wife, Connie, had a number of investment properties. There was no suggestion that they were in it for the money or that there'd been any concerns about the standard of care they'd provided. They'd been given glowing reports at the training they'd completed. There were no red flags in their file. Aside from the criminal charge Trevor had acquired in his twenties for public urination, they were squeaky clean.

She knew that reading reports could sometimes give an entirely different picture from the reality of visiting a carer in person and had a surge of energy as she contemplated what she was about to do. She dragged her notebook from her handbag and called Trevor. Would she be able to come out and see where Jayden had been living? There was a note of apology in his voice when he told her that he was at the mill, but his wife would have no problems with Dana visiting. Once she was speeding down the highway in the work car towards Killarney she immediately felt better.

On her way through town Dana made an impulsive stop at the Killarney Hotel where ten gleaming motorbikes were parked out the front. After wondering whether any of them were responsible for Johnny Buckley's hit-and-run, Dana went inside, passing a trio of men drinking schooners at high stools on the verandah. At the bar, a woman with bright red hair looked up from pouring a beer and gave her a wide, friendly smile.

Dana flashed her work ID. 'I'm Dana Gibson from the Department of Families. I was hoping to have a chat with Brian – sorry, I don't know his last name. Do you know where I might find him?'

The woman's head tilted to the side. 'My son, Brian?'

'Is he friends with Jayden Maloney?'

'He is and, to be honest, I'm glad someone's getting their act together and doing something to find him. I'm Cynthia. Brian's in the dining room. Just head out the back and I'll be with you in a tick.'

Dana walked through the pub and into an extension that served as a dining area. The air was stale in the windowless room. The walls were covered with maps of the local area, a photograph of two craggy bushmen, some mounted saws and bottles, and a spindly plant attempting to climb some lattice. She found herself with a sudden urge to return to the breezy benches on the front verandah.

A boy with neatly combed hair was sitting in the far corner, his head bent over a book and a packet of Smiths crisps in his lap. Cynthia appeared behind Dana and ushered her over to where the boy was sitting.

Cynthia reached into her son's packet of chips and he slapped it away. 'Mum!' he said.

She gave Dana a withering look. 'Honestly, you carry them in your womb for months on end, go through a twenty-hour labour and this is your reward.' She blinked as if she'd suddenly remembered her manners. 'Can I get you anything? A coffee? Glass of chardonnay?'

'I'm fine, honestly. I was hoping to find out more about Jayden Maloney. Whether you had any idea where he might be?'

'We haven't, have we, Brian.'

Brian shook his head, gazing at them with doleful eyes as he sipped his pink lemonade.

'The last time we saw him was two weeks ago – he came in on the weekend and you boys spent the afternoon playing pool – but since then, nothing. For a while there, I was going to take him in, but I'm a single mum and I can barely manage this one on my own. Then he went and stayed out in that caravan at Trevor and Connie's house ' She leant across to Dana. 'I have to tell you, I'm really worried. I've got this bad feeling. I've been thinking I should put some posters of him around town and leave my name as a contact.'

'That's an excellent idea,' said Dana.

'The police are saying they're doing everything they can, but there's no urgency. I keep wondering, would this be happening if he was a middle-class kid who wasn't in foster care?'

Dana could see that Cynthia wasn't a woman to be underestimated. Brian finished his packet of chips and licked the salt from his fingers.

'Did Jayden ever do or say anything to suggest that something was wrong? That he might have been worried?' she asked him.

'He's one of the bravest and kindest guys I know,' Brian said with a lisp. 'There was this one time where this idiot, Rodney, kept picking on me – stealing my tuckshop money and calling me names. Anyway, after he'd stolen my sausage roll and strawberry milk, he was sitting in the grandstand and Jayden walked over to him and they talked for ages.' Brian grinned. 'I don't know what Jayden said to him, but from that day Rodney never bothered me again.' Brian scrunched the empty crisp packet into a ball. 'I hope he shows up soon.'

As Dana drove towards the McClusky residence she detoured past the scene of the hit-and-run. Johnny Buckley only lived a block or two from the pub – she wondered if it really was an accident that had led to his death? As she turned the corner she passed the quaint green house opposite Amber Lanaski's place. The old man was in his usual position on the front stairs, a heavily pregnant red terrier sprawled at his feet. She skidded over to the kerb and opened the car door just as he was launching into a rendition of 'Auld Lang Syne'.

As she picked her way along the cracked red path bordered by clumps of rosemary he stopped singing. 'No offence, but usually a woman like yourself would take one look at a big, bearded man like me and cross the road.'

'None taken. I'm Dana, by the way.'

'I'm Arthur. Arthur Compton.' Close up his hair and beard were snowy white, his pale blue eyes the colour of water. 'What brings you to my humble abode?'

'I work at the Department of Families in Toowoomba. I'm looking for Jayden Maloney. He's sixteen and has light brown hair and blue eyes. Apparently, he's often seen with a Michael Jordan backpack. I was just wondering if you've seen him come past at all?'

'Ah, yes, he's a good boy. Never too busy to stop and say hello.' Arthur's winged eyebrows came together in a way that reminded her of her grandfather.

'I don't suppose you remember when you last saw him?'

'Oh, it would have been over a week ago.'

Her eyes narrowed. 'That's about when he disappeared. Any chance you could be more specific?'

'Oh, well, let's see. It was the same day as my Meals on Wheels comes. I was looking forward to the chicken pie they've been doing lately. So, it would have been a Wednesday.'

'Did Jayden say anything to you?'

'That was it actually, he hardly said anything at all, which was unusual. He's usually quite talkative. But that day he told me he was going to do the right thing. He told me there was no time to chat as he was in a hurry. He seemed very determined.'

'Did he tell you where he was going?' She tried to keep her voice steady as adrenaline raced through her veins.

'He didn't stop, just called out as he passed. I was singing "Greensleeves". There's not many teenagers like him these days. I do hope you find him.'

Dana leant against the railing feeling deflated and hoping that the visit to the McCluskys' house was going to prove more fruitful than her efforts so far. She was about to head back to Susan's car when she thought of something else.

'Arthur, I don't suppose you were sitting out here on the night of the hit-and-run, were you?'

He visibly shrank into himself as he stared up at her. His voice was low. 'I've been waiting for someone to ask me about that.'

'What did you see?'

'I saw Johnny Buckley go past. I knew he'd been at the pub – that's his Friday night routine. He stopped to sing a line of the Men at Work song. That was the joke between us, you see. He was always a bit of a rascal, so I used to sing, *Johnny be good, be good*. And then he'd join in with the chorus.' He tugged at his white beard and stared into the distance. 'After he left I heard an almighty noise. A bike came tearing along the street. Johnny was further up the road when the bike hit him.' Arthur put his hand to his cheek. 'George and Frank ran out to help.'

Arthur's eyes had started watering, but she couldn't help herself. 'Then what happened?'

'The rider got up and started to limp away. He had a motorbike helmet on so I couldn't tell who it was. He pulled out his mobile phone and it looked like he was going to call someone. Maybe the police.' Arthur paused. 'I remember thinking it was strange that he would try to call someone when he still had his helmet on.'

'Maybe he had concussion and wasn't thinking straight?' she suggested.

'You could be right. Such a tragedy. I was praying that Johnny would pull through.'

'You didn't contact the police?' asked Dana.

Arthur's eyes filled with guilt and the dog rose from the ground and licked his hand. 'I would have, but I knew George and Frank would have spoken to them.'

She heard the trauma in Arthur's voice and felt sorry for him. 'Thanks, Arthur.'

As she walked back to the car she could hear the sound of his rich baritone in her ears.

O' Danny boy, the pipes, the pipes are calling,
from glen to glen, and down the mountainside.
The summer's gone, and all the roses falling,
'tis you, 'tis you must go and I must bide.

The McCluskys' house was opposite the church on the hill, making Dana wonder whether its proximity was part of the reason Jayden had been so attracted to the services. The sound of organ music floated from the building as she squeezed past vehicles parked on both sides of the street. As she exited her car, churchgoers were filing down the front stairs and mingling on the lawn at the end of a wedding.

It was like going back in time. Everyone in their best clothes – men in suits and women wearing floral dresses as they clutched their handbags. There were so many people Dana wondered whether the entire town was in attendance. With a pang, she realised that she missed the sense of community the church had provided. Perhaps that's what she should be doing on the weekends instead of working straight through. But the truth was, ever since Oscar's death she'd lost faith. The idea of God who'd allowed her only son to die filled her with ambivalence.

She met Connie McClusky in the front yard of a high-set brick home and followed the rhythmic swishing of her ponytail as she strode down the side of the house, through a side gate and under an arch of climbing white roses. A caravan was parked at the end of their generous backyard. Inside was a small bed and table with a cushioned sofa, which ran around the edges of the van. The velour curtains and brown carpet gave it a slightly dated feel.

'It's not much,' Connie said, as they stared at the *Ace Ventura* and *Friends* posters that Jayden had used as decoration. 'But it seemed to make him happy.' She sat down at the table, then gestured for Dana to do the same. 'I hate to admit this,' Connie said, fingering the small gold cross around her neck, 'but when Trevor told me that he'd offered to let Jayden stay here I didn't want a bar of it. I mean, Phoenix was only eighteen months old and Griffith was three. I already had enough on my plate.'

'That's understandable.' Dana smiled, hoping Connie would take her into her confidence.

'But it was actually the opposite. He was so helpful. He'd look after the kids if I needed to duck out, make sandwiches for them, and he was so good with his hands. He fixed all sorts of things that were broken around here – cupboard doors, leaking taps. I don't know how I ever managed without him.'

'What did he get up to in his spare time?'

'Regular teenage stuff, I guess. He was into basketball and went to youth group and church. He also had a small group of friends he hung out with. They liked to spend their time at the swimming hole near Browns Falls.'

'Was there anything that happened in the lead-up to his disappearance? Anything he was sad or worried about?'

'Well, he used to confide in me sometimes, about how depressed he was that his parents aren't in his life and all the problems he'd had with his aunt.' She hesitated.

'Yes?' prompted Dana.

'I'm not sure.'

'Even the smallest of things can be important sometimes.'

'I wasn't going to tell you this, but on the morning of his disappearance I had a bit of a go at him.' She put a thumbnail to her mouth. 'I was tired and sleeping badly. I was trying to find the camera so I could take some photos at Griff's birthday party and I usually keep it up in the cupboard, but I just couldn't find it anywhere. I'm embarrassed to admit this, but I accused Jayden of stealing it, which is especially shameful after I found it in the glove box of the car a few hours later. Turns out my husband had borrowed it for a buck's party and didn't think to put it back. Anyway, when I found it I just felt like the worst person in the world. You don't think that's why he left, do you? Why we haven't heard from him?'

'I very much doubt it,' said Dana. *Though it would not have helped.* 'Do you mind if I have a look around?'

'Go for it. I'm just glad that someone is taking this seriously.'

On the bedside cabinet was a can of Lynx deodorant and a tube of Clearasil. In the first drawer she found his Game Boy. The second contained a black velcro wallet with Jayden's bank card, bus pass and a condom. *Was he sexually active? Or was it just something he carried with him to make him seem more mature than he really was?*

In the clear insert at the front of the wallet was a Polaroid of a young woman. She was sitting on a swing with her hair in pigtails and wearing a pinafore. There was a similarity to Jayden around the eyes and in her upturned nose which made Dana certain it was his mother. She felt a wave of sadness that he'd lost his mum at such a young age and felt as though she was trespassing on his private pain. A yellow Sony Walkman was on his bed. He clearly hadn't been planning to go for long and now it had been over a week.

She opened the caravan door and thanked Connie for her time. She retraced her steps back to the front yard and found a cameraman setting up a tripod on the perimeter of the property, his ABC News van behind him. Dana headed to her car, deep in thought. As she was starting the engine, she remembered what she'd read in Jayden's case notes. *Jayden had never missed a day of work. He had no interest in drugs and wasn't into absconding.*

She felt a terrible anxiety and a tightness in her chest. When she arrived home at 5 pm she went straight to the lounge room and turned on the TV. On ABC News a female newsreader was addressing the viewers in a serious tone.

The foster mother of Jayden Maloney, a missing teen from the small town of Killarney, has made an impassioned plea for the community to help find him. Connie McClusky last spoke to Jayden on January eight before he left for work.

The segment cut to Connie standing outside her home with her sunglasses perched on top of her head.

'Please, Jay, come home. You're not in trouble and the kids miss you. We all miss you. All we want is for you to come back to us safe and sound, and for this all to have been a huge misunderstanding.'

Jayden's backpack, with a Michael Jordan logo on it, may be a key source of information to finding him. Police have identified a person of interest in Jayden's disappearance, with a name yet to be released publicly. Authorities have ruled out a link between Jayden's case and the hit-and-run accident in Killarney the week before.

When the news program was over it occurred to her that she hadn't had a chance to think about Sean all day. She rummaged through her handbag for her phone, hoping for a message about their date, but her heart swooped when she was greeted by a blank screen. He'd no doubt been just as busy as she had.

She fired off a text asking him what time he wanted to meet at Queen Mary Falls the next day, and hesitated before signing off with a kiss.

When Sunday lunch came and went, and she still hadn't heard from Sean, she started vacillating between despondency and anger. To keep herself busy she whipped up a tuna casserole but didn't feel hungry. At 3 pm she checked her phone, certain he would've been in contact. Once again, the screen was blank.

She was about to force herself out of the house for a run but decided to tackle the problem head-on by speaking with him. Her call went straight to message bank.

Hello you've reached Sean. I'm not around right now but you know the drill ...

She stabbed at the red button on her phone, his voicemail irritating her as much as the fact she hadn't heard from him. Feeling defeated, she ran herself a bath with the Lux body wash she'd been given for Christmas. As she lay back in the water she made some stern resolutions about the next time she found herself dating someone. One, she'd figure out whether the person was worth investing in before getting emotionally involved. And two, she'd make sure they were reliable.

8

On Monday morning Lachlan arrived early in his Range Rover. He jogged down the front path in the drizzling rain, smiling as he met Dana at her front door, droplets of water dripping from his fringe.

'Don't you believe in umbrellas?' she asked him, surprised to find him in a good mood after the tense argument they'd had about Blair the week before. She decided not to bring it up, for fear of upsetting the delicate equilibrium that had been restored.

'That stuff's for wimps.' He handed her a large take-away coffee and a brown paper bag. 'Bacon and egg brekky wrap with special sauce, just for you.'

She breathed in the delicious aroma. 'You're a lifesaver.'

He looked at her as she sipped the warm, strong coffee. 'I don't want to tell you that you look like shit, but ... anyway. How's things with my brother?'

'You know how I told you that I had a date with him on Friday night? Well, he was supposed to take me to Queen Mary Falls yesterday but I haven't heard from him.'

'God, that's poor form – even for him.'

'It's fine, I gave myself a good talking-to last night and I'm pretty much over it now.'

He chuckled. 'I'm sure there's a reasonable explanation – you're the best thing to happen to him in ages. Anyway, we should probably head next door and pick up Angus.'

Dana grabbed an umbrella and they made a dash for the car. Lachlan beeped his horn and after a few moments Susan's door opened and Angus hugged his nan goodbye.

He's forgiven her, Dana noted with relief. She wound down her window and waved at Susan as Angus jumped in the back seat.

'Dinner, if I make it back early enough?' she called out, wondering if Susan could hear her over the din of the rain.

Susan smiled and gave her a thumbs up.

When they arrived in Killarney, Lachlan pulled up at the police station where he'd arranged to meet Sergeant Maretti. After he hopped out, Dana shimmied over to the driver's seat and had just flicked on the indicator when there was a tapping on the passenger window. She jolted with fright then looked up to see Sean signalling her to wind the window down. He was wearing a leather jacket and his hair was dishevelled.

'Hi Dana. Can I jump in for a sec?'

He slid into the passenger seat, the scent of his aftershave curling around her. She turned to him, waiting for him to speak.

His brow was creased with concern as he leant in towards her. 'I'm so sorry I haven't been in touch. I lost my phone right after I got back from Toowoomba and I've only just found it again. Apparently, I left it at the pub and one of the women who works there took it home and has been trying to contact me ever since. You probably thought I was ignoring you or something.'

'It's fine.' She kept her voice casual. She didn't want to have to explain the situation to Angus, or for Sean to know that she'd spent the weekend in a state of confused agitation.

'I'm so sorry. What did we do before mobile phones, hey?'

'Used landlines?' she replied, unable to mask the sarcasm in her voice. 'If you didn't want to talk to me, that's fine. Just be honest about it.'

'I am being honest.' A whining quality entered his voice. 'I know that you probably think that I'm flaky, but I genuinely lost my phone. I don't know what else to say.'

'Uh-huh.'

He looked so stricken that she began to feel sorry for him.

'So, what are you guys up to now?' he asked.

'Angus is going back to his mum's. I'm just about to drop him off at the store at Queen Mary Falls.'

'Oh, great. Look, I've got to pass on a message to Edith, so what do you say I make it up to you and take you up to see the waterfall like I promised?'

'I'm working, Sean. I've lined up some interviews with people from the church who knew Jayden.'

'It'll only take half an hour. And it's not every day that you get to see all that water rushing down the mountainside.'

She hesitated, not wanting to give him the impression that his disappearing act was something she'd condone in the future. 'What do you say we swing by Browns Falls first?' she suggested, relenting. 'Angus says Jayden and his mates spent a lot of time hanging out there before he went missing.'

~

They parked near the falls picnic area and Angus ran ahead, pleased to get out of the car and show her the sights. Dana and Sean followed behind, passing the signs for the scenic walk to Browns Falls. She watched as Angus darted towards the river that flowed through the culvert; two concrete arches with a corrugated iron underlay below a bridge. A strange sense of foreboding came over her as she went down the path and entered the cavernous space, shivering as their footsteps and Angus's calls of delight echoed around them.

When they emerged into the light beneath a canopy of rainforest she stopped, taking a moment to breathe it all in. Angus scrambled over a log that was slippery with moss and leapt from rock to rock across a vigorously flowing stream. Dana clambered over the log, thankful she'd worn sensible shoes. Sean took her hand as they reached the rocks and she smiled up at him.

After a series of smaller cascades they reached the main waterfall, a spectacular sight after the recent rains. She watched as Angus attempted to duck in behind the roaring sheet of water and came out laughing when he was almost drenched with spray. A group of young teenagers, two boys and a girl, sat on a ledge across from them, cheering as one of the males leapt into the deep water.

Her thoughts immediately turned to Jayden. Was it possible he'd been swimming in one of these waterholes the afternoon he disappeared? She tried to imagine him jumping from the rock ledge as this boy had just done. Could he have slipped and cracked his head? Or landed on a submerged object and never resurfaced? It took a moment for her to realise that one of the boys was waving. As he came towards her, she recognised him as the youngest of the group she'd met at the butter factory.

'I remember you!' the boy said. 'You were that lady who came and talked to us with Brother Blair.' Droplets of water dripped down his pale shoulders.

She smiled. 'That's right. Sorry, I don't think I caught your name.'

'It's Tyler. Tyler Henrick.'

'I'm Dana Gibson. What's been happening lately?'

'Not much. I tried to get the gang back together and I even told them I had a whole packet of gobstoppers but no-one was interested. They've been hanging out with other kids since Jayden disappeared.' His face was filled with disappointment and she was tempted to give him a hug. 'It just hasn't been the same without him.'

'You were good friends, were you?'

'Yeah, he was the best. He was four years older than me, but he was always nice. And he didn't care what people thought of him. A lot of people used to call us dorks for going to church, but he never let it faze him.' He let out a loud sigh. 'I've been coming here every day. I keep hoping he might show up for a swim.'

'Well, I really hope he turns up soon. And I'll let you know if I hear anything.'

As Tyler was walking away, Sean sat down next to her. 'Who was that?'

'One of the kids I met when we were looking for Jayden.' She paused, wondering if she should confess that she was thinking about work again. 'I keep wondering if Jayden Maloney got into trouble doing something foolish. Jumping off the rocks and never coming up again.'

He grimaced. 'It's been known to happen. There was this girl in my year, Marnie Lisotte, she—'

'Broke her legs and ended up paralysed?'

'How'd you know?'

'Lachlan told me.'

'Of course.' His face broke into a grin. 'We spent almost our entire childhood out here.'

'Really?'

'It was heaps of fun. We used to do bomb dives off that ledge when the swimming hole was full. We'd run around the rainforest pretending we were in the army.'

'Sounds very wild and free.'

'It was. Not like these days, where everyone's so worried about people hurting themselves.'

'You never injured yourself?'

'Only the one time. I had a few cracked ribs after I swung off a vine and crashed into some rocks.'

'No brain damage?' she teased. She hadn't completely forgiven him.

His eyebrows shot up and he let out a loud and hearty laugh.

She glanced at her watch. 'We should probably head back soon. Tina's going to be calling out a search party.'

They drove beneath a grey sky along a road shrouded by towering eucalyptus trees. At the Queen Mary Falls car park, Dana took Angus's bag from the boot and put a hand on his shoulder. 'Make sure you give your nan a call tonight. She's going through a lot at the moment, so it'll be really nice for her to hear your voice.' She hugged him tight, breathing in the scent of his hair for a moment longer. When she raised her head, she saw Tina lugging a garbage bag along the verandah of the store.

'Bye, Dana!' Angus jogged across the road towards his mum.

Sean got out of the car and stood next to her as Angus bounded up the front stairs of the cafe.

'He found out about Susan yesterday morning,' she said, waving to Tina.

'How did he take it?'

'Not well. He's a smart kid, so he was always going to find out sooner or later. I think Susan made a mistake not being upfront with him.'

'I guess she was probably trying to find the right moment.' Sean took her hand. 'What do you say we start that walk?'

She hesitated, wondering if it was wise to go on a romantic nature walk with him, especially after the promise she'd made to herself over the weekend. Then she reminded herself that she was going to relax and live a little this year, let herself be vulnerable. She fell in step with him as they strolled past picnic tables and barbecues and set off along the track that led to the waterfall.

In front of them a sign said: *Cliff Circuit. 580 m return walk to the picnic area. Please take notice of the safety signs.*

The greenery of the surrounding scrub changed to the pale grey of gum trees as they headed further along a bitumen track. Sean took her hand and a warmth swelled in her chest as bell birds called out around them. A torrent of water roared through a swollen creek under a bridge. The path became steeper as they crossed over and strode up to the lookout. Once at the top, she held onto the railing and stared at the wall of white water running down the smooth rock. Sean put his arms around her from behind and she leant back into him, feeling the firm resolutions she'd made only the night before drift away and float downstream.

'It's not Niagara Falls, but I reckon it's pretty close,' he said.

'It's beautiful.' She could feel his heart beating through his shirt. When they'd stared at the water for a few minutes he took her hand again. As they returned down the hill, Sean gestured for her to follow him along the side of the creek. His face was lit with mischievousness as he stood on the edge of a deck, the water roaring beneath a forty-metre drop.

'Isn't it a bit dangerous without a handrail?' she asked.

He put his head to the side and grinned at her in a way that made her short of breath. 'I promise, I won't let anything happen to you.' He walked out to the middle.

She stepped across and joined him, grabbing him around the waist to steady herself.

'See? It's not so bad,' he said.

Her adrenaline spiked and she suddenly felt out of control. She could be swept away at a moment's notice. She peered over the cliff where the valley spread out below them. Sean pulled her into his arms and kissed her and she held on tight as spray whipped around her face and the water roared in her ears. She reached her arms around his waist and tucked her fingers into his back pockets, dazed by a rush of blood and the scent of his aftershave. She was surprised by how quickly she was falling for him. After Hugh, she didn't think she would feel this way again. But was it real? Or was the intensity of her feelings due to loneliness? The pine trees by the water's edge swayed back and forth, bent over and straining in the wind.

9

Sean and Dana strode hand in hand back to the car park where a rainbow lorikeet was feasting on the blossoms of a bottlebrush tree.

'Do you mind if I just duck in and say a quick hello to Aunt Edith? There'll be trouble if she finds out I've been here and haven't dropped in,' Sean said, giving Dana a quick peck on the lips before they went up the stairs of the store.

The bell chimed above them as the door swung open. Tina was chewing gum behind the counter and moving hot pies around the bain-marie with a pair of tongs. Sean disappeared into the kitchen and Dana smiled at Tina in an attempt to bridge the awkwardness between them. *Surely they had something else in common other than Angus?*

'Can I get you anything?' asked Tina. 'You look like you could use a drink.'

'Orange juice would be great, thanks.' Dana wiped her forehead then handed over a two-dollar coin. 'Where's Angus?'

'In the cabin with his head in a book. You know what it's

like – he chooses books, I choose looks. Or crooks, 'cos let's face it, there's been a few of those in my life.' Her lightning bolt earrings jiggled as she threw her head back and laughed.

Sean came out of the kitchen lugging an enormous cardboard box. He bent over and started restocking the shelves with tins of Milo.

'Not bad, hey?' Tina said, staring at the back of his Levi jeans. 'If you're single there are worse places you could end up than Killarney, isn't that right, Seany?'

He straightened and turned around. 'What?'

'Nothing.' Tina winked at Dana.

'Did you have much to do with Jayden Maloney when he worked here?' Dana asked, trying to change the subject. She wasn't sure what Tina would say if she found out Dana was dating Sean.

'Not really. I'm pretty sure he thought I was just a boring old lady.'

'How long has he been working here?'

'Few months, I guess. You didn't tell me this was going to be a bloody interrogation!'

'Jayden was in foster care so we're talking to everyone who knew him.'

'In that case, you should probably ask Angus. Those two are thick as thieves.'

'I'll do that. And what about Wednesday the eighth of January? Were you working that afternoon?'

'I'm always at work.' She shrugged. 'See, told you I was boring.'

Edith swept through the kitchen door where Sean had emerged from a moment earlier. 'Tina, love, would you be able to go to the co-op and pick up a dozen two-litre milks, please? Oh, hello,' she said to Dana as Tina headed for the door.

'Dana Gibson. Jayden Maloney's caseworker.'

'Yes, I remember. We're all so worried about him, so if there's anything I can do to help, just let me know. Anything. And Sean will help, too, won't you, love?' She placed a hand on her nephew's shoulder and Dana noticed him flinch. Dana had a sudden flashback to the photograph she'd seen at Lachlan's father's house. Aunt Edith, the matriarch of the family who bossed everyone around. It made sense. Sean and Tina were obeying her every command.

'As I said, please let us know if you hear anything,' she continued. 'We're all devastated that the police haven't been doing enough to find that poor boy.'

Dana had the feeling Edith's outrage was rehearsed, a performance to demonstrate how much she cared. To profess sadness over Jayden's disappearance without making an attempt to find him was as pointless as screaming into the wind. Without action her words were meaningless.

Once Sean had finished unpacking the stock, he and Dana said their goodbyes. Outside, dramatic grey clouds hovered on the horizon and a crack of lightning split the sky. Dana's hair whipped around as she jogged down the stairs after Sean. They darted across the road and sprinted back to Lachlan's Range Rover. The clouds unleashed and rain lashed at the windows and beat the roof with a sickening intensity. She glanced through the windscreen at the blackened sky and flicked the windscreen wipers on.

~

Visibility was so poor that by the time they'd made it to Brosnan Road on the outskirts of town Dana was driving at a crawl so they didn't skid off the road. When they reached the main street a group of men were running back and forth between a truck filled with sandbags and the row of shops. Inside, she could see the business owners moving their stock to higher ground. Lachlan was on the verandah of the Killarney pub waving at them. The moment Dana killed the engine the deafening wail of the warning sirens started. Sean and Dana rushed from the car into the pub. Once they'd reached the safety of the verandah awning, she put her fingers in her ears to drown out the noise.

'Flood sirens,' Lachlan shouted unnecessarily. 'Coming from the fire station on Ivy Street. It's been all over the news. The SES has issued a warning and a lot of homes have been asked to evacuate.'

She looked up the street, half expecting a river of water to gush down the mountains. 'What do we do now?'

'We should be alright inside the pub until we get a better idea of what's going on.'

'I really should get home to sandbag the house.' Sean glanced over his shoulder at the darkening skies.

'Don't you dare,' said Lachlan.

'What am I supposed to do?'

'Nothing. Best we can do is go inside, grab a drink and wait for the SES to give us instructions.'

They made their way into the dining room at the back of the hotel where an SES co-ordinator in a black cap was issuing directions to a group of men in fluorescent orange jumpsuits and hard hats. The small army marched past, each one carrying hessian bags over their arms.

Lachlan tapped an elbow of one of the men on his way out. 'Need any help, Mike?'

'Grab some gloves and a pile of bags and come with. We're heading out to sandbag a few of the houses near the bridge.'

Dana watched Sean and Lachlan grab the last two sets of hats and gloves and hurry after the others. She felt a flash of annoyance at their blatant sexism and being left behind, then stalked over to speak to the man in charge. 'Is there anything I should be doing? Anyone I can help?'

His eyes blazed with irritation, making Dana wonder if she'd offended him. 'Cynthia is run off her feet. If you speak to her, I'm sure she'll be able to put you to good use.'

Dana went next door to the bar in search of the publican. People were rushing in all directions, some carrying blankets and heading back outside, others coming into town mud-spattered and soaked, or standing at the bar looking for sustenance. The roar of the rain and wind went up a notch and, for a fleeting second, she worried that the roof was going to be ripped off. She got out her mobile to call Tina and check that she and Angus were okay, but cursed when she realised there was no reception.

Instead, she reached behind the bar to use the landline. When there was no answer, she let the number ring out and put it back on the receiver. She was about to hit redial when the phone began to ring.

'Hello?' The voice on the line sounded desperate.

'It's Dana here. Who am I speaking to?' asked Dana.

'It's Amber from Arbutus Street. There's water lapping at the top step of our place. We're surrounded. Brooke's with me. I don't know what I'm going to do.'

'Have you called the police?'

'I called the SES and told them we'd packed up our belongings and were ready to go, but they said it was too late to evacuate. I've been trying to call the police, but I can't get through. I'm freaking out!'

Dana scanned her mind for information on what to do if your house became flooded then gave up and used her common sense. 'Get to the highest part of the house and take Brooke with you. Is there a manhole up through the ceiling?'

'Yes, but I don't know how to get into it. We can't get there. The water's coming up too quickly, I—' The call cut out.

Dana's heart was in her mouth but luckily the phone rang again. It was Amber, breathing heavily into the phone.

'Amber. What's happening?'

'We're on the kitchen bench. I've got some water and food to keep with us in case the water comes up.'

'Okay, okay, take a deep breath. How is Brooke?'

'She's here with me but she won't stop crying. I'm worried she's going to end up with pneumonia again. She was premature. She's got weak lungs. I don't think she'll cope if we get stuck here.'

'Just hold the line. I'll go and speak to someone to get you some help.'

'Okay, thanks, but hurry. Please.'

Dana rushed out into the crowded dining room and located the SES co-ordinator talking to a group of volunteers.

'We'll be sending rescue teams from the police station and the school is going to be used as an evacuation centre to house people who've been displaced from their homes,' he was saying.

Dana waved at him urgently and he held a hand up to his audience and turned to her.

'What is it?' he asked.

She explained Amber's situation and he pulled a phone from his pocket and made a call. Dana rushed back to the phone to let Amber know that someone was on their way. As soon as she'd hung up another call came through and she was speaking to another women in need of assistance. She spent the rest of the afternoon answering calls and ferrying messages back and forth to the SES coordinator.

When she finally returned to the bar a few hours later it was packed with people. The radio was on full volume and playing the latest news bulletin.

A severe flood warning has been issued for the Condamine River. Major flooding is occurring along parts of the river between the Loudoun Bridge and Cotswold. Evacuation orders have been issued to residents in these areas and police are urging them to make arrangements as soon as possible. For flooding emergency assistance call the SES on 132 500. For life-threatening emergencies call triple zero.

There was a strange buzz in the air, a mix of fear and excitement as a crack of thunder ripped through the sky. At the far end of the bar, a piece of paper with the words *Doctor* scrawled across it had been stuck to the wall under a set of bull's horns. Beneath it a man with a shock of silver hair was talking to Cynthia's son, Brian, while helping to bandage his wrist. There was no hospital in Killarney and judging by the man's age she assumed that a retired GP was the next best thing. A line of people sporting various cuts and grazes snaked out the door.

Dana searched for Cynthia and found her by the dartboard in the middle of an argument with a man whose chin was dotted with white stubble.

Cynthia grabbed the man's arm as he went to leave. 'It's just not safe at this point to go back home. Take a look outside.' She pointed out the window. 'Your health's not good these days, Frank. You should not be traipsing through a storm.'

He stabbed a bony finger at her. 'George is my best mate. I'm not going to abandon him!' He turned and hurried out the front door.

Cynthia shouted after him. 'Don't expect me to save your seat for you!' She gave Dana a withering look. 'He's a regular, comes in every morning and today he decides to be a hero.'

The crowds parted as a teenager with a baby in her arms made her way towards them. Dana gasped in shock.

'Are you okay?' Cynthia asked Dana.

'It's just that he looks like …' The resemblance to her son, Oscar, was uncanny. His blue eyes, the chunky folds of his upper arms.

'He's hungry.' The teen's face was panic-stricken. 'I tried giving him the bottle but he won't take it. He just keeps crying. I think he wants his mum.'

'Where's his mother?' Dana asked, alarmed. The noise in the room had suddenly risen a few decibels. Before she knew what she was doing she'd stepped forward with her arms out.

'She came in here a few hours ago, dropped the baby off, then went straight back out to find her husband,' said the girl.

The baby's cry ramped up to a full-blown wail as a fight broke out on the other side of the room. The couple beside them began to argue with a tall, bearded man who was jabbing his index finger into the woman's shoulder.

Cynthia stormed over to the bar, yanked a stool from beneath the counter and leapt onto it. She put her fingers into her mouth and gave an ear-splitting whistle. A stunned silence fell over the room; even the baby was startled into silence. 'Listen up, everyone. For the next few hours we need you all to remain calm. We're all safe here, nothing's going to hurt you as long as you stay under this roof. But we have a baby up the front here and for its sake and everyone else's we need you to keep quiet. We do not need you screaming at each other and making the situation any worse.'

Cynthia jumped off the stool, beaming as activity resumed at a more subdued level. She took the baby from the teenager and handed him to Dana. 'If you take the bub to the office you should be able to get some peace and quiet in there.' She turned to the girl. 'It's fine now. This woman works for the Department of Families, so the baby's in good hands. Thanks for taking care of him. You don't have to worry anymore.'

The relief on the girl's face was palpable as she passed a shoulder bag to Dana.

Dana cradled the baby in her arms feeling as though she was having an out-of-body experience. The infant continued to cry, his face red with distress, and she pulled herself together, weaving her way through the crowd to find the office as she racked her brain trying to remember what she'd done to calm Oscar down when he was upset.

Once she was safely inside, she grabbed a clean bottle and the baby formula from the bag and rushed to the sink. Using leftover water from the kettle, which she presumed was sterile, she used her spare hand to add a scoop of the powdered formula to the bottle then poured in the water and shook it. Cradling the baby in her arms she was relieved when he started sucking the teat as though his life depended on it, staring up at her with his marble blue eyes. *There you go, sweetheart. That's better.*

She searched the room for somewhere for him to sleep. Improvising, she slid one of the drawers from the desk, lined it with a blanket, then paced up and down the room, rocking the baby gently. When she was satisfied he was asleep, she placed him in the makeshift crib, gently kissing his warm forehead. 'I'll just be gone for a few minutes – just to find out if your mum's come back,' she whispered.

Cynthia was behind the bar filling a jug of water. 'How'd you go?'

Dana sat down and rested her elbows on the bar mat, quickly pulling them away once she realised it was soaked with beer. 'He's fine. I fed him a bottle, made up a crib, now he's fast asleep.'

'I knew he'd be in safe hands.'

'Any news on the mother yet?'

'Nope.' Cynthia grimaced. 'But she's a state swimming champ so she should be able to handle herself.'

Lachlan staggered into the pub, his hair wild and face streaked with mud. Dana caught a glimpse of dark water on the street before the door slammed shut. He slumped on the stool beside her, a musty and putrid smell wafting from his clothes.

'How was it?' Dana tried not to wrinkle her nose.

'Intense. I've never seen so much rain. The SES crew has been helping as many people as possible, but I don't know how much they'll be able to do after the sun goes down.'

Sean collapsed on the stool next to his brother and Dana was relieved to see that he'd made it back safely. 'Just heard that some guy's in trouble. He was calling out for help. They were about to pick him up in the boat, but he got swept away. They're out searching for him now.'

Cynthia was on the other side of the bar. 'That bloody old

fool. That stupid bloody idiot.' She pressed her eye sockets. When she removed them a tear was tracking down her cheek. 'I begged him not to go and now—'

Dana reached over and put a hand on her shoulder. 'We don't know who it is – it could be anyone.' Her bigger concern was that Jayden may also be out there and caught up in the worst flood in a decade. She sent up a prayer that it wasn't him.

She was about to return to the baby when there was a loud bang. A cry of horror went up from the crowd as the room was plunged into darkness.

'We've lost power.' There was fear in Cynthia's voice. 'We'll have to try and get the generator going. Normally Peter would do it but he's out with the SES.'

'I'll give it a go,' said Lachlan. 'Is it still in the same place?'

'Yes, are you sure you can fix it? Peter makes it sound extremely complicated.'

'You were a carpenter for years, weren't you, Lachy?' one of the men asked.

'I should be able to work it out,' said Lachlan.

'You might be able to use the light from your mobile to see what you're doing,' Dana said, taking her own advice and removing her phone from her pocket so she could find her way back to the office.

She turned right using the dim light of her phone to guide her up the hallway. When she reached the office she spent a few tense moments trying to get the key in the door. Finally, she heard the noise of the lock turning and was able to let herself in. When she shone the light over the baby's crib, she was relieved to find him still fast asleep. She sat down beside him, her hand on his chest and sat quietly, enjoying his gurgling and murmurs as he dreamed and the peaceful time alone with him. It was almost 7 pm and the sky outside was dark and shadowy.

Half an hour later the lights flickered on and a loud cheer went up from the bar outside. The baby woke with a startled cry and she gathered him up and took him outside to see what was happening. Lachlan was standing in a group, being patted on the back, a schooner of beer in his hand. She smiled and gave him a thumbs up. A woman in her late twenties came towards Dana from the other side of the room, her eyes wide.

'Oh my god, Teddy! Thank god you're alright,' she said, putting a hand on the baby's back and staring into his face. She stood back and a man appeared beside her. 'I'm his mum, Kathleen. This is his dad, Tom.'

'He's been no problem whatsoever.' Dana glanced at Oscar's doppelgänger. A lump formed in her throat as she cuddled him tight, then handed him back to his mother.

Kathleen held the baby against her chest, her arms strong and brown beneath her mud-splattered singlet. 'Sorry, I didn't catch your name.'

'It's Dana, Dana Gibson.'

'Thank you so much. I'm so grateful. Is there anything we can do for you?'

'Honestly, the pleasure's been mine. He's so beautiful.' She hoped Kathleen didn't notice the tears in her eyes.

'There must be something. At least let us buy you a drink.' Kathleen wasn't about to be deterred.

'A whiskey would be great.'

'I'll make sure it's the most expensive one in the pub.'

Dana propped herself up at the bar with her single malt whiskey and a packet of peanuts.

Lachlan came over and sat beside her. 'What a relief, hey? I tell you, when I heard that she was out searching for the father I had a bad feeling it was going to end in tragedy.'

'All's well that ends well. And such a gorgeous baby.' She took a sip of her whiskey.

'Don't tell me you're getting clucky.'

The front door flew open with a roar of intense rainfall and the crowd parted like the sea. A police officer staggered forward, his expression grim as he held a lifeless body. Dana strained to see who it was, thinking only of Jayden. The policeman laboured towards them, scanning the crowd. Cynthia ran out from behind the bar, a look of panic registering on her face.

'I need a doctor!' The policeman called out, laying the body on the floor. For the first time Dana saw that it was another man and not Jayden.

The GP elbowed his way through the crowd towards them. He knelt, putting his ear close to the man's mouth and nose, then sat up and ripped the buttons of his shirt open. The doctor interlocked his hands, positioned himself over the man's body and began chest compressions. After thirty seconds, he tilted the man's chin, pinched his nose and gave him two short sharp breaths. The doctor looked up. 'Ryan. I need your help down here!'

Dana recognised the name and realised that the policeman was Lachlan's friend, the officer who'd spoken to them on the phone about drug trafficking. The GP kept pumping the man's sternum while Ryan blew into the man's mouth. For a moment he spluttered. Dana held her breath, willing him to wake up.

The doctor's glasses slipped down his nose, perspiration dripping from his chin. 'Come on, Frank!' His voice was laced with despair as he slapped the man's cheek. 'Please, mate!'

Dana glanced over at Lachlan, who now had tears in his eyes. It occurred to her that Lachlan was bound to have known Frank well, given he had grown up in Killarney.

When she looked back to see what was happening with Frank, the doctor was sitting back on his haunches. He glanced up at Cynthia and shook his head.

He said something unintelligible to her and she burst into tears. For the first time, Dana noticed the kelpie. A man from the crowd tried to grab the dog's collar, but it snapped at him and stood by Frank's side.

An eerie silence descended over the pub. The only sound was the wild swirling of the rain lashing against the windows.

A couple of SES workers helped lift Frank's body and took it down the hallway, taking their directions from Cynthia and the doctor, who followed behind.

Ryan stood up and turned to Lachlan. 'We'll have to find out who we need to notify. Cynthia said we can use the phone in the office.'

After they'd been gone for twenty minutes, Dana was in the grips of a crushing anxiety. She'd been left in the lurch and desperately needed to know what was happening.

When she knocked on the door of the office the policeman opened it, towering over her.

'Sorry to interrupt, but my phone and handbag are in here.' She peered through the gap in the door, knowing Lachlan wouldn't want her to make a fuss.

The officer looked down, unsmiling. 'I'm sorry, but you can't be in here.'

Frank's body was in the middle of the room, the blanket she'd used for the baby was now draped over him. The kelpie was on the floor, its head on the hand of its fallen master. The dog lifted its nose briefly, then lay back on the carpet.

The rain continued to lash the window, with rivulets running down the pane as though they'd never end.

10

Dana woke to the chirping of birds and the warmth of the sun on her arms shining through the blinds. She'd managed to get a few hours' sleep on a couch beside the pool table, but her neck had cricked and she winced as she pulled herself into a seated position. She stepped carefully over the sleeping bodies on the floor and made her way outside to the verandah.

The street was eerily calm, light glinting off the murky water that covered the street in front of her. Aside from the stench of raw sewage she could have been looking onto a brown river, the water eddying below her. A polystyrene box floated by. A child's doll came next, its unblinking eyes staring up at the sky. A profound sadness washed over her as she remembered Frank's kelpie. Its refusal to give up on its master, who was never coming back.

Inside, people had started to stir. Cynthia was behind the bar pouring coffee, a bright red scarf tied around her head. She offered Dana a mug then reached down and produced a plastic bag. Dana peered inside and found a fresh t-shirt and a folded pair of jeans.

'These are for you.' Cynthia smiled. 'I reckon we're about the same size and I figured you'd feel much better once you were in clean clothes. Sorry I couldn't come up with something more fashionable.'

'That's so kind.' Dana reached across the counter and squeezed her hand. 'I don't suppose we'll be getting out of here before tonight?'

'That's a definite no. Some of the locals can head out to the school – the SES have organised for a boat to help them out. I'm going to let the out-of-towners stay here free of charge,' explained Cynthia. 'Some of them, like Craig Towns and his mates, I'd rather not have hanging around, but in a situation like this we're going to have to love each other – warts and all.'

The day passed quickly as Dana helped Cynthia clean up one of the back rooms of the pub that had been inundated with water. Sean and Lachlan had rejoined the SES and were responding to calls for assistance. It was 6 pm when they all met up back in the bar. The men she'd seen arguing the day before were getting drunker by the minute. A few of them had made a game out of kicking an orange to each other. A man laughed as his friend's thong flew off his foot and across the room.

Dana tried to catch Sean's eye as he was buying a round of beers, but her stomach dropped when he looked straight past her and paid for the drinks. Once again, she found herself doubting his feelings and wondering if their kiss at the waterfall had meant anything to him.

Blair Hadley staggered into the pub, soaked to the waist. He wandered over to their table and pulled out a stool. Sean joined them at the high table.

'Jeez, mate, where've you been?' asked Lachlan.

'When I heard that the area was being evacuated I wanted to check that none of the boys were in the butter factory, but I got stuck on my way into town. I took shelter on the verandah of an empty house and luckily a kid in a tinnie came by and rescued me about an hour ago. I had no idea how bad it was going to be. I desperately need a drink of water. I'll be back in a sec.'

As he was waiting in line at the bar, one of the men from the group in the corner threw an orange at Blair and it bounced off his head. They roared with laughter.

'What have you done to Jayden, you sick bastard!' one of them called out.

Blair's face was filled with hurt as he turned around to face the culprit. Seeing the group, he quickly looked back to the bar, the tips of his ears becoming a deep scarlet as he hunched over his lemonade.

'I'll talk to them,' said Lachlan.

Sean placed his hand on Lachlan's shoulder and pushed him back into his seat. 'I'll do it.'

'I didn't realise they knew each other,' said Dana, watching as Sean went over to speak to the men.

'We were all mates at school.'

'I would've thought they'd be chalk and cheese.'

'They are, but I guess that was part of the attraction. Sean liked Blair's stability and Blair craved excitement – when we were kids anyway.'

The discussion between Sean and the men in the corner was getting heated. 'For someone who bashes their wife and kids you've got a lot to say for yourself,' Sean taunted, 'How many DVOs has Theresa taken out against you now? Six?'

'Fuck off, Sean.'

'Nice comeback.'

The tall policeman from the night before came through the door and Sean returned to their table.

'Ryan!' Lachlan greeted the policeman, reaching out to shake his hand. 'How's it going?'

'Been a hell of a day. I was only supposed to be back in town for a few weeks. Wasn't expecting a natural disaster! I'm just going to get a drink. Save me a seat,' he said, trying to catch Cynthia's attention at the bar.

'Ryan was our neighbour growing up,' Sean told Dana, turning his attention to her for the first time that day. 'He made a fortune as a stockbroker, then gave it all up to become a copper.'

Dana looked at the policeman who was now lining up at the bar and turned back to Lachlan. 'I'm exhausted. I'm going to ask Cynthia which room I'm in. Do you want me to ask about yours while I'm there?'

'It's fine,' said Lachlan. 'You go on up. I'll catch up with Ryan and sort it out later.'

'Don't leave it too late. You don't want to end up sleeping in the corridor with the fellas over there.' She tilted her head to the group of men who'd started dancing to Slim Dusty on the jukebox.

Dana handed Cynthia her credit card. 'I insist,' she said when Cynthia tried to wave it away.

'Yours is the room in the far corner. Best one in the whole

place and hopefully quiet enough for you to get a decent night's sleep.'

Dana took the key and headed up the carpeted stairs, a rich shade of scarlet under a Tiffany-style lightshade. She opened the door of her room to find a brass bed in the centre of the hardwood floor, the knobs shining a deep gold under a frosted flower ceiling light. On the corner of the shiny maroon doona was a cake of lavender soap and a fresh folded towel. *The country comforts of home.* She'd have to use the shared bathroom facilities down the hall but on the whole she was relieved about the improved sleeping arrangements. She was about to head down to the bathroom when Sean appeared behind her. She was startled but pleased that he'd sought her out.

'Wow, they really rolled out the red carpet for you,' he said, wrapping his arms around her waist. 'I just asked about a room for Lachy and me and she put us in these shitty little beds above the jukebox.'

'Those are the breaks.'

He smiled down at her and a lock of hair fell into his eyes. 'If you need some company I've been told I'm an extremely considerate bedfellow.'

She searched his face, trying to decide whether sleeping with him again was a terrible idea.

As if reading her mind he added, 'I'm sorry about everything. Honestly, if there's anything I can do to make it up to you.' His face was so open and honest she immediately felt bad for doubting him.

As she reached up to kiss him she could feel his bristly stubble. She enjoyed feeling his strength as he pushed her against the wall and pressed the length of his body against hers, moving against her with force. A rumble of thunder sounded overhead and the relentless driving rain pounded on the roof as they moved onto the bed.

In the early hours of the morning, Dana lay awake. The men from the bar had moved upstairs to the balcony outside their rooms. They were playing drinking games and partying like it was New Year's Eve.

She stared at Sean's silhouette, the marble of his physique and the soft sound of his breath as his chest rose and fell beside her. He'd fallen asleep the moment they'd finished having sex and hadn't stirred, despite the noise coming through the thin walls. She shoved the pillow over her head and focused on her breathing, on relaxing all the parts of her body, but gave up after thirty minutes to ruminate – first over Jayden and what could have happened to make him leave town, and then about Susan's diagnosis and how she was coping.

The digits on the clock beside her shone. As they clicked over to 3 am she was filled with misanthropy. *Shut up!* she wanted to scream at the party outside her room. She had visions of smacking the men's heads together and throwing them from the balcony. She was thirty seconds from pounding the window when she heard one of them announce he was off to bed.

Eventually, she drifted into a fitful sleep and woke late, the hot sun lighting the room. She rolled over, ready to snuggle up to Sean, but was surprised to find his side of the bed empty. Plumping the pillow, she fought off a feeling of resentment. Was she just a conquest to him? Was he already losing interest? She closed her eyes, trying to shut out the day ahead.

~

On her way back from the bathroom later that morning, Dana paused in the hallway. The word, *pedofile*, had been scrawled across a door with a thick black marker. *Blair's room.* She ran downstairs, located a bottle of antiseptic spray and a roll of Chux wipes, then sprinted upstairs. She was smudging the letters, swiping the cloth back and forward, when Lachlan came down the hall.

'What are you doing?' he asked.

'Trying to get this graffiti off Blair's door. They couldn't even spell it right.'

'Jesus. Can't they give the poor guy a break?' He ripped off a section of cloth and started helping her. 'I don't get it, I thought you didn't like Blair either. Why are you helping him?'

'Obviously I'm not his biggest fan, but I still think it's unfair to convict him without a trial. And to vandalise the pub in the process.'

'I'm glad you're finally coming around. Blair's not nearly as bad as you seem to think he is.'

'We'll see.'

Once they'd removed the offensive word and returned the cleaning products, they hung over the upstairs balcony, their elbows on the balustrade as they stared across the semi-submerged town.

'I really hope this weather isn't about to set in again,' said Lachlan, looking up at the gathering clouds.

'I know, it's been a nightmare.'

'How did you sleep last night?' he asked.

'Probably the worst sleep I've ever had in my life. You didn't hear them?'

'I've always been able to nod off at the drop of a hat.'

Like your brother. She was silent, wondering whether to broach the subject. 'Where's Sean?'

'I thought he was with you.'

'He was ...'

'Ooh.' His eyes widened, giving the impression he was scandalised that there was trouble brewing between Dana and his brother. 'I hope he's treating you okay?'

'For the most part.'

'What's the problem then?'

'I can't seem to shake the feeling that I'm going to get hurt.'

He shrugged. 'Maybe you're overthinking it.'

Dana reflected on this as a young man trudged along the street below holding his caged cats above his head while brown water swirled and eddied around his calves. 'I hope Angus is alright,' she said, noting the lapse in conversation.

'He's on top of a mountain so he'll be safe. I'm going to head downstairs, see if I can get some up-to-date news from the police on when I'm likely to see Rachel and the kids.'

Dana followed him downstairs and found a crowd gathered at the bar around a portable radio. She poured Lachlan and herself a coffee from the urn that had been set up on the bar and listened to the news bulletin:

Residents of Killarney have been evacuated from their homes, with flood levels peaking at 6.15 metres overnight. Average daily rainfalls over 200 millimetres over the past week have caused major flooding to homes and businesses after the Connolly Dam overtopped three days ago. River levels have since risen by 3 metres, leading to the worst flooding since 1976.

In other local news, sixteen-year-old Jayden Maloney is still missing, not seen since Wednesday the eighth of January, outside the Queen

Mary Falls store. Police have expanded their search to the Warwick area. Anyone with knowledge of Jayden's whereabouts should contact Crime Stoppers.

Someone turned down the volume of the radio. 'They have no idea where that kid is,' one of the men at the bar announced.

'Too true,' agreed the bloke next to him. 'I bet you a hundred bucks he's wandered onto the New England Highway and hitched a lift to Sydney. I guarantee you, the next time anyone sees him he'll be working as a rent boy or in a Hungry Jack's somewhere in Kings Cross.'

'They're right, you know,' Lachlan said to Dana. 'The police are no closer to figuring out what happened. It's been two weeks since anyone last saw him. And the flood will slow everything down. I mean, what hope are they going to have of finding him when all their resources are focused elsewhere?'

'We can't give up hope yet. He's a smart kid. A good kid, despite what he's been through, and he's had to look after himself for a long time. There's every possibility that he's at someone's house, waiting it out until the flooding's over.'

'Come on, Dana. You don't believe that! It's not like no-one knows he's missing – it's on every local news station. It's just so out of character.' A note of panic entered his voice. 'And I haven't been there for him. I haven't managed to lay eyes on him for months.'

'But you checked in with Trevor when he started working at the mill. The reality is, he's in a stable placement and we work in a busy office an hour and a half from where he lives. Nobody will blame you.'

'Don't be so sure. When things go wrong at work, they're

always looking for someone to take responsibility. And it's not the regional director or the manager who gets raked over the coals but the person at the bottom of the food chain – the Department of Families officer.'

'I just wish we could get out there and find him.' She gestured out to the town, inundated with water. 'We were just starting to make headway and now we're stuck here for who knows how much longer. It's so frustrating.' She sighed. 'I'm going to duck upstairs and have a shower. Will you be here when I get back?'

He shook his head. 'I've got to get word to Rachel and the kids and let them know I'm okay. Then I told Ryan that I'd go and help a few of the guys move an old bloke back into his house.'

When Dana came out of the shared bathroom she was surprised to find the hallway buzzing with activity. A group of men were hauling a mattress through a bedroom door. She overheard a policeman instruct one of the officers to gather food, toiletries, clothes and bottled water to take back up to the school. As she waited for them to pass, the door to Blair's room flew open and he came out flanked by Ryan and another policeman, who was carrying a suitcase. Blair nodded at Dana as he was escorted away.

'Where are you taking him?' she asked Ryan.

'To the station.' He glanced at her, then looked at his phone, distracted.

'Has there been a new development?'

The detective slid his phone into his pocket, his face creased with irritation. 'I'm not arresting him. I'm taking him to the station for his own protection. There's no way I can keep him safe here, when half the town are baying for his blood.' He paused, considering her. 'I'm sorry, I don't remember your name.'

'Dana Gibson. Lachlan's colleague.'

'Right. Ryan Kennedy.'

'We met last night.' Up close she could see his dark serious eyes and pale skin.

As Ryan turned and began striding down the hallway, Dana called out after him. 'Before you go. How's Amber doing?'

He paused and turned to look at her. 'She and the little girl are fine. It was a close call – the water was almost at the second level of their house when we arrived. We put her in some emergency accommodation to be on the safe side, but she's back at home now cleaning up. You'll have to get out to visit her as soon as you can. She's got a bloke staying there, Brett Edwards, and I know from personal experience that he's bad news – not someone you'd want around young children.'

By early afternoon the water had subsided enough for her to borrow a pair of gum boots from Cynthia and venture outside. She trudged down the main street slick with mud and headed towards Amber's house, trying to ignore the stench of sewage as she picked her way through the debris. A man lugging his worldly possessions in a laundry basket said hello to her as she passed over Gravel Creek, a swollen torrent of water racing under the bridge. She trudged up Willow Street then turned past the co-op where the shop windows were streaked with mud. When she turned into Arbutus Street Arthur was in his usual spot on the front stairs of his house. The scruffy red dog was curled up on the cement beside him and rose to attention as she came closer.

Once again, Dana noticed the animal's distended stomach and wondered when the litter was due.

'How have you been coping with all this water?' she asked.

'I thought I was a goner when it came up to the fourth step, but luckily it went no further, so I was okay. When the floods went through a couple of years back my landlord got the house put on stumps. My neighbours didn't fare so well.' He shook his head and gestured to the mountain of rubbish piled up beside the house next door.

'Is there anything I can do to help?' Dana asked.

'Not really.' He squinted up at her, his eyes milky in the pale sun. 'It's good to see you again, Dana.'

She smiled, pleased that, unlike Ryan, he'd remembered her name.

He continued. 'You were asking after Jayden the other day. Have you found him yet?'

'I'm afraid not.'

His face darkened. 'It doesn't bode well, that he's been out in this weather.'

The truth of his words sucked the air from her lungs. She looked up at the glass louvres next to Arthur's front door, which was open. She could see a clock and wooden crucifix on the wall. 'I don't suppose you're involved with the church, are you?'

'Involved? I've been going to Holy Cross church since I was a boy. Not only that, but I was the priest at St Mary's until I retired.' His face shone with pride.

'Really?' She wondered why no-one had bothered to mention it to her. 'What can you tell me about Blair Hadley?'

'He's a good lad. I know his mother, Lynette, well. After he started working in the ministry, he used to come to me for advice. We've kept in touch over the years, he always sends a card at Christmas.'

She hesitated, unsure if she should say what was on her mind. 'There's been a few rumours that he's acted inappropriately. That he might be the reason that Jayden's missing.'

'That's not the Blair I know. He wouldn't harm a hair on that boy's head.'

'They're only rumours at this stage. You can never put too much stock in them,' Dana said, attempting to pacify the old man.

'I hope not. The Catholic Church has been caught up in far too much controversy lately – it would be nice if we didn't get dragged into it too.' Arthur looked up at her intently. 'I've had this for a while,' he said, reaching into his pocket, 'and I've been wondering who to give it to.' He pulled out a laminated prayer card and held it out to her.

She hesitated, thinking about what a terrible Christian she was and wondering if she even deserved God's love. She ran a mental checklist of all the awful things she'd done last year – cheating on her husband, slapping a police officer, being instrumental in Lachlan's car crash.

'Go on,' he urged, as if reading her mind. 'Nothing you've done can be that bad.'

She took the card from him, turning it over in her hands and reading the title: *Guardian Angel Prayer for Protection*. An angel dressed in a robe with hands outstretched was pictured inside a border of golden rope. Although she'd struggled to believe in God after Oscar's death, perhaps angels were something she could get on board with.

She placed the card in her top breast pocket and patted it to show she'd be keeping it close. 'Thanks, Arthur.'

'Keep it with you and don't give up hope. A guardian angel will offer you her protection when you need it most.'

She was touched by this gift as she made her way down Arthur's driveway, wading through a puddle of Coke cans then past a Eureka flag that was entangled in a nearby bush. It was only as she approached the house that she could hear raised voices coming from inside. A man and a woman. She waited for five minutes, wrestling with indecision, knowing it wasn't safe to attempt a home visit during an argument, especially when she hadn't even informed Lachlan of her whereabouts.

A child began to wail and she put her doubt aside and hurried up the front path. She gave five staccato knocks on the front door. The house immediately fell silent.

Amber answered the front door with a deep flush on her chest. 'What are you doing here?' Her eyes were wild and accusing.

'Just seeing how you're getting on?' Dana peered down the hall and into the lounge room, trying to get a glimpse of the male she'd heard seconds earlier. 'How's Brooke?'

'Why? What have you heard?' asked Amber.

'When you spoke to me the other day you were in a huge panic about the flood, so I thought I'd see if you were both okay. Do you need anything?'

Amber's shoulders sagged with what appeared to be relief. 'A two-litre carton of milk would be good. And I'm desperate for a bloody cigarette.'

'Well, I'll see what I can do – about the milk anyway.' Dana nodded in the direction of the lounge room. 'Can I come inside?'

'I have a friend here.'

'Brett Edwards?' Dana enquired.

Amber nodded.

'Is he living here?'

'Does it matter?'

'Yes – you're on a support service and we need assurance that any person residing in the house is safe for Brooke to be around. Do you mind if I have a quick chat with him?'

'You're going to anyway.' She stepped aside to let Dana pass. Inside she found Brooke playing underneath the kitchen table and a man standing by the window.

The man pushed up the sleeves of his grey tracksuit top and stared at Dana with the coldest blue eyes she'd ever seen. The air around them seemed to thicken.

'Have a seat.' She pulled up a chair and gestured for Brett to do the same.

'Aren't you going to introduce yourself?'

She smiled at him to show she wasn't intimidated. 'I already know who you are, Brett. But, yes, I'm Dana Gibson. Amber's social worker.'

'What do you want?'

'I was hoping to talk to you about some concerns we've received about Brooke.'

He pulled out a chair but remained standing. 'Why do you need to talk to me? I'm not even the kid's father. I don't have to talk to anyone.'

'Please, Brett, have a seat. Since you're staying here, I need to make sure you're a safe person for Brooke to be around.'

'Safe?' The stud in his ear glittered in the light as he remained standing. 'Why wouldn't I be safe? You should be looking at Amber. All she cares about is where her next smoke is coming from.'

'I'll be assessing everyone in the home, but I've not had the chance to talk to you yet.' She spoke slowly and gently, so as not to enrage him.

'I don't have time. I've got a sick dog at my friend's place that I need to get back to and, as I said, she's not my kid so I don't have to do anything.'

As he stalked out the back door the tightness in Dana's chest began to dissipate. She turned to Amber. 'I'd really like to speak to Brooke for a moment if you don't mind?'

Amber watched through the window as Brett strode away through the backyard, kicking an empty bin across the muddy lawn as he went. 'Brooke.' Amber turned to her daughter. 'Why don't you show Dana the new farm animals in your bedroom? She'd love to see them.'

The little girl with curly black hair piled up on top of her head led Dana down a short hallway and into a room with a single bed covered with an animal-print doona, beneath a sash window. Brooke walked over to a basket on the other side of the room and upended the contents onto a colourful rug. 'Can you play with me?' she asked, picking up a three-legged jersey cow. 'This one broked it's leg. So funny.'

Dana got down on the floor and played until she'd established sufficient rapport to start her interview. 'Brooke,' she began, 'my name's Dana and I work at a place called the Department of Families. Our job is to talk to mums and dads, brothers and sisters, all sorts of people to make sure they're safe and happy at home. And that's what I wanted to talk to you about today.'

Brooke gave a solemn nod. 'Okay.'

'Can you tell me who lives in this house with you?'

'Mum and Brett.' As she laid a sheep on the rug and placed

a small piece of cloth over it, Dana noticed the chipped purple lacquer on Brooke's nails.

'And what are some good things about living with Mum?'

'She plays with me. She gives me cuddles on the couch when we watch TV.'

'What kind of shows do you like to watch?'

'*Rugrats.*'

'And what are some not so good things about living with Mum?'

'Umm. Nothing.'

'And what are some good things about living with Brett?'

Brooke's eyes were dark pools in her small, scared face. 'I don't know.'

'What are some not so good things about living with Brett?'

'He yells at Mummy, and he makes her cry.'

'When did this happen?' Time was a difficult concept for young children, so Dana didn't hold out hope for an answer.

'Every day. And one time when he was being really naughty, he broked the TV.' Her eyes were wide and scandalised. 'I shouted at him, "Stop I don't like it!"'

Good for you, she thought. 'How did it make you feel when that happened?'

'Sad.'

Dana took a deep breath to steady herself. 'Brooke, I'd like you to do something for me. Can you hold up your hand for me and count on your fingers?' she asked, wanting to take Brooke through some protective behaviours. 'Can you tell me five adults you'd talk to if you were ever feeling scared or unsafe?'

'Mum,' Brooke said pointing to her first finger. 'Um, Nanna June, Mrs Ramsey, Hannah.'

'Who's that?'

'Mum's friend.'

'Right. And who else?'

'Um … a policeman?'

'Okay, great. Well, I'm going to have a talk to Mummy for a bit. Will you be okay to keep playing in here?'

Brooke nodded and began to construct a fence for her farm animals.

Dana returned to the kitchen and found Amber sitting at the table.

'Well?' Amber asked, nodding in the direction of Brooke's bedroom.

'Honestly? I get the sense that she's very sad about Brett being in the house.'

A cloud of terror passed across Amber's face. 'You're not going to take her, are you?'

'That's not something we'd ever be doing unless as an absolute last resort.' Dana gave Amber a hard look. 'But you will have to start putting her needs over your need to be in a relationship, or whatever this is.'

'I'd already been planning to tell him it was over. He's always complaining about the meals I make, and I've been thinking why do I put up with this shit? Today was the last straw.'

Dana nodded her head in agreement. 'I haven't been in Killarney for very long, but I've been around long enough to have heard that he's not a good person to have around children.'

'I know, he's still on parole for assaulting that guy who runs the bottle shop.'

'I don't understand – why did you think it would be a good idea to be in a relationship with him?'

'I don't know. We hooked up for a few weeks when we first moved up here and that was fun. I just thought that maybe I'd feel better with some company. Which I did, for about one second ...'

'Have the police made any headway with finding out what happened to Johnny?'

'Not that I've heard. And now with the flood, I wouldn't be surprised if they've forgotten about him altogether.'

'Well, I'm heading to the station shortly, so I'll see what I can find out.' Dana reached for her handbag and stood up. 'And I'll link you in with the domestic violence service in Toowoomba. They'll be able to give you some strategies and support you if Brett gives you any more trouble. They'll also be able to work with you to ensure that Brooke's not being exposed to domestic violence. And don't worry, I'll be following up with Brett as well.'

Amber stared down the path Brett had walked moments earlier. When she turned back her expression was one of unmistakable shame and regret.

Dana found Ryan standing in front of a large evidence board when she arrived at the Killarney Police Station. Detailed maps of both Queensland and New South Wales were pinned under the words *Operation Border Control* and when she looked closely she could see various routes highlighted with the names of trucking companies listed alongside.

Ryan turned around, a look of annoyance flashing in his dark eyes. 'Who let you in?'

'The receptionist said I'd be fine to wander through.' She nodded at the evidence board. 'I would have thought that Jayden would have been your top priority at the moment.'

'He is. There're officers working on it in one of the other rooms.' He led her into his office and shut the door before she had the chance to see anything further. He sat down behind a mahogany desk and gestured for her to take a seat. 'How can I help you?'

'After you tipped me off about Amber's new boyfriend, I paid her a visit. You were right, he's living there. Brooke disclosed that there's already been domestic violence between them.'

'Well, no surprise there. Not with his record.'

'About that. I'd like to get a copy of his criminal history, if possible.'

'For what purpose?'

'So I can conduct a thorough risk assessment of the situation and add the information to the file. I'm just not sure Amber's going to be as willing to cut ties with him as she says she is.'

'No problem.' He tapped some keys on his computer and walked over to where the dot matrix printer was making a high-pitched shriek in the corner of the room. After a moment he handed her a sheaf of paper.

She let out a horrified laugh. 'I didn't realise there'd be so much of it.'

'Like I said, he's got some serious form.'

Dana scanned the criminal history dating back to 1979, which included possessing dangerous drugs, producing dangerous drugs, possessing utensils and pipes, failure to dispose of a syringe, wilful damage and stealing, numerous domestic violence orders and finally the grievous bodily harm charge for which he'd been in jail most recently.

Ryan picked up a stress ball in the shape of an eyeball and clenched it in his hand. 'Anything else I can help with?' he asked.

She smoothed the sheets of paper and placed them in her lap. 'I promised Amber I'd see if the police have made any headway on finding out who killed her ex.'

'When we're ready to charge someone, she'll be the first person to know.'

She was disappointed by his unwillingness to confide in her, but if his current behaviour was any indication of future conduct, it was clear that he was going to be of little help.

After helping Cynthia all afternoon, Dana trudged up the stairs of the pub and headed to the shared facilities for a shower. She stared at spots of black mould in the grout of the tiles trying to banish thoughts of tinea. It was impossible not to think of home, and her own clean bathroom. Her thoughts soon turned to Susan, who would no doubt be worried about her and Angus. When she was done, she dressed and towel dried her hair, remembering how noisy her room had been the night before. She considered rushing downstairs to beg a pair of earplugs from someone but didn't want to give Lachlan any ammunition to bring up her *Princess Diana* nickname which everyone at work had only recently forgotten.

As she padded along the hallway she saw Ryan up ahead, accompanying Blair into the same room he'd vacated only hours earlier. When she passed by, Blair was sitting on his bed, his head bowed. As Ryan attempted to close the door she peered in and he turned to face her.

'Why's he back again?' she snapped, before Ryan had a chance to close the door. 'You only just moved him.' Despite being convinced of Blair's guilt she was strangely outraged by the lack of formal justice he was being afforded.

'We needed the cell after we arrested someone trying to run drugs over the border. Turns out the floods have been pretty useful for the drug task force as its slowing down shipments.' Ryan manoeuvred himself past Dana and into the hallway then shut the door gently to maintain Blair's privacy.

'But what will to happen to him now? You said he needed protecting.'

'The ministry are sending someone over to visit him tonight, but that's about the best I can do in the present circumstances. I'd appreciate it if you didn't tell anyone he's here – especially Craig Towns and his mates.'

'Sure, but I hope I'm not scrubbing more graffiti off his door tomorrow morning.'

'It's only for one night. As soon as I'm able to move the drug perp out of the cells, I'll get Blair back in there.'

Her mind went to Lachlan and how he'd feel if he knew that Blair was going to be holed up in the hotel for another night. 'What are your thoughts on Blair?'

He regarded her with wariness. 'All I can say is the New South Wales Police would not have pressed charges if they didn't believe there was probable cause.'

'My thoughts exactly.' She paused, deep in thought. 'I'm not sure whether you've had a chance to talk to Lachlan yet, but he's adamant Blair's done nothing wrong. That he has nothing to do with Jayden's disappearance.'

'Lachlan likes to believe the best of people. Always has.'

11

The rains returned and continued overnight and into the next morning and Dana lay in bed listening to the water hammering on the roof. She'd always believed that she loved the rain but after three nights in the pub she was starting to feel stir-crazy. Her need to go for a run to blow off some steam was overwhelming. If she could just pound the pavement for half an hour, she was sure that the band of anxiety around her chest would ease and she'd feel like herself again.

She checked her phone, irritated that she still hadn't heard from Sean, then slumped in front of the TV with a bowl of Weet-Bix. The Eurythmics were singing 'Love Is a Stranger'. Annie Lennox was decked out in a suit, jumping in and out of a black limo. *And I want you so*, she sang, *It's an obsession*. She wagged a finger at Dana in warning.

By the time she emerged from her room it was already nine-thirty. She was padding down the hall towards the bathroom and stopped in front of Blair's room, the door ajar. Unable to resist, she gently pushed it open and looked in. The first thing she saw was his feet. The intimate sight of pale spindly toes. At eye-level, where no feet should be. She stepped inside, her eyes tracking upwards. Pressed pants and black belt. Curved shoulders. Blair's body hung from a fan, his back to her, his neck at an odd angle.

Unable to move her eyes from him, her skin prickled. Her thoughts moved sluggishly, sprouting tendrils of horror. Blood roared in her ears and bile soured the back of her throat. Images flashed across her mind. Oscar in his crib. Blair leaning from the tower. Oscar's lips, pale and cold.

She ran from the room, colliding with the edge of a table on her way out, the sharp pain to her thigh barely registering. She froze when she saw Lachlan in the hallway. 'Don't go in there,' she said, unable to offer an explanation.

He pushed past her and went into the room. When he came out again he was silent, the skin on his brow chalk-white. He slumped against the wall, holding his hands behind him for support.

She grabbed him by the shoulder. 'What should we do? Should we cut him down?'

'It's too late. He's already cold.'

They stood together for a long moment. 'Get Ryan,' he said, reaching back to the door and pulling it closed as they heard footsteps on the stairs. 'He's in Cynthia's office.'

Dana bolted down the stairs. When she opened the office door she found Ryan asleep on a yoga mat on the floor. As she burst in, he sat up, dressed in a singlet, a blanket over his legs.

'What?' he exclaimed.

'It's Blair.' She turned away as he reached for his pants. 'He's dead.'

~

The rest of the day passed in a blur of ambulances and police statements. After she'd returned from the station she dragged herself upstairs and knocked on Lachlan's door. He was lying on the bed closest to the French doors that opened onto the verandah. With the exception of a dull green chair pushed against the wall and two single beds, the room was a replica of hers, but far more cramped. On the chest of drawers in the corner was a can of deodorant, a bottle of aftershave and a dark pair of sunglasses that she recognised as Sean's.

Lachlan gave her a weary look with eyes that were red and puffy.

'I thought I'd check on you to see how you're doing?' She slumped onto the cushioned chair, feeling completely hollowed out.

Emotions swept across his face like slow-moving clouds. He sat up on the bed. 'I knew he was struggling after that police interview. I should have gone straight to the church and talked to him when he came home from hospital. I should have made him see sense.' Lachlan put his head in his hands. When he removed them, his expression was blank. 'I should have seen this coming. Once someone makes an attempt on their life, they're always going to have a second crack. The night before last he gave me his Cat Stevens records. He said it was because he didn't have a stereo anymore.' He stifled a sob. 'Could I have been any more stupid?' His voice fell to a whisper. 'He was giving away his *possessions*.'

She drifted over to the tiny kitchenette and opened the fridge, the sight of a tub of yoghurt and half-eaten burger making her feel ill. 'Can I get you a cup of tea? Something to eat?'

He shook his head. 'I just keep asking myself ... why?'

She was silent for a moment before she responded in the

detached and reasoned way she depended on in times of crisis. 'You know, I think it was important to Blair to be perceived as a kind-hearted, compassionate person. Once everyone heard all the rumours flying around about him acting inappropriately, he was in danger of losing his job, his vocation and the respect of almost everyone in Killarney.' She paused, considering her words carefully. 'Has it occurred to you his suicide was the result of his guilt over something that happened with Jayden?'

Lachlan's eyes were almost popping out of his head, she'd never seen him so furious.

'It's not your fault, Lachlan.'

'*Yes, it is!*' The volume of his voice was steadily rising. 'I knew something bad was going to happen. And I did nothing!' He stood up and looked across at her accusingly. 'And if I'm being really honest, Dana, it's your fault too!' He stormed past her into the hallway, slamming the door behind him.

She sat in the chair, stunned, feelings of guilt blossoming by the second. Was Lachlan speaking the truth? Was she partially responsible for Blair's death? Or was he blaming her in an outburst of grief? She considered going after him, calling out, but what could she say? Her stomach ached when she thought about Blair and with it came the raw pain of missing Oscar, the bleakness of his death.

Dana ate dinner alone. A few out-of-towners who were staying in the pub were playing cards in the corner but the mood was sombre. At 7 pm she told Cynthia she had a migraine and went up to her room. Someone in the adjacent room was crying and the jukebox was blasting from the dining room below. Lying in her darkened room, her thoughts turned to Blair and how quick she had been to judge him. Was his suicide really an admission of guilt? Or was he depressed about devoting his life to help others, only to have it blow up in his face? How was his mother coping now her only son had died?

She sunk further down the rabbit hole and started to speculate about Jayden. Surely if he was alive, he would have been found by now? Unless he didn't want to be found? Without thinking she grabbed her phone and did what she'd always done in times of distress – called her ex-husband. For once, the reception was good and Hugh answered on the third ring.

'Dana. To what do I owe the pleasure?' He sounded happy. The agitation of their last meeting, when she told him she was staying in Queensland, had evaporated. 'How's T-bar?' he asked, referring to the local nickname for Toowoomba.

'I'm in Killarney. Trying to locate a missing boy in foster care.' She wanted to tell him about Blair but couldn't find the words.

'Well, I hope you find him. Are you okay? You sound kind of ... flat.'

'We're flooded in. I'm stuck at the local pub until the roads clear.'

'If someone had told me you'd end up living in the country, I'd never have believed them. You used to be such a city slicker with your high heels and designer clothes.'

'Heels aren't really an option for me these days,' she replied. She could hear laughter in the background and wondered if he was at the pub watching soccer. 'How's things?'

'Good, actually. I'm glad you called because there's something I've been wanting to tell you.'

Her heart skipped a beat. 'What's that?'

'I've met someone.'

'Oh, okay.' She tried to think of a response, but her mind was blank.

'We had an end-of-year celebration at work and Angelo brought his sister along. We really hit it off.'

'Wow. So, you're dating again?'

'It's more than that. I've asked her to move in.'

The world slowed down until all that was left to do was breathe. In and out. She felt like she was holding a shell to her ear and had just found out that everyone on the planet was dead.

'That's great. What's she like?'

'Her name's Liz and she's beautiful, smart and has a Master of Commerce. She's actually been helping me with my budgeting.'

'When were you going to tell me about her?'

'I knew you were going to be like this, that's why I didn't want to say anything.'

'Like what?'

'Acting like I've done something wrong for taking a shot at another relationship after you made it very clear that ours was over.'

There was an agonising silence.

'What are you up to on the weekend?' he asked, and she knew he was attempting to steer the conversation towards calmer waters.

'I'm stuck in this pub until the water starts to recede. You?'

'Taking Liz to the new restaurant that's opened across the road.'

A grim urge to laugh bubbled up inside her.

'Look, Dana, we're about to head out now, but my phone's always on if you ever want to talk.'

She hung up, sitting back into the pillows. She felt sick that he'd moved on so quickly and, if she was honest, about how much it hurt.

She pulled the doona cover up over her legs and noticed one of Sean's hairs on the blanket. It was definitely his, impossibly blond in a way hers could never be. It struck her how hypocritical it was to be angry at Hugh when she had done the same thing herself. But it had been so many hours since she'd heard from Sean that the thought of them having sex was impossible – as though she'd only imagined it. Holding the hair up to the light she felt like an archaeologist poring over an artefact of an event so momentous and so unlikely that it could never happen again. Like the Incas creating Machu Picchu or the Egyptians building the pyramids the night she spent with Sean had crystallised in time. A moment of happiness. And now, in the crumbling civilisation of her life, all that was left was the palest of hairs draped across her fingers.

Morning came, despite another night tossing and turning. Dana rose early and went down the quiet hall. She did her best to ignore the police tape and *Crime Scene – Do Not Enter* sign that had been plastered over Blair's room and made her way downstairs. A dog-eared copy of the *Warwick Daily News* was lying on the bar and she read it as she sat at one of the tables and ate her muesli. On the front page was the headline: *Operation Border Control Ready To Blow Lid Off Drug Crime*:

> *Organised crime syndicates moving drugs through the Border Ranges on the New South Wales–Queensland border are being targeted by Queensland Police in Operation Border Control.*
>
> *A twenty-nine-year-old man was the first to be charged, due to face Warwick Court on May 30. He faces two counts of possession and one count of trafficking dangerous drugs.*

Detective Sergeant Ryan Kennedy, a former Killarney resident, is heading up the drug-trafficking task force.

When Dana had finished her cereal, she headed into the kitchen where Cynthia was polishing cutlery, a container of steaming water beside her. Dana pulled up a stool. 'That looks like a lot of hard work,' she said.

'I'm trying to distract myself.' Cynthia swiped at a knife with a starched white napkin looking exactly as Dana felt, her mouth pinched and face drained of colour.

'From what?' Dana asked.

'This place is starting to give me the shits. So many of the people have started treating me like a waitress, expecting me to run around after them, bring them food. If one more person asks me for a cup of tea, I'm going to knock their block off.' She gave a rueful laugh. 'And that's not the worst of it. Ryan made me swear on the Bible that I'm not to talk about what I want to tell you, but I can trust you, can't I?'

'Absolutely.'

Cynthia's eyes were wide as she lowered her voice. 'He's had to store Blair's and Frank's bodies in the coldroom because the road to the hospital's blocked and now every time I go in there to get the milk, I have a major panic attack.'

'Oh my god. I had no idea.'

'Sorry, I just really needed to get that off my chest. Anyway, how are you? Manage to get some sleep last night?'

'I kept having these terrible nightmares of corpses washing up along the main street.'

'Jesus Christ.'

'Not to mention, I've been trying to get in touch with Angus but I can't get through … I hope he and his mother are okay.'

'Well, I'm sure they're feeling cut off from everyone because they're on top of the mountain but with any luck things should get back to normal shortly.'

'Thank goodness.' She made an attempt at a joke. 'Seeing you in the hall every morning is starting to feel like Groundhog Day.'

'Groundhog Day from hell.' Cynthia smiled and poured Dana a coffee. 'Have you heard from Sean?' she asked, sliding the mug across to her.

Dana lifted her chin defiantly. 'No.'

'Before the flood, I was organising an open-mic night. It's a pity it won't be going ahead because I could have found you a new man – one with no emotional issues.'

Dana sipped the coffee that tasted like warm milk and tried not to make a face. 'Thanks for thinking of me, but really, I'm fine.'

'Anyway, he's an idiot. I just hope he hasn't gotten into trouble because he's been larking about in floodwaters and doing something stupid while trying to save the day. That'd be right up his alley.'

They both looked up as Ryan strode past the kitchen, a dark frown on his face. He grabbed a banana from the counter as he made his way to the office. Dana made a mental note to ask him when they were likely to be getting out of there. She picked her next words to Cynthia carefully. 'Does everyone know about the way that Blair died?'

Cynthia poured the container of water out in the sink and returned the knives and forks to the cutlery tray with a crash. 'News spreads like wildfire round here so the whole town knew within hours. Actually, a few of the locals are holding a wake tonight at a friend's house.'

'One minute they're pointing the finger at him and now they're holding a wake in his honour?'

'I think you should come. It's just a few close friends. If nothing else, it might get you out of your head for a bit.'

She couldn't think of anything worse. 'Sure. Come and grab me when you're going.'

Ryan was sitting at the computer by the window, staring at the screen, his face pale as he sipped from a mug of coffee. There were dark circles under his eyes as he turned to look at Dana and she felt a wave of compassion for him. No doubt he was the one who'd had to get Blair's body down from the fan, store it in the coldroom and deal with the paperwork. She stared at the yoga mat on the floor, the tangle of bedding that lay on top.

'Did you sleep in here again last night?' she asked.

He shrugged. 'It gives me a bit of a break from the station.'

'Yesterday must have been really awful.'

His face revealed nothing. 'Perks of the job.'

'Sorry to bother you, but I was just wondering if anyone has been out to Queen Mary Falls? My twelve-year-old neighbour has been staying out there with his mother, and his grandmother will likely be worried about them. I was going to try them again on the landline. I can come back later if you'd like?'

Ryan pushed off the wall and swivelled his chair to face her. 'It's okay. I've been preparing a report for the coroner but I'm done now. And I think the power should be back on out that way.' He shot a look at his watch. 'I'll leave you to it. I'm due to give the morning briefing in a few minutes.'

'At least with suicide it should be a straightforward report,' she said. When he didn't reply she realised he was probably adhering to confidentiality provisions. 'Do you have any idea when we're likely to be going home?' She hated the fact that she was burdening someone who had enough on their plate, but the thought of spending another night at the pub was almost too much for her.

'Your guess is as good as mine.' He stood and removed a jacket from the back of his chair, swiping at a smear of dirt on the lapel before throwing it on. 'I'll leave you in peace.' He shut the door behind him.

Dana dialled Tina's number. She sent up a prayer that this time she wouldn't get the engaged signal. She was about to hang up when she heard Tina's voice.

'Hey ya,' Tina said.

'Hi, Dana here. I was just wondering how you're both coping in the cabin?'

'Bored, is how we are. Climbing the walls. I have to tell you, I'm struggling now that I can't go to my AA meetings anymore. And my little mate over there is the worst. I finally cottoned on to the fact that I just needed to find him some books and that's shut him up completely. But yeah, the sooner we can get into town again, the better.'

Dana picked up a snow dome from the desk and shook it, watching the white flakes settle on Santa's reindeers and the sled they were dragging across the sky. 'I don't suppose you've seen Sean at the shop in the last couple of days?'

'No,' Tina said sharply. 'I heard he was with you.' There was an awkward moment of silence, making Dana wonder if Tina was jealous. 'I guess you'd be wanting to talk to Angus then?'

'Yes please,' Dana said with relief.

There was a rustling noise as she handed the phone over.

'Hi, Dana,' Angus said brightly.

'Angus, it's so good to hear your voice. I've been worried about you.'

'I'm fine. I was pretty bored at first, but then this woman who lives next door gave me this book, *Flowers in the Attic*. There's a whole series and I've been getting into them. They're so creepy.'

Dana despaired over Tina's lack of supervision. 'Well, those books are quite adult so just remember you can always stop reading if they get too much for you.'

'Nothing I haven't seen before.' There was a note of bravado in his voice.

'And what else has been happening?'

'Nothing much. We called Nan last night to let her know what's happening. Then we watched the news in the shop and there was a story about Jayden. The police said they were going to offer a reward to anyone with information on his disappearance. That means they think he's dead, don't they?'

Her stomach dropped. 'I hope not.'

'Well, there's a motorbike in the shed so I was thinking I might head out tomorrow, see if I can find him.'

'Please don't, Angus. You don't have a licence to drive a motorbike, and even if you did, there's so much floodwater that trying to ride a bike will be extremely dangerous.'

'Well, I've got to do something.' Angus paused. 'He's a friend and I think he must be running away from something.'

'Like what?' Someone knocked on the office door.

'I don't know. I just think he was scared the last time I saw him. I think he was running away.'

'Not everyone's running from something, Angus,' she said,

thinking about the number of times he'd run away from Susan's home the previous year.

'Well *he* was.' Angus's voice held a note of defiance.

A woman opened the door, a look of annoyance on her face as she jabbed her finger in the direction of the phone.

'Anyway, I'm really sorry, but I have to go. I'll give you a call tomorrow and hopefully I'll be able to tell you when we can leave. And stay safe. No riding around trying to find Jayden.'

She was about to leave the room when she spied a myrtle green notebook on Ryan's desk. Moleskin, with a number of pages ripped out. She picked it up and turned it over in her hands, trying to imagine him writing in it. Perhaps he was more interesting than she'd given him credit for. She flicked it open to a page that had been dog-eared and began to read the first few lines of a Robert Herrick poem.

Gather ye rosebuds, while ye may.
Old time is still a-flying
And this same flower that smiles today,
Tomorrow will be dying.

Was she making the most of her life, she wondered as she snapped the book shut. Was this all there was trapped in a small town, searching for a lost boy? Wondering what part she'd played in one man's death, while wasting time on another she barely knew.

12

Cynthia and Dana pulled up at a weatherboard house on stumps that were so high it had the appearance of being on stilts. They lugged plastic bags filled with soft drink, potato chips and six-packs of beer through the front yard towards an undercroft filled with junk – old mattresses and broken door frames. Above them, a sheet had been draped across the balustrade with a love heart painted on it.

'Whose house is this?' Dana asked, as they went around the side of the building and into the backyard where a dangerously high bonfire was licking at straggly eucalypts.

'Belongs to Blair's cousin,' said Cynthia. 'I've never met him, but he was the one who put the message on the community noticeboard about the wake.'

They left their bags on the table and joined a small group sitting in a circle around the fire. Dana pulled up a rickety chair next to Cynthia and promptly received an acrid blast of smoke to her face. Lachlan was sitting across from them, and despite the haze in the air, there was no mistaking the anger burning in his eyes. She moved to the left, looking up at the half-dead trees and debris trapped in the branches from the recent flood. A stench rose from the ground as though everything was still wet. She clutched her jacket around her, wondering what on earth she was doing here and how quickly she could excuse herself and return to the pub.

Cynthia passed Dana a beer. 'What's that all about? I thought you guys were friends.'

'We are.' Dana looked cautiously across at Lachlan who was now deep in conversation with the man beside him. 'But it hurts my feelings that he's being this cold. I didn't know he had it in him.'

A short man with dark, shoulder-length hair ambled down the back stairs of the Queenslander with a portable stereo. He placed it solemnly in the centre of the group then pressed play. The synth pop of New Order's 'Blue Monday' filled the air.

A woman on Dana's other side leant in and introduced herself. 'I'm Jessa,' she said. As the flames lit up her face, Dana saw that she had striking green eyes. 'How did you know Blair?'

'Work,' she said quickly, hoping Jessa wouldn't ask more questions. 'What was your connection to him?'

'We were housemates at one point and friends from uni days.' Her eyes misted over and she tugged at the sleeves of her oversized jumper. 'I can't believe he did it. I mean, I knew he was depressed, and he kept saying that he wanted to end it, but I thought it was just a figure of speech, you know? I didn't think he'd actually do it. I mean, I say I want to kill myself all the time.' She began to cry, wiping the tears from her cheeks. A black and white cat crept past and Jessa picked it up and buried her face deep in its fur.

Dana excused herself. While she wanted to help, she was only just keeping a lid on her own emotions. She hightailed it upstairs to the kitchen where she stood under a giant disco ball, near the dips and crackers. She'd been hoping that Sean might be at the wake, but he was nowhere to be seen.

In the bathroom she sat down on the toilet where she could see through the rotting floorboards to the ground below. She reached for the toilet paper, running a hand across the bubbling paint as she stared up at the stained ceiling.

Back in the kitchen, a woman was pouring herself a tall glass of something that smelt of liquorice. Two cats swished around her legs, rubbing up against her ankles. Dana took a beer from the esky, opened it and took a long sip in an effort to dull her growing agitation.

Lachlan came inside and rifled around in the cutlery drawer. Someone turned the music up outside.

'What's the deal with the New Order?' she asked, thinking that if she got him chatting about something trivial, he might forget he was mad at her.

'Blair was a huge fan. A few years ago he made a special trip to England to see them play.'

'I wouldn't have picked it.'

'There's a lot about him you wouldn't have picked.' He turned his back on her and strode away down the back stairs.

She knew he was still angry and wondered why he'd come into the house if he had no intention of being civil. She shivered in her thin coat, grabbed another beer and reluctantly made her way back to the fire.

When she returned to her seat the long-haired man stumbled to his feet and poured his bottle of vodka over the bonfire. It roared to life sending yellow sparks into the heavens, the flames shooting up to such a height she worried the trees would catch fire. Her thoughts turned to Hugh's new girlfriend and whether she was young enough for them to have a child. Then her mind went to Oscar. In the cold light of day she'd learnt to be grateful for his death, the gift he'd given her in getting clear about her life, leaving behind aspects that weren't serving her. But as the flames crackled and her head grew foggy she blinked back tears. She set her drink beside her feet. She'd forgotten how depressed it made her, how it blackened her mood. She leant past Cynthia and held out the other beer to Lachlan as a peace offering.

He shook his head.

On the other side of Cynthia the guy who'd poured alcohol over the fire, reached out his hand. 'Oh, hi. I'm Tony, but my friends call me Shetland.'

Cynthia laughed.

'What's so funny?' He broke into a grin. 'Oh yeah, Shetland Tony. Can I get you ladies a drink?'

'Maybe later,' said Cynthia, turning back to Dana. 'I wonder where Sean is? I haven't seen him in days – which is pretty unusual given he's always at the pub.'

'Who knows,' said Dana, depression crackling through her veins. 'I haven't seen him either—'

'Sean O'Malley?' Jessa interrupted, her face lighting up as she leant towards them. 'Oh, man. He's the best!'

'You know him?' asked Dana, thinking she was a little young for them to be friends.

'Yeah, of course.'

Dana's lips were pursed. 'When was the last time you saw him?'

'Umm, last Saturday. He rocked over to my place for a drink.'

When he told me he'd lost his phone, thought Dana, anger pulsing through her veins. She raised an eyebrow at Cynthia.

Jessa leapt from her chair and raced over to a young man strumming a guitar, enveloping him in a hug.

'I wouldn't listen to anything she says,' said Cynthia. 'Jessa only ever shows up when there's free drinks and she's had so much wine tonight she wouldn't know what's coming out of her mouth.'

But her words held the truth of what Dana had been trying to avoid seeing. *Sean was with someone else.*

When Tony checked if Dana wanted another drink she asked for vodka.

In the morning there was light everywhere and far too bright. It was streaming through windows, reflecting from surfaces. Dana lay in bed feeling like she'd washed up on a shore of jagged stones. Her mouth tasted of gravel and her tongue seemed to take up all her mouth. When she rolled to the side there was an immense pain in her head.

She was shockingly thirsty and remembered the theory of Maslow's Hierarchy of Needs which she'd learnt during her studies. First things first, she needed water then painkillers. She needed to get out of bed.

She could only remember fragments of the night before – everybody singing, texting Hugh, vodka, then more vodka. A tall man handed her a glass from high above as though it had descended from heaven. When the beer ran out they moved on to something sweet: Sambuca?

She remembered an older lady shaking her hand and saying, 'I'm Wendy'. Then meeting her black-haired friend, whose name she couldn't quite recall. Dana groaned. She had told them the story of her life, of Oscar's death and her annoyance over Sean's lack of contact. She remembered being in the back seat of Cynthia's car with her new friends. A wall of fatigue had descended over her and she had rested her head on the vinyl seat. The car interior began to spin. That's right, Tony had been sitting beside her.

'I got called into the cop shop to give a statement about Blair yesterday.'

It was like someone lit a match in an otherwise darkened room. Dana had listened intently, willing herself to take note.

'How'd it go?' asked Cynthia.

'It was weird ... almost like he was accusing me of something.'

'Like what?'

'He said that there was no way that Blair could have hung himself because there was no chair. Nothing for him to stand on.' Tony had paused as though he was processing his thoughts. 'I shouldn't be saying this because I'm drunk, but it was almost as if he thought, I don't know ... that Blair was murdered or something.'

13

A wave of nausea ploughed through Dana's stomach and she took three deep breaths. The retching passed and she staggered back to her bed.

The next time she woke she felt better. She showered and dressed quickly. As she was heading outside, Cynthia called out from the kitchen.

'Heard the good news?'

Dana stopped and turned. 'There's good news?'

'Looks like the worst of the weather is over. There's an end in sight, after all.'

Dana felt slightly more hopeful as she headed down the main street towards the police station. She was still trying to digest these latest revelations. Blair murdered? Right at the moment he wanted to kill himself? Coincidence or divine intervention? She tried to imagine someone getting Blair to unlock his room, murdering him and then managing to stage the crime scene so it looked like a suicide. It was the most outrageous thing she'd ever heard. She weighed up the logic. Blair was suicidal, the entire town hated him, so he hung himself after being locked up in the pub for his own protection. Simple. Why, then, was the chair that he'd climbed on to hang himself found on the other side of the room?

She announced her arrival to the receptionist, swept down the corridors and hammered on the door of Ryan's office.

'Come in,' he yelled. He was sitting down with his boots on the desk and a mug of coffee by his side. He dropped the folder he'd been looking at into his lap.

'You think Blair was murdered?' she asked.

'Who the hell told you that?'

'Why would anyone want to kill Blair? Revenge for Jayden? For abusing other boys?'

'That's what I'm trying to ascertain.'

'And you think it was a murder because there was no chair? No way to climb up and hang himself from the fan?'

'And I'd be letting you in on this for what reason?'

'Because I'm trying to locate Jayden and it's in the child's best interests that we share information about who might be responsible for his disappearance. There's a memorandum of understanding relating to information sharing between the Department and the police, if you'd like me to show you?'

'Seems like a stretch, but I'll take your word for it.'

'So, I'm going to ask the obvious. Why would someone want to kill Blair?'

'The *why* of it is obvious – rightly or wrongly half the town believe that Blair was a sexual predator and that he was responsible for Jayden's disappearance. But the *who* of the matter is far more complex. Jayden was beloved in this town and a lot of the people here played a part in his upbringing because his aunt wasn't able to, so to say that they might be angry enough to kill him is an understatement.'

'So in terms of suspects, the entire town has motive. Are you sure someone didn't just hide the stool or the chair, or whatever he used to hang himself, and keep it to themselves?'

'Why on earth would someone do that? It makes no sense. Not to mention that the only person who went in that room was the local priest and he swears that Blair was alive and well when he last saw him. We're still waiting on forensic tests in terms of the fingerprints on the chair, but that's about all we've got to go on for the moment.'

'Well, I guess that's that then.' She pulled the chair out from the other side of his desk and slumped into it.

'No offence, but you look wrecked. Can I get you a coffee?'

She put her head in her hands. 'There's no good coffee in this town, which is especially difficult if you're hungover.'

'I'll let you in on a secret – there's a pretty solid espresso machine in the tearoom. I can make you a double-shot latte if you like?'

She took her hands away from her face. 'That sounds amazing.'

When he left the room she noticed the folder he'd been looking at. After a moment of indecision – of asking herself whether she was willing to violate Ryan's privacy and breach every ethical boundary known to mankind – she darted around to the other side of the desk. Shoved into the front of the file were numerous colour photographs taken by the Scenes of Crimes officer where Johnny Buckley had died. A black smear on the bitumen was in the multiple frames, yellow paint had been sprayed on it to highlight tyre friction marks, and there were close-ups of black-and-silver scuff marks and blood. The scene portrayed the incident after the body had been taken away.

Dana flicked forward to the autopsy findings. A pathologist, Doctor Letts, detailed numerous abrasions to the back of Johnny's head and to the left side of his body. Johnny Buckley had suffered multiple fractures to his skull and bleeding around his brain. Doctor Letts concluded that the injuries to Johnny's body were consistent with being hit by a motorcycle, as had been reported by various witnesses, and that he was struck on the left leg with the injuries to the back of his skull indicating that his head had then hit the road.

Dana skimmed the pages, her throat dry. She was making a note of the number plate that had been written down by an eyewitness, SJM 007, when she heard the sound of footsteps coming down the hall. She slapped the folder shut and bolted around to the other side of the desk.

Ryan returned with a steaming white mug and set it on the desk in front of her. She took a sip savouring the rich warmth of the liquid as it scalded her mouth. 'You know, this is the first coffee I've had in Killarney that hasn't tasted like dishwater.'

He sat back in his chair and gave her a reserved smile.

'So, how's everything going with the hit-and-run?' The file had piqued her interest. She'd never managed to shake the feeling that whoever was responsible for Johnny's death would lead them to Jayden.

'We're progressing our enquiries.'

She pursed her lips, disappointed. The sound of a motorbike revving outside and roaring down the street triggered her memory. 'Arthur told me that he witnessed the rider limping away from the scene. Do you think that means the perpetrator would have been injured? Did you ever get around to checking the local hospitals to see if anyone presented with injuries consistent with a motorbike accident around the time of the hit-and-run?'

'Of course, we did. I got one of my officers to check with Warwick Hospital, Killarney Medical Centre and a number of local GPs, but I'm afraid none of them reported anyone presenting with injuries of that nature.'

'That's a shame,' she said, trying to keep her thoughts in order. 'Any other developments? What about the bike?'

'I spoke to a witness who had no idea what kind of bike it was but had the presence of mind to write down the number plate.'

'That's good luck.'

'Not really. I did a search of the database and turns out it had false rego plates. The original owner, an old guy called Wyatt Nelson, said the plates belonged to a quad bike he'd bought two years earlier. He'd sold it to his grandson and didn't do the transfer paperwork. One of our officers checked it out and Wyatt said that his grandson had lent the bike out. Wyatt wasn't sure if, or when, the bike would be returned to his grandson.'

'And that's where you left it?'

'Well, how long's a piece of string?'

She was still hungover but, at least if she was in the fresh air, the day would pass quickly. 'I think we should find out.'

14

Dana was surprised when Ryan pulled up outside a tiny church that had been converted into a house. 'Look, I have to warn you,' he had informed her on the short drive across town, 'this address is flagged on our system due to Wyatt Nelson having a propensity for violence against police.' Now that they were parked outside, the place looked innocent enough. A dilapidated dairy was out the back and the lawn was very overgrown.

'We'll have to make it quick. I've got to get back to the station in an hour for a team briefing,' Ryan said. As he strode up the steps and hammered on the front door, Dana lingered behind him in the front yard. A few moments passed before an elderly man stood before them, clutching a tattered brown dressing-gown to his chest.

'Wyatt, is it?' Ryan greeted the man, pulling out his badge and identifying himself. 'I'm Detective Sergeant Kennedy. Just wanting to speak with you about a bike we believe may have been involved in a hit-and-run.'

'Who did you say you were? My hearing's not as good as it used to be because I lost my bloody hearing aids.'

'Detective Sergeant Kennedy. I'm here about the quad bike,' Ryan repeated.

'But I spoke to a young copper about it just last week!'

'We have a few more questions.'

'Can I at least get my tea? I just made it.' He disappeared briefly and returned holding a delicate china cup that was strangely at odds with his demeanour. He leant against the railing of the front steps and took a sip of his drink. 'What did you want to know?'

'As you're aware, we've been trying to locate the bike that was responsible for Johnny Buckley's hit-and-run.'

'I already told you guys, my grandson, Dean, was living here for a few months. His father had had enough of him, so I lent Dean the bike so he could help out for once and spray the weeds up in the back paddock.'

'When would that have been?'

'I don't know, around November last year? He'd been living in the shed out the back because my son couldn't put up with him, and I soon found out why. He was playing loud music, blasting that stereo system of his, and inviting all these delinquents around for parties. Look, I'm pretty deaf, but it was so loud it was even bothering me. Not to mention the neighbours putting up a fuss. One day I found a few of them passed out, paint tins scattered on the carpet and brown marks over their faces. I was so disgusted I kicked him out.'

'And what happened with the bike?' asked Ryan.

'When I realised I hadn't laid eyes on it for a few weeks, I asked him where it was and he said a friend had borrowed it.'

'Who was this friend?' asked Ryan.

'Some bloody drug dealer. I think the girlfriend asked to borrow it and Dean let her have it because he was sweet on her, but then she gave it to the partner. Dean was too scared to ask for it back because he was terrified of the bloke. Daniel Dibello his name was.'

'Did he tell you anything else? Whether Daniel still has the bike?'

'That's the worst of it. He said that this Daniel character didn't even want the bike and that he just wanted the plates. And then wouldn't you know it, just before Christmas I got two speeding fines and I hadn't seen the bike in months. Six hundred dollars I was out of pocket. Dean said he'd help out but I'm not holding my breath.'

'You realise you could have filled out a stat dec. Told the Transport Department you weren't the rider, that you weren't in possession of the bike at the time,' said Ryan.

Wyatt scowled as though the milk in his tea had suddenly turned sour.

'And where's your grandson now?' asked Ryan.

'No idea. Was glad to see the back of him.'

Ryan thanked Wyatt for his time. As Dana followed him back to the car through the long grass she looked over at him. 'Not exactly the caring grandfather figure you'd imagine living in that quaint little house, is he?'

'Sorry, Dana, I'd love to stay and shoot the breeze with you, but I need to get back.'

The wind buffeted her cheeks as she flung the car door open and ducked into the passenger seat. Ryan started the engine and pulled the car onto the road. He was only an arm's length away, but as much of an enigma as ever. Did he want to solve this case?

The mountains on all three sides loomed above them and once again she was unable to shake the feeling that she was trapped in this beautiful town. Going nowhere.

'Do you mind dropping me here?' They were about six kilometres from town and Dana wasn't ready to go back to the pub. 'I think I'll walk the rest of the way back.'

Ryan, who had been fixated on the road ahead, eased over to the shoulder of the road. 'Take my umbrella,' he said, reaching into the side compartment and handing it to her with a half-hearted smile. 'Just in case.' As she opened the door and went to get out, he added, 'If I have a spare moment tomorrow I'll find the address for Daniel Dibello and we can see if he knows where the number plates ended up.'

She thanked him and watched him drive off, then trudged along the road, running her fingertips through the long grass. She felt childish for doubting him. Ryan wasn't trying to stop her investigating, he was just busy. She felt bad that she'd pressured him into helping her find the bike. In the past few days he'd organised search and recovery operations, investigated Blair's death and headed up the drug task force. Not to mention another flooding death, where a woman's body had shown up in a farm paddock, two kilometres from where she was last seen.

She was rounding a bend in the road when a huge semi-trailer roared past, then another in quick succession. She closed her eyes to avoid being blinded by mud spraying from the wheels. She remembered what Lachlan had said on their first day in Killarney: the Feds had cracked down on drug trafficking via the Pacific Highway on the east coast. The trucks had changed their route and many of them were travelling through Killarney to avoid detection. She made a mental note to ask Ryan about it when she saw him again.

She continued along the road for another twenty minutes until she found herself outside the old butter factory. One of the young boys she'd met on her first day in Killarney was leaning against the brick wall, smoking. He dropped the cigarette as soon as he saw her, grinding it into the dirt with the heel of his Dunlop Volley.

He was wearing a striped polo shirt and shorts, which were hiked up all the way to his waist. It occurred to her that perhaps the reason he'd been so keen to hang out with older boys and wag school was because he was being picked on. As Dana drew closer she could see that he was upset.

'Are you okay?' she asked, trying to remember his name. 'I'm Dana, we met the other week.'

'I remember,' he said glancing up at her quickly before looking away. 'I'm Tyler.'

'What's wrong? You look like you're having a hard day?'

'It's Brother Blair.' He burst into tears.

Please tell me he hasn't been abusing you too. She forced herself to keep an open mind. 'What's wrong? What did he do?'

'Nothing! He was my friend. It doesn't matter anymore, anyway – he's dead.'

'I'm so sorry. How did you find out?'

'Brian told me.' The cowlick that hung over his pale forehead made his eyes seem huge.

'Oh, Tyler. I'm so sorry.' It was bad enough contemplating Blair's death as a fully grown adult. She couldn't begin to imagine what it must have been like for a young teenager with no-one to confide in.

Tyler looked up at her shyly. 'Exodus 20:13 says *Thou shalt not murder* so the last thing Blair did was a sin. Do you think there's any way he'll get into heaven now?'

She squeezed his shoulder. 'When I used to go to Sunday School we had a lesson on the book of James. Have you heard of it?'

'I don't think so.'

'In James it says that mercy always triumphs over judgement. For anyone to take their own life they'd have to be in a world of sadness and despair. So, I think that deserves our understanding and our sympathy. And I honestly think that God would feel the same way.'

She looked across town, at the rolling green hills, and was silent for a moment. 'Did Jayden ever tell you that he was scared, or that he was worried about anything?'

He shook his head. 'He's one of the bravest guys I know.'

'Was there anything else going on for him, do you think? Anything that might've gotten him into trouble?'

'I know that one of the men who worked in the shop was asking him to sell drugs.'

The story had a ring of truth to it. She knew of other instances where young people had been used as drug convoys because they were generally able to operate without drawing the suspicion of police. 'Did he tell you the man's name? Or what he looked like?'

'Nah. Do you think Jayden might've changed his mind and ended up selling them?'

'I'm not sure. Everyone has said that Jayden hated drugs. That after his mother died, he wanted nothing to do with them.'

'Yeah, once we had a bottle of bourbon here at the clubhouse, but he refused to even have one sip. He always said that alcohol was for losers.'

'So, can you think of any reason he would change his mind?'

'He didn't like drugs, but he sure liked money. He told me that one day he was going to be rich and move up to Airlie Beach, where one of his cousins used to live. He wanted to buy a house right on the water and was just going to live there and buy a boat, go fishing and camping, and no-one would be able to tell him what to do anymore.'

'So, you think that he might've been likely to sell drugs if there was enough money involved?'

'Maybe.' Tyler's eyes were downcast. 'I've been having really bad dreams about him lately – that Jayden finally got his home at the beach and was diving under the water, but he got trapped and couldn't get to the surface in time.'

'You know it's only a dream, right? That it doesn't mean anything.' She made a mental note to speak to the Guidance Officer up at the school to get him some counselling.

'Sure.' He didn't look convinced. 'I've still got the Elton John tape he lent me. I've been listening to "Song for Guy" a lot lately. He always told me that was his favourite.'

When Dana returned to the pub later that afternoon she went straight to her room. Blair's death, the hopelessness of their search for Jayden, her fight with Lachlan and her suspicions about Sean had finally caught up with her. An aching depression settled in her chest that was impossible to shift. She paid for a glass of chardonnay from Cynthia then sat on the balcony outside her room. When she thought about the events of the past few days she felt as though her brain was going to explode. She thought Blair had suicided but now there was a possibility he had been murdered? But why? Had someone blamed him for Jayden's disappearance? She wondered what Susan would make of it, then realised she hadn't spoken to her friend in days.

She headed straight to Cynthia's office. As she waited for the call to be picked up her eyes lingered on the desk, which was covered in invoices, stained coffee mugs and a curve of stale pizza crust. She was warmed by the thought of the kind, yet disorganised publican, who'd given so much to the town and its people. Her finger was on the redial button when a breathless hello came down the line.

'Susan, hi. It's Dana. Are you okay?'

'A bit worse for wear. I'm in a bit of pain. They've given me medication but all I want to do is sleep.'

'That sounds terrible. I really wish I was there. Angus said he spoke to you. I'm hoping we can get out of here soon.'

'It's been a tough couple of days …' Susan's voice wavered as though she was on the precipice of vast emotion. 'I was almost going to call Jason and ask him to come home, but he just got that new job and I don't want to wreck it for him. Not when everything's going so well.'

A lump formed in Dana's throat and she cursed the universe for trapping her in Killarney when Susan needed her. 'I'm really hoping it won't be too much longer.'

'It's just that I've started to think about what's ahead and I won't lie, I'm absolutely terrified.'

Dana felt panicked to hear Susan so bereft. She was usually so strong, taking everything in her stride. The silence between them lengthened as Dana struggled to find words of comfort.

'What I'm trying to say, is that it's been very quiet without you and Angus around.'

'I know what you mean. I spoke with him yesterday afternoon and he's in good spirits. He misses *you* though and he's very keen to get home.' Though it wasn't a faithful rendering of their conversation, Susan sounded so depressed that Dana would have said anything to lift her spirits. She put the phone on the hook with a sinking feeling before trudging back up the stairs. An oppressive smell lingered in the air – rising damp, cigarette smoke and body odour. As she let herself into her room, she fantasised about being back in Toowoomba under the crisp white sheets of her own bed. Even the thought of returning to the office seemed preferable. She imagined the warm breeze on her face as she wandered across the park for a coffee before work.

A patter of rain hit the window and Dana's heart lurched.

Were they ever going to get out of here?

15

Dana was pleased when Ryan found her in the bar eating breakfast the next morning. As promised, he had pulled Daniel Dibello's address from the computer so they could follow up about the quad bike plates involved in the hit-and-run. They drove to a two-storey brick house with weeds sprouting from the gutters and a wad of letters and advertising leaflets bursting from the mailbox. Daniel's flatmate told them Daniel was in town. Ryan drove the police car up and down the main street three times and was about to return to the station when a man with a goatee and no shoes exited the co-op with a paper bag under his arm. A boy who appeared to be about ten years of age was trotting along beside him.

'That's him.' Ryan swerved to the side of the road and killed the engine.

'Daniel Dibello?' he asked, once they were standing in front of him on the footpath.

'What's it to you?'

'I'm investigating the death of Johnny Buckley. I wanted to ask you a few questions. First of all, what's in the bag?'

'My Subutex,' he replied.

'And where were you on the night of January the third?'

'Tom and I were at home. I remember, because it was my birthday and we were watching the cricket, West Indies versus Pakistan, weren't we, mate?'

The boy nodded and grinned, offering them a gappy smile.

'Look, we have reason to believe that Wyatt Nelson's grandson, Dean, sold you a quad bike, the plates of which have ended up on the bike responsible for the hit-and-run involving Johnny Buckley. Can you tell us how you came into possession of the quad bike and where it is now?'

'Dean owed me some money for work I helped him out with. He gave me the quad bike instead, but I only had it for a couple of weeks. Stacked it heading out to the falls on a bush track one day and it was a write-off. I ended up selling off some of the parts to a guy who worked out at the sawmill. He took the whole thing off my hands for a coupla hundred bucks.'

'Who was the guy?' Dana interrupted.

'Dunno – he dropped the money off at my girlfriend's place. She said he was on a Triumph Thunderbird – didn't even take off his helmet.'

'What do you know about Sean O'Malley?' She put her palms flat on the wooden surface and stared down Ryan, who was sitting behind his desk at the police station.

'I can't talk about it.' He looked at her then, and the sun came out in his usually serious face. 'What do *you* know about him?'

She was silent and he let out a hoot of laughter.

Anger flashed across her face. 'Is Sean a person of interest?'

'You know as well as I do, I'm not allowed to discuss it.'

'I mean, there's got to be a reasonable explanation. Surely, he wouldn't get on his Triumph Thunderbird, mow someone down, then not tell anyone.'

'It sounds like you know him quite well.'

'He's my work colleague's brother, so I have met him from time to time.' She had no desire to admit they had a more personal relationship. 'You do know that nobody's seen Sean for a few days?'

'It has come to my attention, but don't worry about Sean. He'll land on his feet – always has.' There was an edge to his voice that made Dana wonder what had gone on between them, what he wasn't telling her. It reminded her of Lachlan's vague response when she'd asked about Sean's relationship with Edith, when the rest of his family were estranged from her.

She stared out the window wondering what she was missing. The thought of Sean, the man she'd slept with, killing someone on his motorbike made her feel physically sick. She tried to picture what had happened. Could it have been an accident? An act of retribution? Perhaps Sean and Johnny had a falling-out? Lachlan had told her about the drug culture at the sawmill, but she never picked Sean for being involved in any of it. And was Sean's guilty conscience the reason why he'd been so hard for her to pin down, because he couldn't allow himself to get close to anyone? Or perhaps the hit-and-run was simply a variant of the cowardly behaviour he'd displayed towards her so far. By the time she managed to drag herself back from her thoughts Ryan was staring at her. 'Please tell me we're going to be getting out of here soon,' she asked.

'I haven't heard anything, but with any luck it might be tomorrow.'

She pondered the perfectly manicured bonsai tree on his desk and tried to size him up. She'd had him pegged as arrogant and aloof – a modern-day Mr Darcy – but there was certainly more going on than she had first assumed. The more time she spent with him, the more curious she became. He was higher up in the police force than he'd let on, for a start. 'I suppose you'll be running home to your family as soon as the river subsides?'

'Divorced,' he said simply.

'Oh right. I remember now. The difficulty of being a divorced Catholic.'

'And you?'

'I was married too, but our baby died, and the relationship didn't last.'

'Sorry.'

'Yeah, me too.' He was surprisingly easy to talk to she realised as she stood up.

'If it turns out we're still here tonight, I'll be having a few drinks at the bar, if you're interested?' The words came out awkwardly, as though it had cost him to say them.

She remembered Sean and the emotional turmoil and confusion she'd been through during the short time they'd been involved. 'That's very kind. I'll see how I go.'

Dana was making her way back to the pub when she had a flash of inspiration. All of her enquiries were leading to the Queen Mary Falls store. Why *was* Sean close to Edith when Lachlan and the rest of the family wanted nothing to do with her? Had someone asked Jayden to sell drugs at work? And did this have anything to do with his disappearance? Maybe Edith knew where Sean was.

She strode with purpose over the bridge, the Condamine rushing beneath her, and begged Cynthia for the keys to her Toyota Corolla. Once she was in the car, she raced towards Queen Mary Falls where she parked at the picnic spot and took the stairs into the store, two at a time.

The buzzer sounded when she pushed the door open and she found Edith at the front counter reading a copy of the *Warwick Daily News*. The collar on her white linen blouse was impossibly high as she placed her cup on the counter and fingered the fob chain around her neck. 'Dana.' She looked up over her glasses with eyes that were devoid of emotion. 'Can I help you with something?'

'I've come to see Angus. Just having a bit of a browse.'

Edith's brow furrowed but she went back to her paper and Dana went down the aisle to the breakfast cereal section. The boxes of Coco Pops were dusty. When she checked the use-by date she saw that they'd expired in 1993. As she walked into the next aisle she couldn't help but notice the strange array of products on display – toothbrushes with no toothpaste, random packets of children's toys. She had a flashback to what Lachlan's father had said in Stanthorpe; the way the conversation had veered in a different direction when she asked what business the cousins were involved in. Pat had mentioned transport and Lachlan had alluded to drug crime, but she'd assumed they'd been exaggerating because of the falling-out. But perhaps the shop really was a front for something far more sinister.

Dana returned to the counter. 'I have a few more questions to ask you about Jayden Maloney, if that's okay?'

'I'm heading out in five, so you'll have to make it quick.' Edith interlaced her fingers and placed them in front of her. 'This is a delicate issue, Dana. I'm a member of the Queensland Country Women's Association and the RSL Auxiliary. If it gets out that people think my shop is linked with Jayden's disappearance, I'll lose business.'

'Don't worry, I can be discreet.'

'Well, I've been hearing things around town about you.'

'Such as?' Dana knew perfectly well Edith was trying to distract her.

'You've been going around trying to pin Jayden's disappearance on everyone when there's probably a perfectly innocent explanation,' Edith said.

'I'm all ears.'

'Getting swept away in the floodwaters, for a start.'

'Why haven't they found his body then?'

'Goodness, I don't know. Perhaps he was taken by a wild animal?'

Why haven't they found his remains? she wanted to reply, but thought better of it. 'I received some information that Jayden had done a few extra shifts on the days before his disappearance.'

'As I told you before, he's never officially been on the books, so I can't confirm whether that's true.'

'How convenient.'

'For his good as much as mine, he wanted to avoid being taxed heavily.' A smirk played on Edith's lips. 'Anything else you wanted to know?'

'I understand you own a trucking company.'

'O'Malley Transport. Owned by the family since the 1950s.'

'I was listening to a news report the other morning about

another crash on the highway involving a semi and was thinking how difficult it must be to be in the trucking game.' Dana leant in towards Edith, an imitation of deep compassion.

'There's positives and negatives about being in any business,' said Edith.

'But don't you get sick of hearing all the stories of truck drivers speeding? Of driving too many hours, doped up to the eyeballs? I mean, some of those news stories make it seem like breaking the law is a way of life for truckies.'

'There's a lot of pressure on people in the transport industry to maintain their schedules, otherwise they lose work. And some of them use stimulants to get by. It's not something our staff partake in as we treat them extremely well, but that's just the way it is.' She gave Dana a self-satisfied smile, suggesting she had no intention of falling for Dana's attempts to pump her for information.

'And what part does Sean play in your business?'

'What do you mean?'

'He always seems to be helping out, even though I know he has more than enough on his plate with his actual job at the sawmill. Is *he* on the payroll?' She was on the verge of being obnoxious, but she didn't care.

'He's family. We help each other out.'

'Lachlan and his parents don't seem to agree.'

Edith put her shoulders back, bristling. 'Their loss, but blood's blood and I'll always be there for Sean – unlike his alcoholic father.'

At that moment, the double doors from the kitchen swung open and a man with shoulder-length hair under a bucket hat came into the store. She could see a tattoo peeking out beneath his shirt sleeve. She recognised him as the cousin she'd seen in the photo at Lachlan's father's house.

'Who's she?' the man demanded as he stood over her, his pupils like pinpricks, his chest out, challenging her.

'Billy, where's your manners? Have you finished those Anzac biscuits and put them in the oven?'

'No.'

She rolled her eyes. 'Billy's always been my shy boy, haven't you, darling.'

Dana had a flashback to what Lachlan had said about his cousins, about adult men living with their mothers.

Edith placed a hand with blood-red nails on his forearm. 'But before you go, get that bitch out of my shop.'

Dana rushed to the parking area across the road and sat in the car, her heart thumping. She'd been planning to check in and see Angus, maybe even take a look around the caravan park, but Edith's threats had put an end to that. She slumped against the window feeling the sting of defeat as a trio of rainbow lorikeets bickered in a hollow tree beside her. She was about to return to the pub when Edith skidded out of the car park in a white Toyota. Dana ducked below the dashboard so she couldn't be seen. When the coast was clear she crept across the road and snuck up the side road into the caravan park. A large steel shed near the back row of vans caught her eye.

Reasoning that Billy would still be in the cafe manning the till, she yanked the sliding door open and stepped inside. The interior was gloomy despite the heat, and the smell of damp and diesel rose up from the dirt floor. As her eyes began to adjust, she took in a chaotic array of mowers and tools, an ancient Land Rover parked against the back wall. She jumped at a noise to the left of her before registering the rodent scuttle of tiny feet.

'Hello.' She called out, not expecting an answer.

She was about to return outside when a piece of equipment caught her eye. A bike-shaped lump, covered in a dark tarp in the far corner of the shed. She crept towards it and drew back the material, the thrill of anticipation tickling her forearms. A Triumph Thunderbird.

Sean's.

She'd found the bike. Now where was the man?

She traced her finger along a scar on the left handlebar. A weld to fix damaged metal. She knelt at the back of the bike, smoothing her hand across the number plate. SJM 007. She yanked her hand away as if it were on fire. The police would need to take fingerprints now it was clear that this was the bike involved in the hit-and-run.

She stood up, trying to process the enormity of her discovery. Daniel Dibello had told them that the man who'd bought the quad bike had ridden a bike like Sean's, but she'd never allowed herself to believe it. And even if it was the vehicle responsible for Johnny's death, had Sean been the rider? She hurried from the shed and made a call from the public phone box to the police station. She left a message for Ryan about her discovery, he'd need to send a crew out for forensic investigations.

When she hung up she felt terrified about how little she knew about Sean. She tried to remember his actions, concrete gestures of kindness, but all she could remember were his words. Who were his friends? Had he always worked at the sawmill? How could she know so little about a man she'd allowed into her bed? And worse still, her heart.

16

It was almost dark when she got in the car and started back to Killarney. Humidity was thick in the air as she wound the window down and undid the top buttons of her blouse. She pulled the car out of the car park and fiddled with the knobs of the radio, disappointed when there was only static.

She was halfway down Spring Creek Road when she saw it. A massive semi-trailer in her rear-view mirror, its lights on blinding high beam. She shielded her eyes and adjusted the mirror. Moments earlier, the road had been deserted. Now the truck was bearing down on her, getting closer by the second. *Where had it come from?*

Her first thoughts were that it could be Edith's son, Billy. He'd been sent to follow Dana, to intimidate her. She'd asked too many questions about the transport business and now they were trying to scare her off. It was just as Lachlan had said – the dodgy O'Malleys were caught up in low-level criminality and operated behind a code of secrecy, from which Lachlan and his parents were estranged, but strangely Sean had plenty of contact with. Everyone in Killarney seemed to believe that Blair had killed Jayden, but what if Lachlan's family were somehow responsible for the teenager's death. Maybe during all those months working at the shop he'd stumbled on something he wasn't supposed to know. She scanned the road, searching for a safe place to pull over, but couldn't find one. Besides, what if the truck pulled over too? She'd be trapped in the dark with a potential psychopath.

In the next instant, the semi's grate was up against her boot. Her head smacked the side window with a force that made her gasp. She floored the accelerator, willing Cynthia's tiny car to go faster. The truck's horn blared, rocketing her heart rate to a hundred. She turned, trying to catch a glimpse of the driver, but the lights were so dazzling they stung her retinas. She skidded down Border Road, the brakes of the truck screeching from behind. As she rounded the corner the car fishtailed beneath her. Behind her, the trailer leant heavily but righted itself at the last moment. Dana slammed her hand on the steering wheel and swore. There was no mistaking the driver's intention. He wanted her off the road. He wanted her wrapped around a tree.

Her pulse thumped as the lights of another vehicle appeared in the other direction. She flashed her high beams, hoping they might register her distress. If there was a witness to the driver's aggression, maybe he'd be less likely to carry on. The truck drew back, letting her pull ahead, but as soon as the car passed in the other direction, the semi was bearing down on her again. She wiped her palms on her pants, one at a time, and realised she was shaking. By her calculations, she only had another five minutes until she reached the township. Surely she could make it.

She pushed the speedometer to 140 kilometres per hour. The

car began to rattle. Any higher and she'd lose control. The truck revved its engine. Her heart was in her mouth.

The lights of Killarney glimmered up ahead. She passed one house, then another. They were on the outskirts of town. There was no way he'd want the spectacle of driving down the main street.

She was almost there. One hundred metres to the final turn. She sent up a prayer and pushed the accelerator flat against the floor, yanking the steering wheel hard to the right.

When she looked up again the truck was gone, its tail-lights heading left down Violet Street. The moment the danger had disappeared a sharp throbbing started in her head. She reached up to her forehead, pulling her hand away when she felt the warm trickle of blood.

She staggered up the front steps of the pub, ignoring the glances of a group of men on the verandah. Her armpits were dripping with sweat. Her nerves shot.

The pub was busy as she lurched inside. A crowd was watching a game of rugby on a wide-screen TV and cheered as a try was converted between the posts.

Cynthia looked up from behind the bar. 'Oh my god. What happened?' She ushered Dana onto the nearest bar stool. 'Wait there.' She disappeared behind the bar and came back with a washer and a first-aid kit and started tending to Dana.

'Get Lachlan,' Dana gasped.

Cynthia smoothed a bandaid to Dana's forehead then hurried around the corner.

When Cynthia returned with Lachlan he had a schooner of beer in his hand and took the stool next to her. 'Man alive. What happened to you?' he asked.

'Some arsehole tried to run me off the road in his semi. Tail-gated me the whole way back from Queen Mary Falls. Even bumped Cynthia's car.'

'But why? Did you see who was driving? The make of the truck?'

'I couldn't see anything. The high beams were in my face.'

'We'll have to let Ryan know, but I think he's gone down to the border.'

'Anyway, I'm fine. Just a bit shaken. I'm so sorry about your car, Cynthia. I haven't had a chance to check the damage yet.'

'Oh god, don't worry about that old thing. I've been hoping to get an insurance pay-out on it for years.'

A man with a bright red nose and a web of spider angiomas across his cheeks turned around from the bar. 'Would it be too much to get a bit of service round here?'

Cynthia rolled her eyes and hurried back to the counter.

'I need to tell you something.' Dana lowered her voice as she turned to Lachlan. 'I found Sean's bike in a shed behind the Queen Mary Falls shop. With the identical number plate to the one witnesses identified during the hit-and-run. And it's been repaired recently.'

Lachlan took a long sip of his beer, the colour draining from his face. 'Blood-dee hell …'

'I mean, I don't understand, why would he be riding around on an unregistered bike?' Her mind was working overtime. 'And he rode it to visit me after our first trip to Killarney. Would he really be that brazen? To ride it around in plain sight after he killed someone?'

Lachlan stared past her to a couple playing pool by the window. 'I hope not.'

'You said it yourself – the people who live in the cabins at Queen Mary Falls are transient. Truck drivers and tourists – all sorts of people have lived there from time to time. Anyone could have gained access to it if Sean was parking it in the shed and leaving his keys behind the counter. Someone could have gone for a joy ride, killed Johnny Buckley and then returned it without Sean ever having known.' Dana hesitated slightly. 'But the thing that's bothering me the most, is that I don't buy that Daniel Dibello wasn't aware of who bought the quad bike. Everyone in Killarney knows Sean owns that Thunderbird. Are they friends, is that it? And why's Sean associating with a known drug dealer?'

'Sean's always taken short cuts, and I know he's dabbled from time to time. Been involved in distribution for the extra cash. He was trying to distance himself from all that. Things would go well for a while but he had a tendency to blow it all up.'

She put a hand to the cut on her head. It was starting to throb again. 'Perhaps these are things you could have told me *before* we started dating.'

'It's not as though you asked for my opinion.'

'You wanted me to do my social work on him, as your father would have said. You wanted me to fix him.'

'No. I thought it would be good for him to date someone with integrity, a good moral compass.'

'You're just flattering me now.'

'Anyway, he's a good guy at heart. He really is.'

'With a slight predilection for drug use. And for murdering people.'

'Dana.' He gave her a withering look. 'Anyway, there's something else I need to talk to you about.'

'Go on.' She couldn't believe there could be more than what he'd just revealed.

'I know what's been going on with Sean. I just haven't wanted to talk about it because Ryan made me promise not to tell anyone, and I've been angry at you after what happened to Blair.'

'Uh-huh.' Annoyance crackled in her voice. 'So where is he?'

'He went undercover to try and find Jayden. There's a rumour that Jayden was selling drugs from Edith's shop. The cops have never had anything concrete on her and Ryan figured that Sean could use his connections to investigate. Ryan's been trying to figure out who is responsible for the drugs that are now coming through Killarney. And this is the part that I've never mentioned before, but Ryan thinks that the transport company has been doing more than just ferrying drugs on the side. He thinks Edith heads up the whole operation from the shop.'

'You didn't think to tell me that the place where Angus works is the centre of a drug ring? That he might want to find another job?' She was incredulous.

'Ryan said I had to be careful, that telling anyone would compromise the investigation.'

'I'm not just anyone, Lachlan. I'm your work partner. And I could have discreetly removed Angus, brought him back to stay with me and no-one would have been the wiser.'

'Look, Dana. You can't just go rocking up at the shop asking questions, you'll end up getting hurt. But you were right to be worried about Sean. Ryan just told me that he did a wiretap of Sean's phone and he's in real trouble. So, I'm going to start up a search myself, to try to find him.'

'Does Ryan know?'

'No, he's asked me not to interfere. The only reason I'm telling you is in case something goes wrong, and I don't come back.'

'And when, pray tell, is this happening?'

'Tonight. Right now.'

'And what am I supposed to do while you're out investigating? Sit around twiddling my thumbs? We've been stuck in this pub for days. I don't think I can take much more.'

He didn't answer. He was already disappearing out the door where a sliver of light was shining on the darkened shops across the road.

She woke early the next morning, riddled with anxiety about Angus getting caught up in a drug-running syndicate and Lachlan heading out to find Sean in the criminal underworld. She bought two avocado and bacon breakfast burgers from Cynthia at the bar and took them to the police station where Ryan was rushing out the front door.

'I figured you could do with one of these.' She handed him a warm bun wrapped in wax paper.

'Thanks, that's very kind.' His eyes darted around the street as he rifled through his pocket and came up with his car keys.

'It's pretty incredible that the bike responsible for the hit-and-run has been found,' she said, wondering why he was so distracted.

'I suppose so.'

'You suppose so? It's the most significant step forward we've made in relation to finding out who is responsible for Johnny's death.' She had to jog to keep up with him as he made his way to his vehicle.

'I'm just not thrilled with the way you came to have the information about the number plate,' he said, flicking her a look of displeasure.

'Meaning?' She knew what he was referring to but didn't want to give herself away before she knew for sure.

'I know you looked through my files without permission.'

She pulled a face, hoping to redeem herself. 'I'm sorry, I have a tendency to get obsessed with things and I can't let them go.'

'If you weren't in a relationship with Sean, I might've been able to be more open, but since the whole town is aware that you've been together in recent weeks it's out of the question.'

'For what it's worth, I didn't meet him until after the hit-and-run.'

'I still can't discuss it,' he said, opening the car door.

She put a hand on his forearm before he got in the driver's seat. 'I get it. I really do. It's just that the more I look into Johnny's hit-and-run and Jayden's disappearance, the more I'm convinced that the two incidents are linked. Why would Jayden go missing a few days after a hit-and-run in a sleepy town where nothing ever happens?'

'You may be right. When you have a strong instinct about a case you should listen to that. There's often a piece of evidence that doesn't match with what someone's told you, and that's what you need to remember.' He hesitated. 'Has it occurred to you that Jayden could've borrowed or stolen Sean's bike and then suicided because of his guilt?'

'It just doesn't make sense to me. Even if Jayden had been responsible for the hit-and-run, he was only sixteen. People would take into account his age and the fact that it was an accident. He was a minor, so they'd be sure to go soft on him.'

'You know what it's like with teenagers. They're going through so many changes and things can become overblown. It can be a very unsettling time.'

'I hear what you're saying. It's just that from what I've heard about Jayden he was extremely resilient. He'd faced significant adversity in his life, yet somehow he always found the resources to ask for help when he needed it. Have you had any information back from the forensic testing that was done on Sean's bike?'

'They just called. They managed to lift two sets of fingerprints. One lot was Sean's, as it's his bike. But there was also another set of prints we managed to identify.'

'Whose were they?' She held open the driver's side door peering in at him.

'You're not going to be happy about this, Dana.'

She wished he'd hurry up. 'I don't care. Just tell me.'

'They belong to Angus Fitcher. I've got an officer heading out there to speak with him now.' Ryan looked at her apologetically, realising the news had come as a shock. 'Sorry, I've really got to go. I've got a truck trying to cross the border and I need to get out there. Thanks for breakfast.'

'Can I grab a lift to the Queen Mary Falls store? It's on the way.' She needed to ask Angus why the hell his fingerprints had been found on the bike that killed Johnny Buckley. Dana didn't wait for him to answer. She skirted around the front of the vehicle and jumped into the passenger seat.

Ryan started the car and tore open the wrapper of his breakfast burger with his teeth. He steered out of the car park with one hand, then headed south.

'Let me.' She unwrapped it for him and handed it back.

'So, what's the story with the truck at the border?'

'We've been searching a lot of the vehicles for drugs over the last week and apparently the driver of this one is acting suspicious.'

'In what way?'

'Speaking fast, rubbing his nose a lot so they think he's taken methamphetamine to stay awake. But he's refusing to let the officers inspect the load.' Ryan wolfed down his burger in a couple of bites.

'Right. So, rumour has it that you've been using Sean to get you some information as part of Operation Border Control and now he's in trouble.'

'How do you know that?' He frowned as the houses grew further apart and they flew past the industrial area on the outskirts of town.

'Lachlan told me last night, after I was chased back from Queen Mary Falls by a semi-trailer and it tried to drive me off the road. Right about here actually.'

'Seriously? That's terrible. Did you see the driver? Get a number plate?'

'I was too busy fearing for my life to be able to do either of those things.'

'Sure, sorry. But Lachlan shouldn't have told you about Sean and Sean shouldn't have said anything to Lachlan either. It's very unprofessional.'

'Well, as of last night, Lachlan said he was going to head out and try to find Sean.'

Ryan put his head back and let out a groan of frustration. 'I told him explicitly not to do that. I warned him he'd end up a dead man if he did something that stupid.'

The two-way radio beeped. '228 to 97.'

He picked it up. '97 to 228, come in.'

'He's dead!' A voice wailed into the dispatcher.

'Who? Who are you talking about?'

'I don't know. I've never seen him in my life.'

'Calm down,' said Ryan. 'I need you to tell me what's happened.'

There was a static sound on the radio accompanied by a scraping sound.

'Sorry, Boss. We've located a body in the back of the truck.' A new voice on the radio. 'On Border Road just past the Spring Creek Road intersection. White Caucasian. Male. Looks like a drug deal gone wrong.'

Nausea twisted in Dana's intestines. 'Do you think it could be Sean? Or Lachlan?'

Ryan's eyes remained on the road. 'I don't know. I'm more worried that it's Jayden. That he's tangled up with the drug runners.'

Her stomach hurt as she pictured the dead body. She thought about what Lachlan's wife, Rachel, would do if he was dead. After his near miss on the road to Crows Nest it was a miracle his wife let him return to work. If he didn't make it this time Dana knew who'd get the blame.

'Roger that,' Ryan said into the radio. 'I'm on my way.' He turned on the siren.

She covered her ears as he put the car into fourth and sped towards Woodenbong and the New South Wales border.

The B-double truck was parked on the side of the road with a police car in front of it, red and blue lights flashing. Two officers in high-vis vests had handcuffed the driver and pushed him up against his vehicle.

Ryan killed the engine and stepped out of the car. He stuck his head back in.

'Stay in the car. I mean it.'

She nodded. A sickening dread coiled around her throat as the minutes crept by. Ryan and the officers gathered around the back of the semi.

After fifteen long minutes an ambulance pulled up. She craned her neck to see a male and female paramedic enter the back of the truck with a medical kit. They returned for the stretcher a few minutes later.

She chewed her nails. Now there was a possibility that Sean was dead she felt deeply regretful for judging him so harshly. He had been kind to her – when he'd cooked her dinner and shown her Queen Mary Falls.

The paramedics wheeled the trolley down the rear ramp of the truck, the silhouette of the body under a white sheet strapped to a gurney. When the wheels became momentarily bogged in thick black mud it was all she could do to stop herself from sprinting onto the road and demanding that Ryan tell her the identity of the corpse.

After another five minutes passed, she could no longer stand it. She got out of the car and strode over to where Ryan was standing near the front cabin of the truck. He had his back to her and was speaking to one of the officers. She tapped him on the shoulder.

'Just a moment.' Annoyance flickered across his face.

She stood back and listened closely to what he was saying.

'We'll need to contact forensics. Once we have an idea of

who the victim is we'll need to start contacting family members for verification.'

She wiped the sweat from her palms onto her pants.

Ryan swung around, his eyes bright with anger. 'What is it?'

'Who is it?' There was desperation in her voice. 'Is it Sean or Lachlan? Jayden?'

He shook his head. 'It's not them.'

She turned quickly and walked back to the car so he wouldn't see her face, tears of relief in her eyes.

17

It was much later that morning when a police officer finally dropped Dana at Edith's corner store. She passed a dog tied to the front steps, a look of trepidation in its ice-blue eyes as she went inside to find Angus. After being told that he was in Tina's cabin, she strode around the corner and found him on the front deck, reading.

'Still *Flowers in the Attic*?' she asked.

'Yeah, but this is the last one in the series.' He put the book down. 'I don't know what I'm going to do when I'm done.'

'Start a new series?' she suggested, hoping she could steer his interests towards something more appropriate.'

'There's a heap of Stephen King's, so maybe I'll try them.' He stood up to give her a hug.

She stifled a groan and changed the subject. 'Who owns the dog at the shop?'

'Oh, that's Billy's dog. He got him a few days ago. Do you want to come meet him? He's so awesome.'

'Love to,' said Dana, thinking it would be a good distraction while she questioned him about the Thunderbird.

Dana struggled to keep up as Angus jogged over to pat the black-and-white border collie.

'Hey, Rocky. Hey, boy.' Angus pressed his face into the dog's fur.

'I didn't realise you loved dogs so much.'

'I always really wanted one. When I was younger I used to beg Mum for one. She got me a toy poodle one Christmas, even though it wasn't what I wanted and I'd spent the entire year begging for a border collie. But then we only had it for two months because it got a tick and died.'

'That's a sad story.'

'Oh well,' he said philosophically.

She sat down on the step next to the dog. 'There's been something I've been meaning to ask you about actually. That bike that's been in the shed for the past few weeks – did you ever end up riding it?'

'Nah, Jayden and I used to sit on it sometimes and pretend we were in the Grand Prix. I can't ride it myself, it's too big. But Jayden took me for a ride.'

She breathed a huge sigh of relief. She'd come to know when he was lying and he hadn't exhibited any of his usual tells, such as not meeting her eyes.

'And besides,' he went on, 'I knew that Mum would have hated it.'

'Really?' she said with surprise, thinking motorbikes were right up Tina's alley.

'She had a boyfriend once who had a really bad motorbike accident where he fell off and cut up his leg, so she made me promise never to get one. She calls them donor cycles – because people who die on them get head injuries but their bodies are usually intact so they can donate their organs.'

'I got the inference.' She hid a smile over his need to explain it to her. 'By the way, did Jayden ever ride the bike on his own?'

'Yeah, all the time. Jayden was good at fixing stuff. He used to work on the bike and make sure it was running well. Sean said he could just take it whenever he wanted. He didn't even have to ask.'

'That was nice of him.'

'Anyway, I already told all of this to that copper who came out earlier today.'

'It looks like the bike was involved in the hit-and-run.'

'I know. They thought I ran over Johnny, even though I have no idea how to ride it and I've only ever sat on it. I told him he was clutching at straws.' Angus shrugged. 'I said he could cross me off his list of suspects. When I told him that we solved the Sandra Kirby and Debbie Vickers case last year he was really impressed. He asked me questions about it for, like, forty-five minutes.'

'Well, I'm glad you enjoyed being interrogated.' She was relieved that there was a reasonable excuse for Angus's prints to be on the bike and that, for once, she had agreed with Tina's parenting advice.

'I did.' He grinned. 'Hey, let me show you the tricks Rocky can do. Sit boy. Shake hands.'

The dog obediently put out its paw and Angus shook it.

Dana spent the remainder of the day trying to distract herself by helping Cynthia serve up food and drinks to the volunteers who were helping to clean up the streets. There was excitement in the air, a local covers band had been arranged to play for the Australia Day public holiday and while most of the other festivities had been postponed due to the floods, Cynthia felt that the celebration might help raise everyone's spirits. Despite the fact Dana was keen to get home, her main concern now was the whereabouts of Sean and Lachlan. Why the hell hadn't they gotten in touch?

It was 3 pm when the landline behind the bar rang. Dana made a dive to pick it up.

'Two people have turned up at Glengallan House, an isolated homestead. One of the builders called it in,' explained Ryan. 'There's a good chance it might be them. The rescue chopper will be landing behind the pub in five, if you want to come?'

She didn't need to be asked twice. Dana slammed the phone on the receiver and raced outside, through the car park and into the wide expanse of grass behind the pub. Minutes later the silence was broken by the deafening whirr of propellers as the helicopter landed. She clambered into a seat beside Ryan. The pilot talked into his headphones and flicked the controls. The roar of the engine crescendoed as the chopper tilted backwards and rose into the air. Large drops of rain began to hit the windscreen as they flew over crops and farms, heading north. The Condamine River, brown and swollen, coiled towards Warwick, and the acres of green plains sprawled towards the distant peak of Mount Sturt. Twenty minutes later, a sandstone mansion appeared below. Ryan turned around and mouthed the word *Glengallan* over the din.

The homestead was the epitome of a haunted house – fire damage had warped the front verandah. A cypress tree grasped at the roof with branches like skeletal hands. As they descended, the grass parted and Sean and Lachlan darted out from the lower level of the house, shouting and waving their hands in the air. A surge of emotion hit Dana squarely in the chest as they came closer. The helicopter hovered a few metres above the ground. Their faces were lined with exhaustion as they rushed forward.

The band members were dragging PA equipment towards a makeshift stage and the locals were lined up in rows in front of the bar when she got back to the pub.

'So, what was it like going up in that chopper. Was it exciting?' Cynthia asked her and Lachlan.

'A little bit too exciting, if you ask me,' said Dana.

'You can fill me in on everything when I finish work tonight,' Cynthia said, and hurried back to the kitchen.

'Sean should be down in a minute – he's just having a shower,' Lachlan explained, taking a long sip from his schooner and wiping the back of his hand across his mouth when he'd finished. 'I don't think I've ever needed a drink as much as I've needed this one.'

Dana leant forward. 'Don't hold out on me. What happened?'

'It was the craziest thing ever ... I can laugh about it now, but at the time I wasn't sure I was going to make it out alive.' He appeared to note Dana's look of frustration. 'Anyway, I went searching for Sean at this property which was owned by a friend of my cousin. We'd gone to school with this guy years ago. But when I showed up one of them recognised that I worked at the Department. They quickly realised that Sean was an informant and he wasn't there to buy drugs after all. They called three of their mates and, long story short, ended up holding Sean and me at gunpoint with a sawn-off shotgun.'

Dana's face filled with horror. 'Then what happened?'

'There was a bit of a scuffle. Sean got a black eye and they locked us in a side room while they figured out what to do. I was sure we were goners. But then they tied us up and shoved us in one of their big four-wheel drives and dropped us in the middle of nowhere. I guess they figured that it was going to be easier to make us disappear for a bit than actually murder us. Anyway, we wandered around in the dark for a few hours until we stumbled across Glengallan House. Thank god for that, otherwise we wouldn't have known where the hell we were. We ended up sleeping there, which was seriously creepy, and then in the morning one of the builders who was doing repairs took pity on us and called the police.'

'Wow, that's quite a story.' She had to yell over the top of the music as the band started up. Cynthia delivered their bowls of nachos. 'And did you manage to get any more information on Jayden? Whether he was distributing drugs for them?'

'No, I really think he had way too much decency to be involved in anything like that.'

Dana sat back in her chair. 'I'm so relieved we found you. When you were gone, I started thinking about what a good friend you've been to me since I moved to Toowoomba. I was so upset when I thought about how bad things have been between us lately.'

'It's all good. It'll take a lot more than a few arguments to stop us being friends. Besides, who else would I get to type up my case notes for me?' He grinned.

Sean came towards them with two schooners of beer and placed one of them in front of Dana.

'You're looking good.' He touched her upper arm as the strains of White Town's 'Your Woman' drifted through the speakers. His eyes were unnaturally blue and he'd amassed extra facial hair while he'd been away.

Lachlan finished his drink and stood up. 'I'm going to hit the shower myself. I'll be back soon.'

'How've you been?' asked Sean once they were alone.

'Fine, thanks.' She knew she should ask a question in return but remained silent, waiting for him to explain himself.

A look of confusion clouded his face over her apparent lapse in manners. 'What have you been up to?' he asked.

'Just work and being trapped here in Killarney.'

He frowned at a group of young women dragging each other onto the dance floor. 'Do you want to go outside for a bit? It's hard to talk in here.'

'Sure,' she said in a resigned way, following him through the French doors and onto the verandah.

His words came in a rush. 'Sorry I went off the grid again. It's just that Ryan was putting pressure on me to help find that kid and I couldn't say no. And I thought if I told you, I'd put you at risk.'

The anger that she'd been building up over the past few days evaporated and settled into something more benign. 'I know, it's just been incredibly hard not knowing if Lachlan was okay.' She wasn't about to admit that she'd also been worried about his safety.

He put a hand on her shoulder. 'I get it, I really do. And hopefully you'll let me make it up to you.'

She shrugged off his touch, not allowing herself any further weakness. 'There's one thing I need to ask you first. What's the story with your bike?'

'What do you mean?'

'The Triumph Thunderbird. It was the bike used in the hit-and-run.'

He blinked and sat back on his stool. 'I left the keys behind the counter at the shop that night so anyone could have ridden it. You have to believe me; I had no idea that it had been used in the hit-and-run that killed Johnny Buckley.'

'What about the damage to the bike,' she shot back. 'You must have noticed the repairs on the handlebars?'

He ran a hand through his hair. 'I did, but whoever borrowed it did the right thing to fix it. I didn't see the point in tracking down who'd ridden it, I thought it was probably a kid and didn't want to get them in trouble.'

'You didn't think to mention it to the police?'

'No, because not in my craziest dreams could I ever have imagined it being involved in the hit-and-run.'

He was getting defensive she thought, watching the fear in his eyes. 'So where were you on the third of January? Were you responsible for the death of Johnny Buckley?'

'What?' he cried. 'That's insane. And besides, I have an alibi.'

'Who is it?'

'I'd tell you, but I can't. There's a lot of awkwardness tied up in it for some people.'

'You didn't tell the police about the repairs because you knew how bad that was going to look?' The image she'd had of Sean being a good and decent person had slipped through her fingers. Lachlan had been right. Sean wasn't a bad man, he was just a weak one. She was relieved to see Ryan striding towards them.

'Good news,' Ryan said. 'I've just had word that the water has receded and the bridge in Warwick is now clear. You'll be able to drive home tomorrow.'

'That's wonderful news,' said Dana, blinking back sudden tears of happiness.

'And, Sean, I'll need you to come with me to the station.'

'Come on, man, can't we do it tomorrow? I didn't do it. I swear to god. And like I said, I've got an alibi.'

'No can do, I'm afraid,' said Ryan.

'I know what you're doing. Being the big, strong man. Trying to show off in front of her.'

'Don't make this any harder than it has to be.' Ryan grabbed Sean's upper arm and steered him towards the door.

Sean called back towards Dana as he was being led away. 'I'll call you when you're back in Toowoomba. We'll go for coffee.'

Lachlan returned just in time to see them heading out the door. 'Where are they off to?'

'Questioning.' She was thankful that she'd almost finished her beer and her inhibitions were disappearing. 'What's the story with Sean's alibi for the hit-and-run.'

Lachlan groaned. 'Someone has to tell you. It may as well be me.' He hesitated. 'Sean left the motorbike at the shop because he went to visit a woman named Emma who lives at a nearby property.'

'I thought he was with Jessa.'

'Who?' His forehead creased with confusion then a light came on. 'Oh, her. She's always had a thing for him, but he's never gone there.'

'So, who's Emma?'

'The woman he's been having an affair with. He didn't want anyone to know because she's married.' He was silent for a beat. 'With kids.'

She was so incredulous she laughed and returned her glass to the table with a loud clink.

'But he wasn't responsible for Johnny's death!' he called out, as she stalked away up the stairs towards her room.

18

Dana felt a complicated mix of emotions as she tidied up her room, straightening the shiny maroon doona across the brass bed one last time. She'd spent eight days at the hotel but it had seemed like a lifetime. Soon she'd be back in her own home, with Angus and Susan next door, the hum of bees in the mock orange tree and everything in its right place.

Downstairs she found Angus and Tina at the bar, chatting to Cynthia's son, Brian. Dana gave Cynthia a hug and said her goodbyes with a sharp twinge of affection as she promised to keep in touch. She accompanied Angus and Tina outside to Lachlan's Range Rover.

Tina ruffled Angus's hair as they stood beside the car. 'Good luck starting your fancy new school, kiddo. And I'll chat to Nan and see if you can come and live here with me, like we talked about.'

Dana stowed his bags in the boot and tried to ignore Tina's emotional blackmail. When she looked up Ryan had appeared with Lachlan.

'Last day, hey?' Ryan said.

'I was starting to think I might be living above the pub forever.' She looked into his brown eyes thinking how much time they'd spent together over the past week. She'd almost come to regard him as a friend.

'Keep in touch. And I'll be sure to give you any updates on Jayden as they come in,' he said.

'Thank you. And I'm sorry we never got around to having that drink.'

'Oh, well. I'm in Toowoomba occasionally so I can always look you up. And you never know, you might be back here sooner than you think.'

'I doubt it.' She stared up at him, trying to decide whether to hug him or to shake his hand, then settled on a warm smile. As Lachlan pulled onto the road, going faster than she was comfortable with, she waved out of the passenger window.

'I can't believe I'm finally going to see Rachel and the kids. They're going to be ropable.'

They flew down Ivy Street as the sun broke through the clouds. For the first time, the tops of the mountains ringing Killarney were visible and not shrouded in fog. As they turned onto the highway, passing fields of luminescent green, she felt the tug of opposing emotions. Sadness about the loss of Blair and their inability to find Jayden, but relieved she'd soon be in the comfortable familiarity of home.

In Godsall Street the white roses were in flower on either side of the front steps and the heady scent of blossoms filled the air. The lavender was growing wildly in the front garden, alive with the droning of bees. As Lachlan pulled up on the street, Angus leapt out and used the knocker to hammer on Susan's front door.

'Not too loudly,' said Dana, 'she might be sleeping.'

Susan opened the door.

'Nan!' Angus threw himself into her arms. Dana was struck by the change in Susan's demeanour – her collarbones stood out prominently making her look frail and withdrawn.

Dana hugged Susan close, feeling her bird-like shoulders through her thin cotton t-shirt. She blinked back tears knowing there was no way Susan would want her feeling sorry for her.

'Lachlan.' Susan beamed up at him. 'How've you been?'

'What can I say. I'm very happy to be heading home.'

'Well, I hope you can stay for five minutes. I've made my world-famous lemonade scones with cherry jam.'

'Okay, five minutes.' He grinned.

They sat on the verandah in wicker chairs as Susan set a plate of scones and a pot of tea in front of them.

Angus took two scones and wolfed them down. 'Nan, can I go on the computer please? I've had my afternoon tea now.'

'You've only just got home!'

'But I'll have loads of emails to check.'

'Oh, I suppose so. It has been a week since you've been on it.'

He dumped his plate and raced inside.

'Some things never change,' said Susan.

'If it makes you feel any better, one of my friend's kids is only six, and they're already having arguments over the computer,' said Lachlan.

They waved at a neighbour walking her dogs down the street and Dana felt a sense of peace wash over her. She sliced a scone in half then slathered it in cream and jam. She was about to take a bite when her mobile started flashing; she'd silenced the ringtone when Angus had fallen asleep in the car. Her stomach dropped as she stared at the screen now, not daring to pick it up.

Lachlan gave her a questioning look. 'Aren't you going to get that?'

'We just got home. And besides, I'm sure they'll ring back if it's important.'

The phone started flashing again.

Dana sighed and picked it up. 'Ryan, I didn't expect to hear from you quite so soon.'

'They've located a body in a culvert at Queen Mary Falls.' He was in full police mode – no niceties. 'It's Jayden.'

Dana leapt up, turning her back on Lachlan, her heart in her mouth. 'What happened?' She had to lower her voice and walk out into the garden so the others couldn't overhear.

'It's unclear at this point, but we can talk more when you get here.'

She hit the red button and realised Angus was standing behind her.

'Who was it?' he asked, a strange expression on his face.

Lachlan and Susan were staring over at her expectantly and for a moment she wondered whether she should tell them in front of Angus.

He was going to find out one way or another.

'I'm so sorry, but it was about Jayden. His body's been found in Spring Creek out near Queen Mary Falls.'

'Is he dead?' he blurted.

'I'm afraid so.' Her heart went out to him. So many people taken from him, now he was chalking up another loss.

He was quiet in his grief. A single tear ran down his face and he went over to Susan and lay his head on her shoulder. Dana turned away, blinking the tears from her eyes. *Soon his nan will be gone too.*

Lachlan swore and dumped his plate on the table. 'Give me a moment to tell Rachel and the kids, then we're good to go.'

'Are you sure?' asked Dana, noticing that he suddenly looked very pale. 'At the very least we can drop in so you can see your family before we head back out.'

The sun was slipping towards the horizon by the time they reached Allora. Lachlan gripped the wheel with grim determination, steering through sections of road that were still waterlogged. They drove on past sheds filled with bales of hay and fields hidden deep in shadow. When they reached the valley of Killarney the mountains were ringed with dark clouds. Killarney was breathtaking, thought Dana as she stared out the window, but its beauty was dangerously deceptive.

It was dusk by the time they reached the Falls. The play equipment was deserted, and police cars were haphazardly parked in the picnic area. A light mist felt chill on her skin as they made their way down the slope towards the twin-arched culvert. Dana felt the weight of inevitability. Now that they were here, finding Jayden's body in the river seemed somehow predestined, a trajectory they'd been on since they drove to the sawmill two weeks earlier. *Of course, he hadn't just gone missing.*

As they went further along the path, she could see a flood light had been set up to illuminate the tunnel where police tape cordoned off the scene. Shadowy figures were rushing in and out of a forensic tent that had been put up to assist the investigators.

She followed Lachlan into the culvert, noting the sinister way it amplified every sound, from the surge of the river to the monumental rumble of a car passing on the bridge overhead.

Each step brought a rising anxiety. One part of her had no desire to see Jayden's body, yet another could not turn away. How else would she accept his death and help others to do the same?

She fell in behind Lachlan as he weaved through the officers and paused at the entrance to the tent where Ryan was on the phone. He snapped it shut and met them at the police tape barrier.

'Stay there – otherwise you'll contaminate the scene.' His voice echoed as though they were standing in a hollow tin can.

'What do you think happened?' Lachlan asked, as Dana craned her neck to see past a group of officers gathered around the body.

'Hard to say at this point. Could be anything from a drowning to something more suspicious. Up to the coroner to decide.'

The officers moved aside and she had a clear view. Jayden was on his back in the water, pushed up against a log, his knees buckled. The skin on his torso had darkened, deep gouges from where he'd hit the rocks. His bloated body was unrecognisable from weeks in the water. His face was turned away from them, his arms outstretched in a final embrace. The river his cold grave.

By the time Dana and Lachlan returned to the picnic area, two policewomen were holding back a small pack of journalists. The bright flashes of a dozen cameras went off, illuminating the surreal beauty of the eucalypt trees towering above them. Dana blinked, holding her hands up to shield her eyes and ward off a sense of rising disconnect.

'Dana Gibson,' one of them yelled. 'Were you Jayden's case worker?' The questions came thick and fast as the reporters shouted across the car park trying to make their voices heard. 'What can you tell us about his death? How did he die? Is the Department doing enough to protect our kids in care?'

An officer cleared a path as they were pushed and jostled all the way to Lachlan's car.

They divided up the tasks when they got to the Killarney Police Station. Lachlan phoned the Regional Director and typed up case notes while Dana wrote a ministerial briefing, a critical incident report and talked to a woman from Crisis Care. By 3 am she was so exhausted she was prepared to sleep on the floor, but one of the officers directed her to a camp bed in Ryan's office while Lachlan went off to nap on the lounge in the tearoom.

She was woken a few hours later by Ryan gently shaking her shoulder. She dragged herself up and replied to a number of emails, then staggered to the pub, got the keys from Cynthia and made her way up the stairs to the room which she'd now come to think of as her own.

The next three days were spent chained to the desk at the station as Dana tried to organise a memorial service. She was grateful his religious views were well known and so it was a straightforward matter for the ceremony to take place at the church where he'd served as an altar boy.

On the night before the funeral, she turned on the TV and flicked on the ABC News coverage of Jayden's death. The female news reporter stared the audience down with bulky shoulder pads, her voice burying deep into Dana's psyche.

A leaked internal memo from the Queensland Police Service has revealed the body of Jayden Maloney, a missing teen from Killarney, has been found almost three weeks after he is believed to have died. The body was found downstream from Queen Mary Falls after heavy flooding inundated the area in recent days.

A limited post-mortem showed injuries to Jayden's head, chest and limbs consistent with a fall from a great height.

The memo revealed Jayden had been experiencing feelings of guilt about a recent hit-and-run accident in the small community on the day Jayden was last seen alive. It is believed Jayden had helped repair the bike involved in the accident. There were no witnesses to Jayden's fall, but ABC News has been informed that his death will likely be ruled a suicide.

Dana was incensed, jumping up from the bed and pacing around the room as she tried to recall if Jayden had given any indication that he was experiencing suicidal ideation. All she could remember was the endless evidence pointing to a young man who was driven, grabbing at life with both hands.

Jayden's foster carer, Connie McClusky, then gave an interview, her face awash with tears as she spoke to the camera:

'He was such a good boy.' Connie wiped her cheeks. 'I can't believe this happened. He always had a kind word for everyone and helped out wherever he could. The whole town was his family.'

Dana felt emotion welling inside her until she couldn't stand it anymore. She grabbed the remote control, stabbing at the off button.

~

On the dawn of the memorial service Dana lay awake, feeling apprehensive. She wondered how it was possible to feel such intense grief for a boy she'd never known, but reasoned that she was still coming to grips with Blair's suicide and the death of Oscar eighteen months earlier.

It was an impossibly bright morning as she headed up the hill to the Holy Cross Catholic Church, stepping past a marble statue of Mary and groups of journalists gathered out the front. The scene was one of chaos, people spilling out onto the lawn from a church that was unable to contain the community's grief.

What she glimpsed inside was no different. The entire town was jammed into the pews and along the aisles, while ceiling fans whirred overhead. As she was walking up the front stairs she ran into Angus, Tina and Susan. Dana was relieved to see Angus and drew him to her for a long hug. When she let go, Tina was waiting by the entrance looking pale. Dana wondered if Tina was beginning to grasp the reality of Susan's death, how painful it was going to be when the mother she'd taken for granted had passed on.

Dana squeezed into the back row behind a group of teenagers in Killarney State School polo shirts. Two girls at the end of the pew were being reprimanded by a teacher in an otherwise silent crowd. How must it feel to be at a memorial service for someone their own age? How would they cope, or even come to accept it?

She gazed around, trying to locate Lachlan, Sean or Ryan but gave up, assuming they were somewhere up the front.

'It's so sad they can't release his body until the coroner finishes the autopsy,' said one of the women beside her.

'I know,' agreed the other. 'But given that he killed Johnny

Buckley then took his own life, there's not much that can be done.'

Dana realised that most people in the town likely believed the theory that Jayden was responsible for Johnny Buckley's hit-and-run, then suicided because of his guilt. Two deaths tied up in a neat little bow. For the most part, she understood the need to explain Jayden's death away, the psychological safety that came with no longer having to worry about a murderer on the loose, but something about it felt wrong.

A whispered hush fell over the crowd as a woman with a messy brown bob settled herself at the piano, propping a sheet of music in front of her. When she started to play the familiar refrain of 'Song for Guy' Dana was completely undone. The anguish she'd been bottling up since witnessing Jayden's body in the culvert overflowed. She pictured his wide, open smile, and remembered his friends' love for him.

The ceremony passed in a daze of tears. Towards the end of the formalities the sun streamed through the stained-glass windows and a line of white birds flew across the sky. For a moment it felt like a release. That despite the terrible pain to be endured, there was also immense beauty.

When the service was over, she stumbled through the heavy wooden doors into the bright sunlight. The first person she saw was Ryan, in full police regalia. A hot rush of tears streamed down her cheeks and when she let him put an arm around her shoulders she knew she must be learning. To show her emotions and not bottle everything up.

19

'Hey, Dana. It's me, Lachlan. How are you coping during this whole enforced leave thing? What's been happening?'

'Very little, actually.' Dana had been sitting under the peach tree in her backyard reading a brochure Shivani had sent about accommodation in Noosa when her mobile rang. 'I tried to call a few times after Jayden's funeral. How've you been feeling about everything?'

'Oh, you know.' Dana could hear the catch in his throat. 'It's been hard. Jayden was my shining success when I started work. He made me feel like becoming a social worker was worth it, though the fact that he was doing so well was down to him, I probably had very little to do with it.' He was silent for a moment. 'Over the past few days I've been giving a lot of thought to whether I want to continue at the Department. I mean, what's the point if you can't even keep your most resilient kid alive?'

'You can't quit, Lachlan, you're really good ... maybe even

better than me,' she said, knowing he was more likely to be honest if she could get him to laugh.

He chuckled. 'That's a huge concession coming from you.'

'I'm serious. You're incredible with the clients, you've got great rapport and you get them to open up and tell you things. I have no doubt that Jayden loved having you as his caseworker.' What Lachlan said about leaving the Department had spooked her. She couldn't imagine any way in which it would be possible for her to work in the Toowoomba office if he wasn't there.

'Anyway, I'm hoping that this is just a rough patch. Rachel thinks I should just ride it out.'

'Well, you've been through a really tough time with Jayden's death, not to mention your childhood friend just died as well.'

There was an awkward silence, the old ghost of the Blair argument that lingered between them. 'Actually that's the reason I'm calling. I just had a phone call from Ryan,' he said.

Her pulse quickened as she sat up straighter in the cast-iron chair. 'Go on.'

'The fingerprints from the chair in his room came back and after some further investigation they identified that someone had tampered with the scene, making it look like Blair was murdered.'

'What?'

'A local kid – Tyler Henrick.'

She gasped. 'The one who was hanging out at the old buttery?'

'Correct.'

'Why on earth would he do that?'

'He was concerned that if anyone found out that Blair killed himself he wouldn't get a church funeral. According to Tyler's statement, suicide is considered a sin.'

'I was only chatting with him a couple of days after Blair died. I should've realised he was trying to tell me something.' She paused, trying to process the fact that Blair had taken his own life. 'I'm so sorry that Blair had to die like that. Do you think this had anything at all to do with Jayden?'

'Honestly, Dana, I don't know. All I know is that some mysteries in life will never be solved.'

She plucked up a blade of grass from the lawn and twirled it around her finger. 'Really? Do you truly believe that?'

'Well, we can't keep funnelling all our energy into this one case. It's time to focus on other parts of our lives.'

She sighed. 'As you well know, once I get my teeth into something I find it hard to let go.'

'I get it, I really do. After Kate died, and before I met Rachel, all I wanted to do was get on the tools, but eventually I realised that I'd become a workaholic. Even if I did manage to put a cabinet together in record time, my grief was still going to be there waiting for me. I was using an external solution to solve what was actually an internal problem.'

'I've been thinking about taking a drive out to the farm near Queen Mary Falls to speak to Sean's alibi.'

'Were you even listening to anything I said?'

'It's just, I'm not convinced he's telling the whole truth.'

'You must genuinely dislike my brother.'

'It's not that. They do boxes of fresh fruit and veg and I'd like to pick one up.'

'Give me a break.'

'What? I love organic produce.'

He took a long breath down the other end of the line. 'You're a grown woman, Dana, but I'd strongly advise against it. It really is none of your business.'

After Dana hung up she went next door and found Susan in the hallway, rugged up under a layer of cardigans as though the breeze shaking the rose bush would blow her over. The pigmentation on her face had yellowed and the tremor in her hands belied a fragility that was unnerving.

Susan kissed Dana's cheek and she was enveloped by the scent of Nutrimetics cream. 'Come in. How are you?'

'Fine thanks,' said Dana, as they went into the kitchen and Susan switched on the kettle. 'How are you feeling today?'

'Dreadful. I feel like I could just go back to bed and sleep the rest of the day.'

'Why don't you?'

'I've got so little time left, I want to make sure that I don't miss anything.'

Dana was silent, unable to argue with Susan's logic. 'How's Angus?'

Susan set a mug of tea in front of Dana then sat down opposite. 'He's been a bit down in the dumps, but there's so much going on for him that he has good reason to be depressed.'

'Has he mentioned Jayden lately?'

'Not really.' She put her head in her hand and closed her eyes.

'Are you sure you shouldn't lie down? Even if it's just for twenty minutes? It might make you feel better if you have a nap.'

'I think I will do that, actually.'

'Would you mind if I borrowed your car for the rest of the day? I was hoping to take a trip out to Killarney to tie up a few last threads with Jayden.'

'No, that's perfect – it needs a good run, and I'm not going to be using it.'

An hour and a half later, Dana pulled up alongside a timber fence where clumps of white and yellow ox-eye daisies grew on either side of a gate announcing *The Falls Farm*. She strode up a dirt road past a yard of brindle cows chewing clover. Further along was a small shed and fenced-off area where chickens and geese pecked at the dirt. As she approached the house, she admired a couple of enormous pumpkins arranged on a table out the front. A woman in a floaty dress wandered down the stairs carrying a couple of cartons of eggs.

'Hi, I'm Emma,' she said, by way of a greeting as she placed the eggs on the table with a *For Sale* sign. 'How can I help?' She had blue eyes, porcelain skin and was at least a decade younger than Dana.

'Hi,' said Dana, not wanting to give her name. 'A friend mentioned that you sell boxes of fresh fruit and vegetables. I was hoping I could buy one from you?'

'Oh great, come on through. They're in the shed out back.'

As Dana followed her around the side of the house, she noticed a sandpit filled with a small trike and kids' toys. It took all of her self-restraint not to be appalled by Sean's behaviour. 'So, how long have you lived here?' she asked casually.

'About five years. We're a family-run organic retreat and we practise regenerative agriculture, grow all our own herbs and vegies,' Emma said, sounding like she was reading from a script. She lifted a heavy box full of leafy cabbages, potatoes and pumpkin. 'We sell fresh, non-pasteurised milk too, if you're interested?'

'That sounds wonderful.' They headed up to the next paddock where three black-and-white jersey cows lay on emerald-green grass. If it wasn't for the mission at hand, Dana knew she would have been entranced by the idyllic beauty of the place. 'Do you get any help running the farm?'

'My husband, Max, does all the hard labour. He's at the sale yards at the moment, trying to buy us another bull.' Emma led the way into the dairy with a ponderous gait. She knelt in front of a small fridge to retrieve a bottle of milk.

'Actually, you probably know the friend who tipped me off about this place. Sean O'Malley.'

Emma blinked rapidly as she looked up at Dana from behind the fridge door. 'Yeah, right. Sean.'

'I work with his brother, Lachlan.'

There was silence as Emma buried her head in the fridge and began to rearrange its contents.

'So how do you know Sean?' Dana asked.

'I don't know, I guess we had like a mentor–mentee relationship.'

Laughter bubbled up inside her as she imagined Sean attempting to charm Emma. Charm she'd fallen prey to herself. 'What was he supposed to be teaching you?'

'Design.' Her head was still behind the fridge door. 'He is a stylish guy. Had lots of good marketing ideas he thought we could incorporate into the business.'

'Interesting,' said Dana wishing she could see Emma's face. 'It's a pity about his bike.'

'How it got all dinged up?'

'Yes.' Dana felt as though she was addressing a young child. 'Did he tell you how it happened?'

'He said that someone borrowed it. He was really angry, actually.'

'Did he tell you their name?'

'No.'

'And how did it get fixed?'

'Some kid who was good with their hands.' She rose to her feet and handed Dana a bottle of ice-cold milk.

'Well, it's lucky you were together the night Johnny Buckley was hit, otherwise he would have been in real trouble.'

'Yeah, I picked him up from the shop on my way into town. We had a really nice roast dinner. I haven't heard from him in a while actually.'

'That's a shame,' said Dana, feeling relieved that Sean's alibi was standing up to scrutiny.

'The weird thing about it is, the police keep dropping by to ask me about him.' She pulled a face. 'My husband is super annoyed. He talks about free love and everything and how we have this amazing open relationship, but when I show interest in other people he seems to change his mind.'

'Relationships can be very complex,' said Dana, knowing the platitude was unhelpful. 'How much do I owe you?'

Emma looked at Dana unflinchingly. 'Fifty dollars.'

Dana cringed as she handed over a fifty-dollar note. She'd come all this way for a very expensive box of vegetables, milk and almost no new information. She accompanied Emma back through the paddocks towards the car.

'Do you know where Sean is at the moment?' Emma asked, as she stacked the box of produce in the boot of Susan's car.

'I imagine he's still in Killarney.'

A lost expression swept over her face. 'I've been waiting for him to get in contact with me, but I think he might've lost his phone again.'

'Ah yes, the lost phone,' she said with disbelief.

Emma stood at the gate, a vacant expression on her face as Dana reversed down the drive.

20

Dana's next port of call was the police station, but when she arrived she found Ryan's office door firmly closed. A junior officer with a shiny head glanced up at her from a desk by the wall. He reclined in his chair as he stared over at her, rotating his pen between his fingers.

'He's in a meeting if you'd like to wait?' He stared at her legs until she slid into a vacant desk and tucked her ankles beneath it.

A wall map outlining the Australian states caught her eye and she had a flash of inspiration. Maybe she could get Blair's interstate child protection history from when he'd worked in New South Wales. She rested her head in her hands. *Surely there must be someone willing to give it to her?* There were two women from Dana's former team in Sydney, one called Kimberly and another woman whose name Dana couldn't recall. It was a long shot, but one of them might be willing to help.

The young officer was now flipping through his desk calendar.

'Would you mind if I made a quick work call?' asked Dana.

He grinned. 'Go for it.'

She dialled the number of her old office in Sydney and held her breath. After being on hold for a few minutes there was a click and the sound of the receiver being picked up. 'Department of Community Services, this is Kimberly speaking.'

Dana couldn't believe her luck. 'Oh, hi, Kimberly, this is Dana Gibson.'

'Dana! I heard you'd moved up north. What can I help you with?'

'I'm working in the Toowoomba office in Queensland these days and was hoping you might be able to share some information with me about a case I'm working on?'

'No problem.'

Dana was pleased to note that Kimberly's attitude to information sharing was the exact opposite to some of the colleagues she'd worked with in the past. 'We've received information about a local, Blair Hadley, who was facing charges in New South Wales and I wanted to know what was happening with that?'

'Just a sec, I'll look it up on the system.'

After Dana provided his date of birth there was a pause.

'I'm just reading what the investigating officer had to say in their initial assessment. Apparently, the teenager retracted his allegations a few weeks ago and confessed he'd made it all up.'

A few weeks ago. *Prior to Blair's death*. Dana was dumbfounded. All of her scepticism of Blair had been based on those charges. 'It still could have happened though, right? I mean, it's not unusual for young people to make allegations and retract them after they succumb to the pressures of having to appear in court, or having to tell their family.'

'I'd usually agree with you, Dana; children rarely have anything to gain by making allegations of sexual abuse, but in this case the police located a number of items in his bedroom that he wasn't able to provide an explanation for. The teenager's girlfriend disclosed that he'd been boasting about how he'd ripped off the brother and had been blackmailing him for money.'

Dana thanked her and hung up. She was still staring blankly into space when Ryan opened the door of his office. His expression was questioning. 'What's happening?'

'We should go to the pub for that drink. There's a lot to talk about.'

Half an hour later Ryan and Dana were sitting at one of the outside tables on the verandah of the Killarney pub, two Guinness pies with chips and salad on plates in front of them.

'So, how was the trip to the farm?' asked Ryan, after Dana had filled him in on her morning's work.

'I got some good produce.'

'Anything else?'

'No. Sean's alibi checks out – he was with Emma the night of the hit-and-run.'

'The one who's married to Max?' he asked, his face a picture of innocence.

'Of course, the one who's married to Max. You already knew that.'

He smirked. 'Just checking.'

He dipped one of his chips into a silver jug of gravy and she realised she'd spent so much time with him recently that their being together felt completely natural. After a waiter took their plates away, they ordered cake and coffee and she filled him in on the information she'd been given about Blair.

He stroked his chin. 'I spoke to the commissioner yesterday and we decided to draw a line under the investigation. It's abundantly clear that the evidence against Blair has been nothing more than rumour and innuendo.'

He was right, she thought, raking a hand through her hair. The Blair angle was a dead-end. Even if Blair had been responsible for Jayden's disappearance, the truth would feel hollow now he was no longer around to defend himself. 'Are you going to tell Lachlan about all this?'

'Yes. He's been talking to Blair's mother on the phone and she's still very distressed. Lachlan, Sean and I have chipped in to buy her something nice.'

It occurred to her that Ryan had a whole backstory with Lachlan's family that she wasn't privy to. It was of little matter. The only thing she was capable of thinking about was how an innocent man had come undone on the basis of a false allegation.

And how she'd believed it wholeheartedly.

After Ryan had returned to work Dana took a walk to clear her head before the drive back to Toowoomba. At the Gravel Creek Bridge she rested her elbows on the railing and gazed down at the water. She tried to work out the precise moment her analytical skills failed her. Blair had presented as a good person. He'd helped Lachlan get his car fixed when he was younger, mounted a search party for Jayden, and spent endless hours serving his family and community. His responses during his interview were believable.

Not to mention, he'd never lied to them. Why then hadn't she believed him when he said he was innocent?

She knew it was because she had believed the child. Because that's what she'd always done. And as everyone knew, children had very little to gain from making up stories of abuse – which meant that this case was a true anomaly. Still, it didn't make her feel any better. She couldn't imagine what it must have been like to have been in Blair's position. To be minding your own business, lending a hand to the people who needed it the most, and be hit by a wall of horror – an entire town wanting revenge.

She kept walking and eventually she came across Killarney State School. On impulse, she ducked inside. After speaking to the Principal and announcing her intention to research the area for a book she was writing, she was directed to the library.

At the front desk a woman with a jade pendant around her neck was stacking piles of books to return to the shelves. 'How can I help you?' she asked.

'This is a bit unusual.' Dana suddenly felt self-conscious, hoping the woman wouldn't ask her for details. 'I was just wondering whether you had any copies of the high school yearbook from 1976?'

'We should do.' The librarian closed the book in front of her and stood up. 'Follow me.'

They walked all the way down one of the aisles and the woman pulled down a large folder. 'You're in luck. They go all the way back to 1964. Prior to that it was called the Rural School; the boys were taught manual skills and girls learnt home management.' She handed the heavy folder over to Dana. 'Yell out if you need any help.'

Dana set herself up at a table in the back corner. On the

front of the 1976 yearbook was a grainy photo of the school – a central wooden building with a large extension built onto the side. She flicked through the pages looking at old photographs. In one photo a group of younger students were lined up in rows out the front of the schoolhouse. The boys and girls in the front row sat on the ground with their arms and legs crossed, the majority of them not wearing shoes. She recalled Lachlan saying that Killarney had been a different place when he was younger. Rougher, with violence breaking out in the pub on a regular basis.

In the Principal's report she was intrigued to read that Ryan Kennedy had been the Head Prefect and Dux of the year. It went on to say that he'd passed junior with eight A's and had won an open scholarship to study at Toowoomba Grammar School.

A few pages further in was a note about the annual athletics sports day with pictures of students holding their ribbons. Ryan had been age champion and Sean runner-up. She knew that going through old archives to find information on Sean, Ryan and Blair was a massive waste of her time, but so far it had proven to be a useful distraction from having to think about her own guilty conscience.

She tried to imagine what their relationship had been, and wondered how Sean would have coped with losing to Ryan. Not well, she speculated, thinking about the dynamic between them. Ryan had been serious, studious and athletic. Sean was social and good with his hands. Perhaps high school had been the start of Sean and Ryan's animosity towards each other, where the competitiveness between them had ignited.

In the centre of the book was a collage of candid photos – teenagers with their arms around each other doing peace signs, staring into microscopes, clutching musical instruments and participating in all manner of school events.

The last thing she saw before she closed the book was a small photo of Blair bottle-feeding a black lamb as he cradled it in his arms. The label underneath read. *Blair Hadley. Agriculture excursion to Toowoomba Royal Show, March 1976.*

The look he was giving the creature was one of such love and tenderness that her eyes brimmed with tears.

21

Back in Toowoomba that night, Dana invited Susan and Angus over for dinner. When they finished their gnocchi with lemon and sage, Susan volunteered to make a cup of tea while Dana and Angus watched *The Mighty Ducks* in the lounge room. Dana moved over to be closer to him on the couch as he finished his last spoonful of hokey pokey ice cream.

'So how have you been feeling about everything since Jayden died,' she asked him.

'Okay, I guess. I've been having dreams. In one we were drinking Cokes and feeding the birds like we used to on our breaks.'

'That's understandable. It's hard to get closure when someone disappears from your life unexpectedly.' She took his bowl from him and stacked it with hers on the coffee table. 'Did I tell you that I took a trip out to Falls Farm today?'

'Where's that?'

'Near Edith's shop. It's where I got the fresh vegetables that we ate with dinner.'

'Why did you go all the way out there?' His eyes narrowed as though he knew what she'd been doing.

'I wanted to talk to a woman who had some information about the bike used in the hit-and-run. Sean's Triumph Thunderbird.'

His eyes were intent on the TV screen but she knew he was listening.

'The woman who owned the farm, Emma, told me that a kid helped Sean to fix his motorbike. She thought it was someone who was good with their hands. Angus, are you listening to me? Do you know who it was?'

'I guess so.'

'Well, who?'

'Jayden told me that he'd been the one to fix it up after it was in a crash.'

'So, why didn't you tell me?'

'I didn't want him to go to jail.'

'But what about Johnny's family? What about his little girl?'

'I don't know. I didn't think about it like that. Johnny was already dead. It's not like anything was going to bring him back. He was still going to be dead and Jayden was going to be in jail. Just for hitting a guy who ran onto the road like a crazy person.'

'Well, this changes a lot of things. There's now a direct link between Jayden and the hit-and-run. It implies that he was part of the incident, or at least knew who was responsible.' She stared at the side of his face in the flickering light of the TV screen. 'I would have thought you'd have cared a bit more.'

He shrugged. 'Johnny's dead. Jayden's dead. But Nan's still alive. You should be paying attention to her before she's dead too.' He jabbed at the power button on the TV remote, flicking it off and throwing it onto the lounge. Before she could say anything more he got up and stormed down the hall, slamming the front door behind him.

Dana looked after him in shock, it was impossible to deny the truth in what he'd just said – that life was for the living. She got up and went to find Susan in the kitchen. 'I'm really sorry, but I just tried to have a chat with Angus about Jayden and he got mad. He's gone back to your house.'

'Don't worry about him, he'll get over it soon enough. He's angry at everyone at the moment, it's just part and parcel of him knowing I'll be gone soon.' She shrugged. 'Anyway, what do you say we take our cuppas outside?'

They sat on the verandah with cups by their side, leaning back into the sofa with their feet up on the outdoor table. Susan reached into her pocket for a packet of cigarettes and lit one. 'You don't mind, do you?'

'Not at all.' Dana reached for the cup beside her and took a sip. 'Have you always been a smoker?'

'I smoked for years and I used to really enjoy it, but I gave it up when I got pregnant with Tina. Now that I'm not going to be around for much longer, I figure, why deny myself? What about you?' asked Susan. 'Have you ever tried it?'

'Once or twice during high school, but I never really got into it. I was a runner, so it wasn't very compatible.'

'That's very sensible of you.'

'Have you heard from Tina lately?'

'I called her last week. She's refusing to visit me after I told her that she couldn't have Angus when I die. I wanted to sit down and talk to her properly but in the end I had to tell her over the phone. Not the way I was hoping to give her the news …'

She shrugged as though she didn't have the energy to continue.

'And how did she take it?'

'Hard to tell as I couldn't see her reaction.' She shifted on the couch, grimacing. 'I'm worried she's going to become a vulture after I've gone, picking over my belongings. And I'm really sorry, but you're going to have to deal with that. I've been very clear in my will, about who gets what, so hopefully she can't wreak too much havoc.' She glanced over at Dana. 'It's the drugs again. She's back on them, I know it. Whenever she's using, she disappears for weeks at a time and only gets in contact when she needs money – like I'm her personal ATM.'

'And how's Angus coping with everything?'

'I think he might finally be old enough to accept the reality of who she is. But there's a good chance she's going to keep disappointing him. Over the past day or two I've really sensed a change in him. I think he's incredibly angry that she's not here spending time with me. Anyway, enough doom and gloom. How's things with that dashing man?'

'Sean?' replied Dana, wanting to delay the conversation.

'Yes, the one with the motorbike.'

'Not so good. Turns out he was seeing someone else at the same time and there were a number of other things that happened, which has led me to believe that he isn't entirely trustworthy.'

'How disappointing, he seemed so nice. Young men today have too many options. It takes forever for them to settle down. But if you want me to boil his bunny for you, just let me know – I'll do it for you.' She gave Dana a wicked grin. 'And are you excited about the trip to Noosa tomorrow?'

'I am. I've been fantasising about lying on the beach doing nothing for weeks.'

'Well, you've earnt it. There're very few people who work as hard as you do.'

They sat shoulder to shoulder for the next hour talking and laughing. Dana stared up at the star-speckled sky as she walked Susan to her front door. The air on her back was soothing and benevolent. The same feeling she had whenever she was with Susan.

Shivani dropped by early the next morning to pick Dana up and they drove to the coast without stopping. Three hours later they arrived in Noosa. Shivani pulled up outside a five-star hotel nestled in lush rainforest and a porter took their bags. Once in her room, Dana drew back the curtains and stared at the ocean. She collapsed onto her pillowy white king bed complete with a soft feathered doona and wondered why she hadn't thought to do this earlier. She deserved a holiday. In fact, she'd been screaming out for one. It was such a relief not to be thinking about the investigation.

The first thing they did after they'd finished unpacking was head for the pool – a glistening lagoon fringed with palm trees. They lay on sun lounges, the scent of coconut oil lingering in the air as Bob Marley tunes wafted gently through some speakers. Dana lay with her eyes closed, letting the sun warm her skin.

Shivani sipped on a pina colada and turned to Dana. 'I definitely think we should go to dinner tonight.'

'Sounds good to me,' she said without opening her eyes.

'I was thinking of booking Bistro C. The view's great and they make the most amazing whiskey sours. Not to mention, I've spent many hideous London winters dreaming about their seafood.'

When they'd finished their meal that night, they strolled back up the hill to the hotel, breathing in the salty air. Dana fell asleep listening to the slow rotations of the ceiling fan and the distant hush of waves on the beach.

As the days went by Dana found herself letting go, thinking less and less of Jayden and who killed Johnny Buckley, and simply enjoying the moment. She wore sarongs, cut her hair and developed the beginnings of a tan on her milky white skin. As she lay on the sun lounge next to the pool she finally felt as though she'd learnt the secret to life. To relax and not to succumb to endless obsession and burying herself in work.

Towards the end of the holiday they followed the signs to the coastal walk through the national park. With the sea to the left they hiked past the thunderous waves crashing into the rocks at Boiling Pot Lookout. On the high bluff at Hell's Gate they stopped for a drink of water and took in the spectacular views of the turquoise sea. As they were heading back along the path it began to spit. Dana turned her face to the sky, enjoying the rain and salt spray on her skin.

The sun was intense by the time they arrived back at Little Cove so they stripped down to their swimmers and waded into the water. Dana let the choppy waves bounce her up and down with the current then duck-dived under the waves. The water offered a cooling respite after their long walk.

They asked another tourist to take a photo of them when they were back on the beach. With their arms gripping each other tightly they stood framed by pandanus trees, surf and sand. Their faces were filled with joy as they grinned at the camera.

A man in a tan linen suit with a gold name badge ran out from behind the reception desk when they got back to their hotel.

'Dana Gibson?'

She nodded.

'There's someone on the phone for you. Says it's urgent.'

22

When Dana stepped into the hospital room she found Susan propped up in bed on a nest of pillows. A patchwork quilt had been spread over her legs and her breathing was laboured behind an oxygen mask.

Susan removed the mask and Dana could hear the low hiss of the gas. 'Thanks for coming.' Susan's voice was weak as though it had taken tremendous effort to speak.

'You don't need to thank me,' said Dana reassuringly.

'But your holiday—'

'Don't be silly.'

Susan winced as she tried to sit up in bed.

'How are you feeling? Do you want me to call one of the nurses? Get you more pain relief?'

'There's just one last thing I need to do.' Susan paused, taking a painful gasp. 'I need to see Tina.'

'No problem. I can pick Angus up from school. We'll drive down and get her.'

'Take my car.' She nodded to a cupboard to the right. 'Keys are in the handbag. Oh and Dana ...'

Dana sat down and put her hand over Susan's.

'I don't want a funeral. I don't want the kids to make a fuss.'

Dana nodded, not trusting herself to speak.

'A garden party,' her voice rasped. 'Sprinkle my ashes in the backyard, near the mock orange tree. That's when I was my happiest, when I was gardening. Okay?'

Dana could feel tears stinging her eyes. She bit her lip, trying to keep it together so she could be strong for Susan. 'Okay.'

'And promise me. That you'll be the one to look after Angus. Not his mum – she's had her chance. Not anyone else, but you.'

'I promise. You don't have to worry.'

Susan put the mask on and lay back into the pillows. She closed her eyes. It wasn't long before her face went slack and her heavy breathing resumed.

Dana leant over and kissed her on the forehead. She reached for the keys in Susan's handbag and let herself out the door. When she stepped into the long white corridor she saw a nurse exiting the room opposite.

'Excuse me?' said Dana. 'I'm a friend of Susan Fitcher's. I was wondering if I could have a quick chat?'

'Sure?' The nurse held a clipboard to her chest and gave Dana her full attention.

'Susan seems to have deteriorated very quickly in the last week or so and I was just wondering ... how long she has left?' Dana said awkwardly. 'It's just, she's asked to see her daughter. I'll have to drive down to Killarney and pick her up, but I'm worried I mightn't have much time.'

'It's something we can never really know for sure, but Susan's a fighter so I'd say you have a few more days.' The woman smiled sympathetically. 'But you wouldn't want to leave it any longer than that.'

Once again Dana found herself in Susan's car with Angus in the passenger seat as they drove to Killarney. It was a quiet trip and he spent most of the time listening to his Walkman and fixating on the scenery, thoughts of his nan clearly playing on his mind.

It was mid-afternoon by the time they reached the outskirts of Killarney. She pulled in at the petrol station to refuel and as she was replacing the hose in the pump, Angus stuck his head out of the car.

'Dana, can you get me an icy pole? I'm feeling a bit car sick.'

She doubted his excuse, but was relieved that he appeared to be cheering up.

She heard the roar of a motorbike as she was paying at the cash register. Coming out of the service station doors, she saw Sean parked behind her car, removing his helmet.

'Dana!'

Her stomach lurched when he smiled at her.

'I was going to call tonight to see what you were up to.'

Yeah, right, she thought, noting that she didn't feel in the slightest bit disappointed about his lack of contact. Susan's illness and her time in Noosa had forced her to reconsider her priorities. She'd come to the realisation that reliability in a partner was high on the list. She turned her gaze to his bike.

'You've gotten rid of the Thunderbird?'

'It lost its appeal after I found out that it was involved in Johnny's death. Like it had bad juju or something.'

'I can see how that might happen.' She pursed her lips as something else occurred to her. 'Did you ever lend the bike to Jayden Maloney?' she asked, already knowing the answer, but curious to see whether Sean would be honest with her.

'He was a good kid, good with his hands too. Whenever I had a problem with the bike he was the first person I'd take it to. I told him he could ride it whenever he wanted.' He squinted his eyes as though he was trying to gauge her expression. 'But don't worry, I've told Ryan all about it.'

The passenger door of the car flew open and Angus stormed over. 'You promised you weren't going to do that anymore,' he said to Dana.

'Do what?'

'Keep investigating Jayden's death. All you keep doing is bringing back everyone's bad memories.'

'Oh, Angus sweetie, I'm sorry.'

He turned and stormed back into the car, slamming the door behind him.

Dana looked up at Sean. 'He's pretty upset. Susan's taken a turn for the worse and is in hospital. I don't think she has much longer now.'

'That poor kid. He can't seem to catch a break.'

There was silence and Dana glanced down at the strands of pale grass growing through the cracks in the cement. 'So, what have you been up to lately?'

'Nothing much. Work mainly, we've been really busy at the mill – still understaffed.'

'Maybe you should think about visiting your dad? It's just that when I saw him at the farm with Lachlan, he seemed really lonely.'

'Yeah, sure.' He hesitated. 'Do you want to meet for a drink in Toowoomba tomorrow night?'

'I don't think so.'

His brow scrunched with confusion. 'Is something wrong?'

'I'm fine.' She smiled at him. 'Just fine.'

'Okay. Well … I'll catch you around.'

She watched in the rear-view mirror as he became small to her. No more than a speck on the horizon.

They drove along Warwick Killarney Road past newly ploughed fields and telephone lines stretching all the way to the horizon. The plane trees Dana had admired on her first trip to this small rural town were blossoming with fruit against a backdrop of blue-grey mountains and she was relieved to see the Condamine flowing at a normal level again.

When they reached the main street Angus pulled off his headphones and turned to her, eyes pleading. 'Can we say hi to Arthur? Please?'

'Sure,' she said, in the hope that this would resolve some of the tension since his blow-up at the petrol station.

True to form Arthur was sitting on the front steps in a straw hat. 'Angus, my boy, how've you been?' A yellow scab on Arthur's forehead indicated a recent brush with skin cancer. 'Still working at the store?'

'Yes, I'm hoping I'll be able to work there every holidays.'

'It will be good experience to know how to run a shop.'

'I'm not in charge of it, just helping out,' Angus explained as Arthur's dog ambled up the front path. 'Oh, wow! When are the puppies due?'

'Any day now.'

The dog came over wagging its tail and lay heavily on the concrete beside them.

'And how are you, Dana?' Arthur asked politely.

'I'm well. It's good to see that the town's bouncing back after the floods.'

'Well, everyone tries to pull together when something like that happens. Do you still have the prayer card I gave you? The one with the angel?'

She smiled and patted her handbag. 'Right in here.'

'That's good. You never know when you're going to need it.'

Dana bent down to examine a small concrete statue of the virgin Mary on the top step. 'Is this new?'

Arthur nodded. 'Blair's mother, Lynette, gave it to me as a gift for going though Blair's things after he passed. She wasn't feeling up to it and I was happy to help.'

'What kind of things did you have to sort through?'

'Mostly just religious books and papers. A notebook with personal correspondence, but don't worry, I gave it straight to Ryan.'

'A notebook?' Dana felt a jolt of recognition.

'Yes, Blair wrote poetry and the like.'

'What kind of poetry?'

'I'm not even sure. Works with a biblical bent.'

'Like Herrick?'

He looked up sharply. 'Yes.'

The green notebook she'd seen on Cynthia's office desk hadn't belonged to Ryan after all. It was evidence. 'But there were pages ripped from that book,' she said.

He hung his head between his knees then stared up at the

street behind her as though the wind had gone out of his sails. 'Tell me your favourite song, Dana. Choose anything, I'll sing it for you.'

'Arthur, can you answer the question.'

'Angus, lad, why don't you go out the back and fill Tara's water bowl. It's getting low.'

Angus gave Dana a dark look as though he knew she was still following a lead, but did as Arthur asked and sloped away towards the back of the house.

'From what I could gather he used some of the paper to write letters,' said Arthur, his voice low.

'And that's what you ripped out of the notebook – letters?'

'One letter, which I ripped into tiny pieces and threw into the wheelie bin.'

'Who was it addressed to?'

'The Queensland Police.' Arthur sighed heavily. 'He said that when he worked at the Rose Bay parish there were allegations about the brothers abusing children. One of the kids in particular had complained to him, but he'd turned a blind eye. He was being eaten up with guilt. Felt that God was punishing him when people up here got wind of it and started speculating.'

'I don't understand, why did you rip up the pages?'

'I didn't have the stomach to make a big deal out of it. There'd already been so much ugliness written about the Catholic Church. And Blair had passed.'

'Arthur, you have to tell Ryan.'

'I'm not sure what he'll be able to do. There were no names, no dates. It was as though Blair was being deliberately vague. Like he was drafting the letter but wasn't sure if he was going to send it.'

'Still, it's the right thing to do. It might help other children who could be at risk.'

Angus rounded the corner, stepping gingerly with a full bowl of water in his hands. He placed it down for Tara and looked up at her expectantly, reminding her that Susan was waiting for them at the hospital.

'It was lovely to see you again Arthur,' she said. 'But we need to head off. We're picking up Angus's mum and giving her a lift back to Toowoomba.' She gave him a pointed look. 'And remember what I said about speaking to Ryan.'

Arthur nodded and tipped his hat. 'Well don't be a stranger, and make sure you say hello to that mother of yours for me, laddy.'

As they returned to the car Dana mulled over this new information from Arthur. Blair wasn't responsible for Jayden's disappearance, but he was guilty of another crime – failing to protect a child. Her mind swam with a mixture of sadness and frustration as she realised that he'd carried that guilt with him, the corrosive weight of it, right to the day of his death.

'I've just got to run in to see Detective Kennedy for a minute,' Dana said as she pulled up in front of the police station. 'I'm just dropping something off. I promise,' she added when she saw the flame of annoyance in his eyes.

'I'll stay here,' he said, flatly. 'I'd prefer to read my book. At least that's interesting.'

'Sure, I won't be long,' she said, choosing to ignore his sarcasm.

She hurried up the stairs of the stone building and into the reception area. The administration worker gave her a suspicious look but, after a quick phone call, led Dana through to Ryan's office.

He was finishing up a phone call when she was shown in and his face softened. He gestured for her to take a seat. He'd had his hair cut since she'd last seen him and she was thinking how much it suited him as he returned the phone to its base.

'Sorry about that,' he said.

'No problem, Angus and I are picking up Tina, so I thought I'd just pop in and drop this back to you.' She placed his umbrella on the mahogany wood of the desk in front of him.

'Thanks for that. Hopefully you won't be needing it quite so much from now on.'

'I know, that rain was something else.' She paused. 'How've you been?'

'Busy. We've been ramping up Operation Border Control and have made quite a few arrests in the last couple of days. I'm just preparing a few affidavits for court next week.'

She smiled, thinking about Lachlan's earlier advice. 'Has it ever occurred to you that you might be seeking out external solutions rather than dealing with your internal pain about the divorce?'

'I have been daydreaming about having some time off lately. Maybe getting another dog.'

'You do strike me as a dog person. Very loyal and dependable.' She smirked, surprised to realise that she was flirting with him. She steered the conversation back to the reason for her visit. 'So, any news on the Johnny Buckley case?'

'The trail's gone cold. Completely cold actually. I've transferred the case to one of my colleagues. He said the Commissioner's putting a lot of pressure on him to wind it up.' He leant in towards his computer and clicked the mouse. 'Actually, you've just reminded me – I keep getting these messages from Toowoomba Base Hospital saying that they've got some information for me. I'll have to get back to them and let them know it's with Dave now. So, how's things with you?'

'I'm well, I just got back from a holiday at the beach so I'm feeling much calmer. More relaxed.'

'Are you still investigating?'

'Now that it's clear that Jayden's dead I've been trying to let it go – which has been hard, but necessary. Besides, I'm about to be given a whole new bunch of cases to work on.'

She was enjoying speaking with him and had no desire to leave. It occurred to her that she was probably just delaying the inevitable difficult conversation she was about to have with Tina about visiting her mother. She filled Ryan in on what Arthur had said about Blair, then dragged herself up from the chair. 'Anyway, Angus is in the car so I should probably get going.'

He gave her a self-deprecating smile. 'Well, drop by any time. I'm always here.'

'You should really get out more.'

'Same could be said for you.'

'Let me know if you end up getting a dog,' she said with a grin. 'I'd love to see it.'

'Will do.'

Emotion welled in her chest as she let herself out. She paused on the front steps of the station, her hand to her cheek. Had he been really happy to see her? Or had she imagined it? Something significant had happened but she didn't know what it was, or where it would lead.

23

The chime over the door rang as Dana stepped into the shop. Tina, who was standing behind the cash register and talking to a customer, paused and looked over with surprise. Dana was relieved Angus had chosen to stay in the car as she wanted to warn Tina about how angry he was with her.

While she waited for Tina to finish at the counter, Dana strolled around the store looking at the heavily discounted Christmas decorations that were now on sale. She had a flashback to the first time she'd been to the store, when Angus had proudly shown off his new skills behind the till and filling in the staff logbook.

As Tina walked the customer to the door to give them directions, Dana reached past the cash register and grabbed the logbook. She flicked through the pages to find the date she was after: Friday 3 January 1997, the date of the hit-and-run. She ran a finger down the lined page to see which staff were on duty. Familiar names appeared before her. All but one.

Her heart sank when she realised there was no documentation of Tina being at work on that date. Dana considered that there may be a good explanation for Tina to have lied to her about it. She was probably involved with drugs and didn't want to get in trouble with her parole officer. Even so, Dana knew she'd have to ask about it at some point.

The man Tina was talking to thanked her and left without buying anything. As soon as the door closed Tina let out a sigh. 'Finally.'

Tina came closer, her shirt was covered in tiny retro-style lips. She gave Dana a strange look. 'Why are you here? Is Angus okay?'

'He's fine, he's in the car.' She slid the book beneath the register.

Tina stared at the space on the counter where the book had been. 'And what were you looking at that for?'

Dana squared her shoulders, figuring there was no point in lying about it. 'I've been trying to figure out why you told me you were working on the day of Johnny's death when, according to the logbook, you weren't.'

'Look, can we talk about this later?' Tina's face was etched with irritation. 'If Angus is okay, why did you drive all this way to see me?'

'Angus is fine, but your mum's not.' Dana placed her palms on the counter. 'She wants you to come home, Tina. This could be the last chance you get to see your mother while she's still alive.'

Tina breathed in, then let out a long exhalation. 'Can we just go for a walk and get out of this shop? I'm starting to feel seriously claustrophobic.'

'Sure,' said Dana, thinking that she'd probably have much

more of a chance of Tina being honest if she wasn't feeling threatened.

Tina yelled out the back for Billy to cover the counter then took her apron off and hung it on the hook by the kitchen door. 'Let's do this,' she said, with what sounded like false brightness.

They walked across the road and into the Queen Mary Falls car park where Angus was still in the back seat engrossed in his book. He gave them an absent-minded wave and they set off on the circuit walk.

Dana followed Tina's lead and they strode through the clearing past the barbecue area. Tina's hands swung back and forth under the towering eucalypts, the sunlight shifting on her hair. As they headed down the path to the waterfall Tina finally slowed her pace, allowing Dana to fall in step beside her.

'I know my mother wants you to look after Angus after she's dead but I want you to know, I am not okay with that.'

'Tina—'

'Just let me speak.'

'Okay.'

'I know Susan loves the fact that you have all the status symbols – the massive diamond ring and that stupid Mercedes, but Angus and I don't need any of that. We do free stuff. We go to the park and have fun. We pat the dogs at the RSPCA. I don't buy the idea that you need loads of money to raise a kid.'

'For a start, I don't even own any of those things anymore.'

'But she has talked about it, and I know she thinks you'd make a better mother than me.'

'Look, Tina. No-one is arguing that you're Angus's mother. You'll always be his mother and I'd never stop you from seeing him. But rather than worrying about who's getting custody of

Angus, right now we need to focus on your mum. She's only got a few days left and she wants to say her goodbyes to everyone, so she can be at peace.'

The sound of a whipbird cracked through the trees as they continued along the track. Up ahead a young girl balanced on a log as she waited for her family to catch up. Tina shook her hands out in front of her as though she was trying to compose herself. 'The thing none of you people seem to remember, is that I had him as a little baby. I used to carry him around in a Baby Bjorn across my chest when he was the size of a loaf of bread. You don't understand how much I love him. None of you can understand. I love him so much. I'd be willing to do anything so we could be together.'

Dana's mobile vibrated in her pocket. Ryan's name came up on the caller ID. She picked it up.

'How are you?' she said as she answered the phone.

His voice was urgent. 'Dana, where are you?'

'Just on a walk.' She smiled at Tina as they continued along the path towards the top of the waterfall.

'With Tina?'

'Yes,' she said, not wanting to let on who she was speaking to.

'You're not alone, are you?'

'Uh-huh.'

'Jesus Christ.' He breathed heavily into the receiver. 'Dana, you need to listen to me. I spoke with a liaison officer at Toowoomba Base Hospital. They said that Tina came in on the fourth of January – the day after the hit-and-run. The notes say that she was hypertensive and tachycardiac. That she presented with multiple lacerations on her arms and legs. Initially, when the doctor asked what had happened to her, she said that she'd rather not say, but when a nurse spoke to her in the early hours of the morning, she let it slip that she'd been in a recent MBA.'

Static crackled down the line as the reception started to break up.

'A what?'

'MBA. Motorbike accident.'

A shiver passed through Dana's body. She had a nightmarish flashback to Tina visiting Susan in hospital, an image of Tina wearing long sleeves and harem pants. Could that really have been to cover the wounds on her arms and legs?

'Do you understand?' asked Ryan.

'I think so … yes, that sounds good.'

'Dana, can you keep her talking until we get there?'

'Lovely. I'll talk to you next week and we'll decide where to go.'

'I'm sending a unit out now.'

They reached the bridge and stood side by side, staring across the valley, Tina's anger palpable. The waterfall below roared like a tap on full blast and Dana felt the feathering of white mist on her face.

It was like standing at the edge of the world and looking down. The shocking beauty. A sharp intake of breath. And the realisation that Tina had killed Johnny Buckley.

24

Tina walked further along the bridge, to the exact spot Sean had taken Dana on their second date. 'If you stand over here, you'll get the best view.'

Once again, Dana felt terror tingling in her body even though there was no rational reason for it – Ryan had told her Tina had been responsible for the hit-and-run. But surely it was an accident?

Tina leant down to tie her shoelace. 'So, who was that?' she asked, staring up at Dana, her eyes full of mistrust.

'Mum,' said Dana. 'She always calls at the worst times.'

'No, it wasn't.' Tina stood up so that they were face to face. 'The problem with you, Dana, is you think I'm so fucking dumb.'

'Honestly, I've never thought that.'

'So, come on then. Out with it. What was the call about?'

Dana hesitated, pretending she was in deep emotional turmoil about whether to tell Tina the truth, and milking each second for everything it was worth. 'It was Shivani from the Department, asking for advice about a court matter. But I didn't want to talk about it in front of you. It's confidential.' Tina's eyes narrowed as Dana continued. 'I thought we came up here so you could tell me why you said you were working on the night of Johnny's death?'

'I don't know where you were brought up, but where I'm from that's called a lie.'

'I see.' Dana was taken aback that Tina was being so honest with her.

'No, you don't fucking see. You're about to steal my child. You're going to put him in a blazer and send him to some preppy private school and call him your own. And on top of it all, you expect me to be okay with that.'

'I know it's hard.'

'No, you don't. You've never had one day in your entire rarefied life that's been one-tenth as hard as mine.'

'I had a son once.'

A light of curiosity came on in Tina's eyes. 'What happened to him?'

'Died. Eight months old.' The old sadness rose up, radiating through her body. 'I checked on him and—' She shook her head.

'It's not the same, you know. You can't compare losing an eight-month-old baby to losing a twelve-year-old. It's apples and oranges.' Tina's eyes were like fire. The flame growing brighter and brighter.

'I don't really understand,' said Dana, aware of Tina's mounting rage and desperate to keep her talking. 'If you weren't at work, then where were you on the night Johnny Buckley died?'

'It's not my fault he ran onto the road like an absolute fucking lunatic.' Tina was clearly getting more distressed. 'But let's face it, if anyone finds out, that's it for me. Once they realise I was high, that I had the tiniest bit of meth in my system, I'll be back in jail.' She stared down at Dana with unnatural intensity. 'There's no way I'm going to be separated from Angus again. Ever.'

'If what you say is true,' Dana said, thinking quickly, 'that Johnny ran onto the road without warning, then it was obviously an accident.'

'If there's even the tiniest chance that I'll be charged with murder, that's what will happen. They'll say it was intentional. That I mowed him down because I had some weird agenda – drug related probably. Because there's nothing that makes you more of a pariah than having drug charges in your criminal history.' She took a breath. 'Truth is, I'm unlucky,' Tina said, repeating Susan's words from earlier in the year. 'Always have been. Anyone else in the world would have ridden the bike that night and nothing would have happened, but with me, some poor bloke stumbles out onto the road and ends up dead. Born under a bad star. Been like that all my life.'

A movement behind a eucalypt caught Dana's eye and she glimpsed Angus's face, shocked and white, before he darted back behind the tree. From his expression, he'd heard everything his mother had said.

She strained to hear for the police sirens, but there was nothing. *Where were they?*

'I know you think I'm crazy, that I've lost my mind,' said Tina. 'But I haven't. It's just that lately I've been watching you with Angus, picking him up, driving him around in Mum's car. I saw how happy you all are without me in his life. It's like being stabbed in the heart. Over and over until there's nothing left. I know if I go back inside, Mum will have finally managed to replace me with the daughter she always wanted.' Tina was pleading now. 'That's why I need you to do something for me.'

'What's that?'

'I need you to promise that the only people who will know about this whole hit-and-run incident are you and me.'

Dana had a flashback to Susan's advice about meeting a hurricane head-on. 'I'm sorry, Tina. There's no way I can lie for you.'

What happened next played out in slow motion. Her legs lifted from the blow and her body followed. She was in shock and felt no pain, although a part of her knew that was what would follow. Instinctively she threw out an arm, grasping the wooden sleeper that ran along the bottom side of the bridge with one hand. She swung in space momentarily and looked down. Using all her strength she grabbed on with her other hand. The wooden paling was splintered and rough under her fingers. And then she felt it, heavily winded by the blow to her solar plexus, each breath was fire. The water roared below her and confusion seeped through her brain as she tried to figure out what was happening. An image of Jayden flashed through her mind. The wounds on his body from the fall. *This scenario has played out before.* Tina luring Jayden to the top of the waterfall, and pushing him off, just like she'd pushed Dana. His body weaving its way downstream in the weeks before he was found.

With her life flashing before her, Dana couldn't believe how stupid she'd been. Tina was right. She was the dumb one. She'd followed Tina to the top of the waterfall like a lamb to the slaughter. In the ominous silence Dana tried to imagine what Tina was doing and pictured her sitting on the bridge, staring over the valley. A statue.

The sound of sirens wailed in the distance, becoming louder and louder. With a surge of adrenaline Dana tried to pull herself up. If she waited any longer she'd lose her grip.

Tina came closer. She flicked a glance down at Dana then ground down hard on her fingers with the heel of her shoe.

Dana cried out, red-hot pain shooting through her hand.

'Mum!' Angus was suddenly beside them, yanking Tina away by the shoulders and screaming at her. 'Stop it!'

The pain in Dana's hands was unbearable. She pictured Oscar. Holding his warm body again. The thought was irresistible, the need to be close to him, so intense it was visceral.

All she had to do was let go.

Dana felt herself starting to drift and knew it was over. Knew she couldn't hold on any longer.

So much for my guardian angel.

Angus was reaching down. She looked up towards his hand, then at the water below. It was hopeless. She didn't have the strength. She had a vision of herself falling through space. Down an endless vortex. Lost forever.

She let go.

When she looked up again Angus was holding onto one of her hands. He was surprisingly strong, his sinewy arms gripping hers.

'Mum, help me! Mum!' The outrage in his voice unmistakable. In the next second, both Tina and Angus were dragging Dana upwards until the solidity of the bridge was beneath her.

When she opened her eyes Tina's hands were in fists by her sides. Her face was like stone as she stared out to the horizon.

She's going to jump. The thought passed through Dana's mind, but she was too weak to do anything. She tilted her head in Tina's direction. 'Your mum,' she whispered to Angus.

He turned to her and started screaming. 'Don't you think you've already done enough, Mum? Nan's about to die and now you're going to make me watch you jump off a cliff?'

'There's no point anymore!' she shot back.

She watched on as Angus cried out, sprinting over to his mother and reaching for her hand. He led her back to the rock ledge where he pushed her into a seated position.

The next thing Dana saw was Ryan's face in front of her, close enough to see the flecks in his brown eyes. He took her injured hand, splaying her bleeding fingers as he checked for broken bones then helped her into a seated position. His face was full of concern. 'Looks like you got lucky this time.'

Over by a hoop pine two of his officers were standing over Tina. 'I've got to get over there and oversee the arrest. I'll be back soon,' said Ryan.

Dana sat on the bridge, numb with shock. An officer cordoned off the crime scene with tape, turning back a group of hikers on their way to the lookout. A policewoman was talking to Tina: 'Place your right hand behind your back.' There was a scuffle and one of them snapped a pair of hand cuffs onto her wrists.

'Mum,' Angus yelled out as they were about to go. 'Did you kill Jayden too?'

Tina stared at the ground, unable to meet his eyes.

'If you don't tell me the truth, I'm never talking to you again.'

Dana couldn't believe how calm he was being, as though he was growing up before her eyes.

Tina broke down. 'I didn't want to, but he was going to tell the police. I couldn't bear to be parted from you. You've got to believe me—'

She was still pleading with Angus as she was being led away, her face a mask of agony and defeat.

Dana had no idea how she was going to break the news to Susan. Dana's phone started to ring in her pocket. Her hands were shaking as she attempted to pick it up. 'Hello?'

'Dana Gibson?'

'Yes.' Her voice was unsteady.

'Dr Halliday from Toowoomba Base Hospital.'

Dana remembered the voice. The kind woman who'd sat on the bed and told Susan she had cancer.

'I'm sorry to tell you this, but Susan's passed away.' The doctor waited a few beats, then continued. 'She'd just had her medication and looked very peaceful when the nurse found her. I don't think she suffered.'

'Thanks for letting me know,' Dana said mechanically.

'We'll be in touch about the official formalities, but for now it would be helpful if you could inform her children and any other family members.'

A tear slid down Dana's cheek as she hung up the phone. How had such a lovely woman, who'd been a beacon of light in Dana's dark times, been fated to such misfortune? She tucked her legs into her chest and wrapped her arms around them, staring out across the valley in the golden light of the late afternoon. She thought about the pain and anguish Susan would have felt once she realised Tina had been responsible for the deaths of two people. The living nightmare of knowing her only daughter would spend the rest of her life in jail.

EPILOGUE

Dana brought her cup of tea out onto Susan's verandah and sank into the sofa. She sipped the steaming liquid as a pair of white butterflies flitted in and out of the rose bush to the sounds of birds chirruping in the trees. The leaves on the camphor laurels in the park had turned a deep maroon and once again everything was changing.

In the dog park across the road Ryan jogged up and down the bike path with an Irish terrier puppy behind him. The dog's ears were pinned back and its tail wagged as it bounded back and forth.

Angus came through the door in a Bart Simpson t-shirt and collapsed onto the couch beside her.

'No fair,' he said, gesturing across to Ryan in the park opposite. 'How come he got to have one of Arthur's puppies?'

'He's a grown man. He can do what he wants.' Dana gazed over at Angus as he bent down to tie his laces. His fringe was getting long and she'd need to take him for a haircut now that it was school holidays again. 'Is that what you really want? A dog?' She pictured it chewing on the furniture. Digging up Susan's beloved garden.

'That's what I've always wanted. Ever since I was six.'

'We'll have to see then. I'll just have to figure out how I could make it work. And whether I could take time off to make sure I'm at home while it's a puppy.'

Ryan flung a tennis ball across the park and the dog bolted after it. Once it had the ball in its mouth the pup dropped it and started sniffing the ground.

Angus slathered sunscreen on his arms. 'So, is he your boyfriend now?'

'I guess you could call him that.'

'Are you in *love*?' he asked in his usual blunt manner.

'I am.' She was surprised at how clear her feelings were, after years of ambivalence with her ex-husband. This was how it was supposed to feel. A rush of warmth on an otherwise dull day.

'Dana and Ryan sitting in a tree. K.I.S.S.I.N.G.'

'Okay, Angus. That's enough.' She couldn't help but smile.

He glanced at his watch. 'Oh, crap, I told Michael I'd be at the courts by two.'

'It's just a casual game, isn't it?'

'Yeah, but he beat me in nearly every game last week and this time I'm playing to win.'

He stood up to grab his racquet and his head almost touched the hanging basket. She couldn't believe how tall he was getting. She felt a sudden surge of emotion as she realised there were only a few more years until he was a man.

'Have you put sunscreen on your face too? We don't want you getting any more freckles.'

He swiped a stripe of white across his nose then jogged down the stairs.

'Angus,' she called as he reached the front gate. 'The paperwork came through today.' She'd wanted to tell him while they were eating his favourite dinner – chicken fettuccine – but she couldn't wait any longer.

His nose wrinkled in confusion.

'The judge signed off on the guardianship order, so it's all organised. I'll be looking after you until you're eighteen.'

'Good-o.' He bounced back and forth on the balls of his feet then opened the gate. He paused. 'And I still get the house when I'm twenty-five?'

'Yes, Susan left it all to you. Her final wish was that you always knew how much she loved you.' Now she paused. 'And how much your mother and I love you as well.'

For a split-second pain flickered in his eyes. 'I'll be back in time for dinner,' he said with a smile. He sprinted along the fence line, a blur of skinny legs and hair flying in the breeze as he disappeared down the street.

Dana remained on the verandah a while longer, listening to the rustle of the grass, the long sigh of the wind in the trees. As she closed her eyes, she heard the whisper of the angel on her shoulder.

The promise of only good things to come

ACKNOWLEDGEMENTS

This book wouldn't have been possible without the help and support of so many wonderful people:

Thank you to my publisher, Aviva Tuffield, for your insight and wisdom and bringing my books into the world. A huge thanks to my talented editor, Jacqueline Blanchard, who worked tirelessly and patiently on the editing for *Killarney*. Also to Lucy Czerwinski, Daniel Seed and the staff at UQP for your hard work and skill.

Thank you to Benjamin Paz at Curtis Brown. Your support and enthusiasm for my books has been wonderful – I've been incredibly lucky to have you as my agent.

Thanks again to my incredible writers' group, the Dead Darlings Society – Deanna Antoniolli, Mary Chan, Dan Fallon, Karen Hollands, Kaja Holzheimer, Nicky Peelgrane, Isabel Prior, Fiona Reilly, Fiona Robertson, Paul Thomas and Warren Ward – who've been on this writing journey with me for over a decade; where did that time go? Thank you for teaching me so much and for sharing the ride.

A special thanks to my family: my parents, Barry and Frances Mottram; my brothers, Brent and Sam; and Natalie, Amity and Rainey and Baz Macintosh for all your support. Thank you also to the longtime friends I neglected to mention the first time around – Fae Ballingal and Anna Hollindale.

A huge thank you to all the readers of *Crows Nest* who embraced the story and the character of Dana Gibson, and those of you who got in touch.

Thank you to the talented Caroline Lee for your excellent narration of my audiobooks.

Thank you to the community of Killarney and the surrounding areas of Warwick and Queen Mary Falls for proving a stunning backdrop to my novel and for providing such happy memories. All characters and events in this book are fictitious with some creative licence taken with place names and settings.

Special thanks to my kind and generous work colleagues in Systems and Practice Review. Thanks for being such wonderful people to work with and for being so supportive of my writing.

To Fiona Robertson, thanks from the bottom of my heart for being such a kind friend and provider of excellent writing critique.

And last, but not least, a big thank you to Alex, Emily and Jack, my light and loves. None of this would be possible without you.